Jess rested her palm on her stomach.

"Did you hear that, Baby?" she asked. "Grandparents are in your future."

For the first time, Duffy understood Jess. She had no parents. She didn't want to let her child down as her mother had. What to him was a casual mention of his mother's involvement was the promise of a special gift to her: *family.*

"I'm taking this pillow from the bed for me," Duffy said carefully. "Don't get any ideas."

She blinked at him. But it wasn't the *I'm remembering something* dazed look he'd seen her get every once in a while. Jess looked at him as if seeing him for the first time. As Duffy, not Greg's mirror image.

That look touched something deep inside him, something that warmed and eased, something he'd kept locked away and refused to name.

Dear Reader,

Welcome to Harmony Valley!

Things aren't as harmonious here as they once were. Jobs have dried up and almost everyone under the age of sixty has moved away in the past ten years, leaving the population...well...rather gray-haired and peaceful.

But things are changing since three hometown boys made good. They've returned home, started a winery, and now the economy is inching its way forward.

Jessica Aguirre has come to town, but not for a job. She's looking for someone from her past, someone who might help her remember. When she sees a photo of Michael "Duffy" Dufraine in a local newspaper, she's convinced he has the answers she's seeking. Duffy is afraid he knows the answers, but Jessica won't want to hear the truth.

I hope you enjoy Jessica and Duffy's journey, as well as the other romances in the Harmony Valley series. I love to hear from readers. Check my website to learn about upcoming books, sign up for email book announcements (and I'll send you a free sweet romantic comedy read), or chat with me on Facebook (MelindaCurtisAuthor) or Twitter (MelCurtisAuthor) to hear about my latest giveaways.

Melinda

MelindaCurtis.com

HEARTWARMING

A Memory Away

———

USA TODAY Bestselling Author

Melinda Curtis

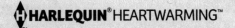

Recycling programs
for this product may
not exist in your area.

ISBN-13: 978-0-373-36751-1

A Memory Away

Printed in U.S.A.

HARLEQUIN®
www.Harlequin.com

Award-winning, *USA TODAY* bestselling author
Melinda Curtis lives in California's arid Central
Valley with her husband, an ancient Labrador, a
"Shorkie" princess and a cat who would be queen
of them all. Their three kids are all in college (not
in California) so you're more likely to see posts
regarding Melinda's pets than her kids on social
media (for which her progeny are thankful).

Melinda enjoys putting humor into her stories,
because that's how she approaches life. She writes
sweet contemporary romances as Melinda Curtis
(Brenda Novak says of *Season of Change*, "found
a place on my keeper shelf"), and fun, steamy
reads as Mel Curtis (Jayne Ann Krentz says of
Cora Rules, "wonderfully entertaining").

Books by Melinda Curtis

Harlequin Heartwarming

The premise of this story was born at a bar with senior editor Victoria Curran and polished from the brilliance of Kathryn Lye (thanks, ladies!). Margie Lawson challenged me to bring more quirk to Harmony Valley (thank you, Margie!). And Mr. Curtis literally kept me fed as I put the finishing touches on it (thanks for letting me have the "Follow your instincts" fortune cookie fortune, babe, even though that isn't really a fortune).

CHAPTER ONE

DID HE LOVE ME?

Jessica Aguirre didn't know if he loved her. She didn't know if he *knew* her.

She stood on a gravel drive in the midst of a vineyard in Harmony Valley. Heart pounding. Head pounding.

Did he love me?

The man in the photograph would tell her.

Jess clutched a newspaper photo, and stared at the group of men and women in front of a two-story farmhouse with a vintage weather vane. There was a man in the back row on the left. He was the one.

She recognized him right away. Recognized dark hair with a curl at his temple. Recognized a straight, no-nonsense nose. Recognized caramel-colored eyes. Those eyes. If only she could remember...

What if it wasn't him? What if this was a dead end? What if...?

Jess drew a steadying breath against the

panic rising in her chest and lifted her gaze to the well-looked-after farmhouse. The day the picture had been taken there'd been big fluffy clouds in the sky above the cupola. Today the sky was clear and blue. The late January air was crazy cold, stinging Jessica's toes in her sneakers.

The slender woman who'd greeted Jess on this Monday morning hurried down the front porch steps. "He'll be here in a few minutes. Come inside the tasting room." Christine was the winemaker for the newly opened Harmony Valley Vineyards, which was headquartered in the farmhouse, the subject of the newspaper article, and where *he* worked. Christine's carefree smile told Jess the woman had never lost a moment, a day or weeks from her past. "We have all the amenities inside—hot tea, a bathroom and a place to sit down."

"I don't want to be any trouble." Jessica resisted glancing at the clipping again. Would her unannounced appearance be welcome? Or create mayhem?

"It's no trouble. *You're* no trouble." Christine had the kind of smile that invited you to relax, to open up, to be part of the family. "Come inside. It's cold out here."

It was cold. Jessica's jacket wouldn't zip up anymore. And family…

In no time, Jessica was sitting at a table cradling a cup of hot tea. The tasting room was elegant in a simple way that fit the farmhouse. Dark wood, intimate tables for two, out-of-Jessica's-price-range granite slabs on bar tops. But the room was oddly empty.

"Where's the wine?"

Christine followed the direction of Jessica's curious gaze to the bare shelves behind the bar. "Barrel aging. I'll be blending some for limited release soon. But most of our harvest will age another year."

"Aging wine is all about patiently waiting, isn't it? Even when you don't know how it will turn out." Jessica had become good at biding her time. "Making wine is like waiting for bread dough to rise." Or babies to be born.

"Exactly." With a contented sigh, Christine's gaze lingered on the room as if seeing it filled with bottles of her making.

Outside, the wind whistled past, drawing Jessica to the window in time to see a muddy gray truck pull into the gravel drive.

"There he is." Christine gave Jessica's shoulder a sisterly squeeze, and then headed toward the door. "I'll be upstairs if you need anything."

Did he love me?

A man got out of the truck. Dark hair. Straight nose. Familiar eyes.

It's him.

She leaned forward, peering through the paned glass, her heart sailing toward him, over ever-hopeful waves of roses and rainbows.

Jess didn't usually let herself dream. But now…today…him…

And yet…

He wore a burgundy vest jacket that clashed with a red long-sleeve T-shirt. Worn blue jeans. A black baseball cap.

Instead, she saw him in a fine wool suit. Black, always black. A navy shirt of the softest cotton. A silk tie in a geometric pattern. Shiny Italian loafers…

He took the stairs two at a time, work boots ringing on wood.

Jessica's heart sank as certainly as if someone had drilled holes in the boat carrying her hopeful emotions. Clouds blocked the sun. The rainbow disappeared. Unwilling to sink, Jess clung to joy. To the idea of him.

He entered without a flourish or an energetic greeting. He entered without the smile that teased the corners of her memory. He entered and took stock of the room, the situation, her.

Their eyes met. His were the same color, same shape, so heart-achingly familiar.

It was the cool assessment in them that threw her off. Not a smile, not a brow quirk, not an eye crinkle.

He came forward. "I'm Michael Dufraine, but everyone calls me Duffy."

His name didn't ring true.

Had he lied to her?

She couldn't speak, could barely remember her name.

The wind shook the panes. The house creaked and groaned.

He smiled. A polite smile, a distant smile, an I-don't-know-you smile.

Disappointment overwhelmed her. Jess resisted the urge to dissolve into a pity puddle on the floor.

"And you are…?" He extended his hand.

On autopilot, she reached for him. Their palms touched.

Jessica's vision blurred and she gripped his hand tighter as clips of memory assailed her—his deep laughter, him offering her a

bite of chocolate cheesecake, his citrusy co-
logne as he leaned in to kiss her.

It is him.

Relieved. She was so relieved. Jessica
blinked at the man—*Duffy*—who she vaguely
recalled and, at the same time, did not.

She'd practiced what to say on the hour-
long drive up here from Santa Rosa. Ran
through several scenarios. None of them had
included him not recognizing her.

She should start at the beginning. Best not
to scare him with hysterics and panicked ac-
cusations, of which she'd had five months
to form.

*Don't raise your voice. Don't cry. Don't
ask why.*

*And don't lead the conversation with the
elephant in the room.*

Despite all the cautions and practicing and
caveats, she drew a breath, and flung her
hopes toward him as if he were her life pre-
server. "I think I'm your wife."

DUFFY RELEASED THE woman's hand as if he'd
accidentally grabbed a rattlesnake. "I'm not
married." And he'd sure as hell remember if
he had been.

"Or I was… Or I was your girlfriend…

maybe?" She glanced down at her belly. Her very pregnant belly.

Holy in-need-of-a-handrail.

Duffy sat down heavily across from her, still chilled from the winter cold. Chilled now to the bone. "I haven't… You couldn't…" He swiped a hand over his face, very much aware that his boss was upstairs and the walls in the century-old house were very thin. "Who are you?"

"Jessica… Jess Aguirre." There was a quiet beauty about her. Long dark hair, big dark eyes, a smooth olive-skin complexion. Many women shared her physical features. Few carried themselves with a combination of contained dignity and edge-of-her-seat intensity. "You…um…don't know me?"

"You or your passenger."

Reality was returning. He could see it in her face. Jessica seemed stricken that she wasn't his significant other, but otherwise she appeared stable. She didn't wield a knife, didn't draw a gun, and she wasn't screaming to high heaven that he should know who she was.

"But…you have to know me." Jessica leaned over the table—or as far as she could with that baby bump—and whispered, "We've kissed and…" She glanced at her stomach.

And here Duffy had thought he'd taken care of all of his brother's loose ends. "I'm not Greg."

"Greg." She murmured his brother's name, then repeated it—stronger.

"My twin." Duffy took out his wallet and handed her a picture he'd only recently started carrying—him and Greg before a Little League game.

She placed the photo on the table next to a crumpled newspaper clipping of the winery staff, her smile as soft as morning dew on a grape leaf. "Greg." She said the name as if testing it with her tongue and finding it acceptable.

He felt compelled to explain. "We were identical."

"Were?"

"He died nearly six months ago."

"No." She moved a hand to her belly.

"Struck by lightning." Yes, there was a God. Although, "He was killed instantly and didn't suffer." Duffy was proud of the detached way he delivered the news. His brother had been a greedy piece of trash, which some siblings may have forgiven, but not when the target was Mom and Dad. "So if you're looking for the man who did you wrong, it was him." Duffy gazed out at the cold, dormant vineyard, which felt much like his heart. "My brother was no saint."

"I don't believe that." She slid Duffy's picture across the table. "Or you wouldn't be carrying his photo."

He wasn't going to rehash the painful details of his life with this stranger. "Why are you here?"

Jessica closed her eyes. "I came looking for closure."

"Did Greg steal from you?" The question had to be asked, and he didn't hide the bitterness. Greg had taken every penny of their parents' retirement fund. Luckily, Greg hadn't spent it all before he died. "Did he promise you he'd love you until the end of time?"

"I... I... I can't remember."

HE WAS DEAD.

Whatever Jess had been expecting to find by coming here, it hadn't been this.

He was dead.

Whoever Greg had been.

He was dead.

There'd be no tearful reunions, no admissions of mistakes, no offered apologies. How foolish she'd been to expect to show up here and find a man who loved her, one who'd fall to his knees as he held her hands and begged for forgiveness.

Sadness for Greg's death mired her insides, more for her baby—who'd never know his or her father—than for the man she barely remembered. It seemed wrong somehow. The day. The news. The man she was left facing.

The baby kicked her ribs.

"What does that mean?" Duffy asked, pulling her back to the present. "You can't remember."

Flashes of memory shuttered in her head with every word Duffy uttered, every shrug of his shoulders, every nuanced flick of his brow. His face was austere, where Greg's had been amiable. His eyes were care-lined where Greg's had been carefree. And the clash of burgundy vest with a red-sleeved T-shirt? Greg would never have paired those two colors. Of that, she was certain.

"I was in a car accident five months ago." Jessica dropped her gaze to her baby barge, needing to swallow twice before she could get more words out. "I have retrograde am-

nesia. I can remember growing up. I can remember how to make sugar cookies from
scratch." She swallowed again. "But I haven't
been able to remember anything about my
baby's father." She couldn't even remember
whether they'd once been married or in love.
"Not until I saw you."

"So Greg's the father?" Even Duffy's voice
was different. His words spoken slower. His
tone deeper and filled with cynicism.

"I'm certain of it...now." She took a drink
of her once-hot tea, feeling as cold as the
green beverage. How much should she tell
Duffy? He wasn't coming across as the most
supportive listener. But what had she to lose
by holding back? "You seem so familiar. I
remember you kissing me—"

"Greg," he inserted tersely, staring at her
hard. Not only had Greg been unwelcome
here, Jess was, as well.

She strengthened her voice. She'd lived
too long without answers to walk away from
his obstinacy. "I remember us—*him and I*—
laughing." It was hard to imagine her laughing with Duffy.

"Well, I'm glad he made someone happy."
He'd perfected that unforgiving look.

Greg, what did you do? "But...you were twins...brothers. You didn't get along?"

"Greg would steal the belt from your waist if he could make a buck off it." So much anger. It vibrated in the air between them, pressing her back as if he'd pushed her.

Snatches of images. Smiles and laughter. Tender touches and endearing words. She couldn't believe Duffy's opinion of Greg. Still, doubt crept up her throat, closing it off.

"Greg took all your money, didn't he?"

So much weariness in his tone.

It weighed on Jess. She'd felt burdened for so long, she wasn't sure how much more she could take.

It couldn't have been Greg who'd taken her money. There'd been love between them. She just knew it. Every time she began to question it, a feeling of love would rise up. That feeling was conspicuously absent today. "I can't prove he took anything."

"Fess up. There's something missing." His gaze probed for the truth, but there was a reluctant slant to his eyes, as if he didn't want to know.

I'm so sorry, Baby. Jessica's hand drifted to her stomach. "The only thing I know is that a week before the accident, my bank account was drained."

"He did it." Duffy was maddeningly certain.

Jessica shook her head when instead she wanted to shake him. "I can't be certain of that."

"I am. I know my brother better than anyone." His lips pinched upward at the corners, so tense she wouldn't have called it a smile. "Twins, remember?"

She didn't want to believe him. There were the recently remembered smiles and kisses.

Duffy stood. His gaze cut toward the door. His feet pointed that way, as well. "Sorry about the memory thing, but I need to get back to work."

She should never have gotten her hopes up. She should have accepted that the father of her baby was gone and his family wouldn't want anything to do with her. Being unwanted was her reality.

But something inside of her wouldn't settle. Not this time. "Wait. Can I see you again?" At his frown, she rushed on. "I've recovered quite a bit today just by listening to you talk. For five months, I've had nothing." Desperation seized her and squeezed. "Please. It's important to me that I remember."

His jaw worked. He didn't look at Jess. Clearly, he didn't want to see her again and be reminded of Greg. But his hesitation meant he wasn't as cold and uncaring as he might want her to believe. That perhaps somewhere in that closed-off heart of his were memories of Greg he cherished.

Above them, the ceiling creaked.

"There's no point." But he didn't leave or ask her to go.

Hope flooded her chest. "There is. There's every point. Up until today, I couldn't remember how I got pregnant. If I'd been abandoned by my husband or raped…" *Steady, girl.* She squared her shoulders. "I grew up without knowing my father, not even his name. All I'm asking for is a little of your time."

"I know I'm going to regret this—"

"You won't." Jessica gathered her things, anxious to leave before he changed his mind.

"Come back Saturday at six. There's a restaurant in town, El Rosal. I'll be having dinner there." She wasn't entirely sure she'd heard him because it sounded as if he'd added the words *Whether you're there or not.*

CHAPTER TWO

THE ONLY THING worse than finding out your brother had left a bun in the oven? Duffy's new boss hearing all about it. At least Ryan, the assistant winemaker, was off today.

"Sorry for the lack of privacy. That was pretty heavy." Christine stood in the doorway between the tasting room and the kitchen. "How are you doing?"

Duffy shrugged, watching Jessica walk to her car with carefully measured steps. She tugged the ends of her jacket, trying unsuccessfully to wrap them around her belly, hunching her shoulders against the cold.

So frail. So fragile. Duffy wanted to believe her.

She didn't remember Greg? How was that possible?

Christine came to stand next to him. "I'm not sure how I'd react to knowing I was going to have a niece or nephew soon."

I'm going to be an uncle.

Duffy hadn't processed Jessica's news in that light. He'd been blindsided by her presence and her pregnancy and her claims of amnesia. He supposed that as the child's uncle, he had a responsibility—to be a fatherly influence since Greg wasn't around, to teach the little tyke how to throw a ball and swing a bat, to make sure the kid had some money socked away for college.

Money?

Recently buried worries resurfaced in his gut, sour and unpleasant.

After Greg swindled their parents, Duffy had helped support them. Since Greg's death, he'd sold and liquidated all his twin's assets, and given everything to his mom and dad. He'd set them up in a senior living apartment complex, one that could help his mother take care of his wheelchair-bound father. For the first time in what seemed like forever, Duffy's paycheck was his own. His weekends were his own. His life was his own. All because of the money Greg left behind.

Did Jessica and her baby deserve a share of Greg's money?

Morals dictated he give Jessica something. But what if she was lying? What if she was exactly like Greg?

Jessica drove away in a dinged and dented four-door sedan. Everything about her said *trust me*. That's how he'd felt about Greg, too.

His gut continued its churning. Duffy couldn't shake off the feeling of being sucked back into a Greg-induced vortex of financial folly.

Trust Jessica? Give her money? She claimed she had amnesia. Greg would have told her that was a hard scam to sell. And Greg had been the king of con artists.

Christine glanced up at him. "You think she's lying." It wasn't a question.

"You know how when you meet someone you give them the benefit of the doubt? How you trust what they tell you is the truth?"

"Yes."

"You could never trust a word that came out of my brother's mouth." Duffy barely recognized his own voice. It was as thick with emotion as the day he'd learned of Greg's death. "If she and Greg…"

"Don't judge her so quickly," Christine said. "If only for the baby's sake."

Duffy nodded, but the desire to convict outweighed the compulsion to trust.

Thankfully, Christine's work ethic intruded. "You mentioned on the phone that you wanted to show me something."

He had. "Let's take a drive." He needed a distraction and he needed to show Christine the extent of the threat on the hill.

The winery had recently purchased several small vineyards around town, ones that had been lying idle and untended for years. One of their properties was on the slopes of Parish Hill and might have a problem. As the winery's newly hired and first-ever vineyard manager, it was Duffy's responsibility to restore the vineyards to optimal production.

A few minutes later, Duffy drove them down Main Street. There was little traffic. With a population just reaching one hundred, and barely twenty of those residents below the age of sixty-five, there weren't many cars around.

Nearly two decades ago, the largest employer in town had burned to the ground. Younger Harmony Valley residents had moved closer to civilization, leaving the town on the brink of extinction. And then three local boys made it big in the dot-com world, returned home to decompress and decided to save the town by starting a winery. The jury was still out on the saving part, but those employed at the winery were optimistic.

"It's sad about Jessica, isn't it?" Christine waved to the elderly barber, standing on scarecrow-like limbs in front of his shop.

"I suppose." Duffy drove slowly around the town square with its ancient oak tree, and took the turn toward Parish Hill and its steep switchbacks.

"I was trying to imagine how I'd feel if I couldn't recall a part of my life. It must be frustrating and terrifying not remembering who the baby's father is." How quickly Jess had pulled Christine into her camp. A strike against her.

Duffy navigated a tight turn. "Can we talk about work?" Always? He liked to keep his private life separate from his professional life.

"You're one of the few people in town who doesn't want me to stop talking about the winery." There was no change in Christine's voice. No indication that she felt snubbed by his request. "Promise me you'll never change."

"Never." Of course, she might not like what he was about to tell her.

Duffy turned onto a dirt road that led to a

small vineyard clinging to the hillside. According to their records, the Cabernet Sauvignon vines had originally been planted in the 1990s. Their trunks were thick and twisted. Duffy parked and led Christine down the vine-tangled hill. The vineyard had shriveled, unharvested grape clusters on the ground.

He stopped at the bottom row of leafless, wintery plants. "Look at this. See how these vines have produced fewer shoots and canes than the next row up?"

"Yes." Christine's gaze moved with a scientist's deliberation. "What do you think? Soil composition? Water drainage?"

"It could be those things. But we also have to consider leaf roll virus." A grapevine disease that delayed maturity and lowered grape yield. Saying it out loud was like telling a child there would be no Christmas this year.

Christine didn't like the news. She frowned and shook her head several times before she said anything. And when she did speak, her tone had the serious quality of a winemaker twice her age. "You can't know that. You'd either have to see it in their leaves come spring or have tested the vines."

"True." But he knew the signs, had seen

them on his last job, where the winery owners hadn't wanted to hear the news, either. "Look at this." He crouched next to the rotted remains of a withering grape cluster. "There are others like it all along this row." He moved to a row farther up the hill, carefully making his case. "Now look at this cluster."

"Almost twice the size," she murmured. Then she shook her head again. "Leaf roll has never been documented in Harmony Valley."

"I was exactly where you are. Drainage, incline of the hill, even the fact that these vines haven't been harvested or trimmed back in years." Duffy tugged on a bare branch. It snapped free, another indication of the poor health of the vines, weakened by years of drought. "I had Ryan pull the data. The last row was planted ten years ago after a fire destroyed part of the vineyard. I couldn't find any confirmation of it being certified virus-free stock." He tossed the vine to the ground. "I'd rather err on the side of caution, wouldn't you?"

After a moment, Christine nodded. "We should test for red blotch disease, too."

"Agreed." She'd taken the news better than he'd expected.

They hiked up the hill, the biting wind at their backs.

"I walked the vineyard last fall when we decided to expand." Christine paused on a rise to take in the rest of the area, sounding resigned, as if she were to blame. "But I can't remember going that deep into the rows."

"It's okay. Maybe I'm wrong." Duffy prayed it was so.

"If they are diseased," she said softly, more to herself than to him, "we'll have to take them out right away. Both leaf roll and red blotch dilute the taste of the grape." Christine opened the truck door and inspected the bottom of her boots one at a time. "Check for bugs on the bottom of your shoes. Mealy bugs—"

"Spread the disease," Duffy finished for her, already examining the crevices in his boot lugs. He added in a neutral tone, "You hired me because I know things like this."

"I'm sorry. It's a shock." Her apology was as arrow-straight as the worry furrowing her brow.

"With your approval, we'll have Ryan take samples and send them to the lab."

A beat-up green truck backfired as it trundled down the dirt road behind them.

"Rutgar," Christine said. "I…uh…told you about him, right?"

Sounded like she hadn't told him enough. "Used to own this property. Likes to know what's going on."

"Everyone in town is a bit of a gossip," she said apologetically. "It's not something I divulge during a job interview. You're in the grace period of being new to town." Christine hesitated, and then her smile turned as apologetic as her tone. "Or you were. Now that Rutgar's showed up… Well, let's just say folks' curiosity can sometimes be trying. Be patient with them. They mean well. And they grow on you." She quickly transformed into a confident, friendly winemaker greeting the previous owner. "Rutgar! What a surprise."

A bear-sized man stood beside a rusted truck fender. His gray-blond hair hung inches from his chin and draped thickly across his shoulders like a long, matted mane. "What are you two doing out here?" His accent was European. All he needed was chain mail and a sword to carry off the Viking vibe. "That's the second time I've seen *this one* up here today."

This one being Duffy. "We're discussing the condition of the vines." Duffy didn't feel comfortable sharing his suspicions. Instead, he introduced himself. Duffy wasn't a small man, but Rutgar's hand swallowed his.

"I want to be informed about what goes on. This is my land—"

"Was." Christine stepped up to hug Rutgar. "Was your land. You sold it to me, remember?"

"I sold it to your fiancé." The older man made a noise that sounded like a territorial growl. "I live on top of the hill. Everything that goes on here is my business."

"Of course, it is," Christine soothed. "And just so you're aware, there'll be workers up here sometime in the next few weeks."

Rutgar's sharp blue eyes narrowed. "Workers won't go any farther than this driveway."

"The view from the top is spectacular." Following Christine's lead, Duffy kept his voice kiss-butt polite. "You can see the entire valley. Why limit access on a public road?"

"Because the top of Parish Hill is my home." Rutgar's features twisted into something no one would call a smile. It involved drawn-back lips and bared teeth. "I've seen you up there wasting the nice lady's time."

"Surveying the land." Duffy's patience

held. Barely. "It's easier to keep all the properties straight with a view from above."

"Wasting time," Rutgar scoffed. "Winemaking takes months and years, and a lot of effort."

As did placating former landowners. "Since you're so interested in what's going on, can I count on you to help cane?" Given the vineyard hadn't been cut back in what looked like nearly a decade, Duffy was betting the answer was no.

"You can count on him to watch," Christine ribbed.

Rutgar shook a finger the size of a sausage at her. "I like you."

"You'll like him, too." Christine gave Rutgar's shoulder a gentle nudge that didn't move the large man an inch. "Now back out. We've got other vineyards to inspect."

"HOW DID IT go yesterday?" Vera yelled over the sound of the mixer's grinding motor.

It was 4:00 a.m. and the owner of Vera's Bakery in Santa Rosa was preparing the batter for red velvet cupcakes. They sold hundreds of them in the weeks leading up to Valentine's Day. The large industrial kitchen was already filled with welcoming, sugary smells from cinnamon rolls and various breads and cookies of all kinds. At the next worktable, several bakers were chattering in Spanish. Jessica's maternal grandparents had emigrated from Mexico, but Jess didn't speak more than a handful of words in their native tongue.

Normally, Jess couldn't wait to begin baking. Contributing to a busy kitchen always made her feel as if she belonged. Not today. Today she felt as if she'd never belong. Not with her coworkers, not with Greg's family, not with anyone.

"Did you find your baby daddy?" Vera's white hairnet covered her unnaturally red hair like snow on a high desert mountain.

"He's dead." Jess was saddened by Greg's death. Sad, yes, but since her memories of him were like dandelion fluffs on the wind, it was a detached sadness. If they'd been in love, wouldn't she feel broken?

For what must have been the thousandth time since she'd woken up in the hospital after the accident, Jess wondered if her baby was a creation of love. But now the wonder-train was on a new track.

What if Duffy's words were true? What if Greg had used her?

What if? What if? What if? She was at square one again. Too many questions. Too few answers.

"Your baby daddy's a deadbeat?" Vera shouted, sending her dangling silver cupcake earrings swinging over the tattoo of a rose on her neck.

"No. He's *dead*."

"What?" Vera promptly switched off the mixer and came around to Jessica's side of the prep table. "Dead? So who was the guy in the photo?"

"His twin brother. Duffy." His handsome and bitter twin brother.

Vera's brows shot up accusingly. "You're sure he didn't just make up the twin angle? Some guys will do anything to avoid paying child support."

Jess tied her apron on as she weighed what she'd been told. The man she'd hoped she might be in love with wasn't Duffy. She was sure of that. "I believe him."

"That's a shame. If you can't find a baby daddy, you'll need a sugar daddy." Vera shook a finger in Jessica's face and asked her something in Spanish she didn't understand. When Jess stared at her blankly, Vera said,

"How can you raise a child alone? Without a man's steady head and regular paycheck?"

"Women raise kids by themselves all the time." Jess was more interested in providing Baby with family roots than a secure bank account—although that would be nice, not to mention having a father figure around.

"Yes, but women shouldn't bring up babies alone. You're a smart girl. All you need to complete the package is to learn your native tongue to catch a good man." Her smile and nod indicated Jess was *this close* to attracting the right guy. "Smart girls always find sugar daddies."

"I'd just like to find my memories," Jess said.

Vera muttered in Spanish again and then stared at Jess as if she were a problem child. "I said memories won't keep you warm at night, but maybe your baby's uncle can."

"I have an electric blanket," Jess deadpanned. "And to be clear, even though I'm having dinner with Duffy this weekend in Harmony Valley, I am *not* planning on a brother swap so that I can have an insurance policy."

"You should listen to me. I know what I'm talking about." Vera laughed and turned on her loud mixer. "You be careful driving out there. Big storm coming in with flooding predicted. It's bad enough you'll be on leave soon. I need you every day until that baby is born."

Given Harmony Valley was sixty miles northeast and at a different elevation, Jessica wasn't worried about the weather. That was days away. Storms sped up or slowed down, and forecasters often predicted flooded roads during rainstorms and nothing ever happened. Jessica hadn't seen any roads under significant water since she'd moved to Santa Rosa from Sacramento last summer.

No. Jessica was more concerned with Duffy. Was he going to show up for their dinner? And could his presence help reveal more of her lost memories?

Would she ever know if Greg had loved her?

CHAPTER THREE

"HOW CAN I tell you this, Eunice?"

Eunice Fletcher braced herself because Agnes Villanova—town councilwoman, president of Harmony Valley's widows club, manager of the boutique the women in town ran and general town cog—was often the bearer of bad news.

"Who died?" Eunice clutched the yellow cotton pieces of a baby quilt she'd been cutting when Agnes stopped by her house. "Mildred? It was Mildred who died, wasn't it?" Another town councilwoman.

"Mildred is fine. It's—"

"It's Rose." The third councilwoman. It'd been years since a spot on the council had opened up. "I knew the poor dear was on her last legs mentally."

"Rose is fine. Sharper than ever." Agnes ran a hand through her pixie-cut gray hair, and pressed her lips together as if trying to stop herself from saying more.

"Quit beating around the bush and tell me who died. I'm very busy here." Stitching quilt pieces together at the window that faced the old Reedley place. The two-bedroom bungalow next door was being rented by one of those winery employees. A tall fellow named Duffy, who rose early, made eggs for breakfast with a sprinkle of cheese and liked cream in his coffee.

"It's *you*, Eunice. I came to talk about you."

The yellow blocks fell to Eunice's lap. "*I'm* not dying."

Agnes sighed. "It's *about* you."

Eunice stacked the blocks on top of each other, smoothing out the creases with her liver-spotted fingers. "You need to work on your delivery, Agnes. I thought someone had died again." Mae Gardner had recently passed. Eunice hadn't even realized Mae was sick. "What about me?"

"It's your baby quilts."

"Are they selling? I'm making them as fast as I can." She'd make them faster if Duffy was home more often. Sewing gave her an excuse to sit by the window.

"Maybe you should slow down." Agnes pulled the pink sunflower quilt Eunice had made from her tote and unfolded it. "We can't sell a baby quilt with Frankenstein stitches."

Eunice squinted at where Agnes pointed to the fabric. *"Frankenstein stitches,"* she harrumphed. "Have you seen the way my corners meet? They're perfect. And my stitches are wonderful." Her grandmother had taught her how to sew by hand, back before they made fancy machines.

"You can't see your stitches, can you?"

Eunice didn't want to admit she couldn't. The comment about Frankenstein hurt.

A truck pulled into the driveway next door. Agnes turned, blocking Eunice's view.

"Is that Duffy?" Eunice craned her neck. "His license plate has two eights at the end."

Agnes gave Eunice a chastising look over her shoulder. "How can you see across the yard and not see the stitches on your quilt? Have you tried reading glasses?"

Eunice suppressed a gasp. "No one in my family has ever needed glasses." The Fletcher women were beauties, every one.

"You can deny needing glasses all you want—"

"And I will."

"But until your stitches improve, I need

you to make something else for the shop."
Mae's Pretty Things was a boutique that carried handmade gifts for the tourists, the ones everyone was sure would start showing up soon. Or as soon as there was wine to sell.

Eunice narrowed her eyes. "What *other* things?"

"That's why I'm here. To see what other things you can make that aren't sewn together."

If that wasn't the most infuriating statement. "I don't make other things. I sew." Over the years, she and Mae had stitched together everything from pot holders to placemats.

"Eunice, you taught kindergarten and youth Bible study. You have to be crafty to have worked with kids all those years."

And she had been. "We colored. We fingerpainted. We glued things." Not fine art by any means, but it qualified as crafty.

Agnes frowned. "Oh."

"Yes, oh." Eunice looked at the sunflower quilt block she'd meticulously pieced together. The corners were square. The angles perfect. She'd never worn glasses in her life. "You want something else? I can color you a picture with crayons. Or create turkey portraits made from painted handprints. Or glue Popsicle picture frames decorated with colored glitter."

"You need glasses." Agnes's words were as short as she was.

"I'm not going to hide my eyes behind a pair of homely frames." Her mother would spin in her grave at the thought.

"Don't be vain, Eunice."

Too late. "My cousin Kim had a great body. My sister Julia had beautiful red hair. Kim gained weight. Julia went gray. But I still have my peepers." Eunice had violet eyes like Elizabeth Taylor. And Eunice was still alive. "My eyes are my best feature. Everyone says so." She'd made a good living modeling with those peepers. She wasn't about to cover them up.

"And yet you can't see." There was sarcasm in her friend's words. And impatience. And exasperation. "I'm not asking you to wear glasses all the time. Just when you're sewing. I'd rather have one of your quilts to sell than an arts-and-crafts picture frame."

"Oh."

"Yes, oh." Agnes carefully folded the baby quilt and set it in Eunice's lap. "I'll make an appointment for you with my eye doctor in

Cloverdale. In the meantime, you can borrow my reading glasses and see if that helps." She dug in her tote and handed Eunice a pair of black rectangular frames.

Eunice accepted them with a two-finger hold, as if they were slimy creatures who might sting. "They're—"

"Hideous. Yes, I know. But they work. Put them on and see for yourself."

Reluctantly, Eunice did as Agnes asked, but not before looking up to see if Thelma across the street was sitting at her front window. Thankfully, she wasn't. Glasses on, Eunice glanced down at the pink baby quilt. The stitches were monstrous. "Blast."

"Exactly."

DUFFY PREPARED HIS coffee by the small light over the stove. He hadn't slept well. Thoughts of Greg's baby and Jessica had him counting alarm-clock clicks.

He was thickheaded tired. But it was a workday. He'd rely on his morning ritual to get him going. Drag himself out of bed, check; grind fresh coffee beans, check; make a pot of coffee, check; and stand there waiting for it to brew. The standing and waiting was a waste of time, but he liked not doing anything. He liked the quiet. He liked—

Snap.

Duffy startled. The two-bedroom Craftsman house was ninety years old and prone to the creaks and groans of an older property in California. But this wasn't a creak or a groan, and it had come from outside.

His entire body tensed as he strained to identify the sound over the hiss of the coffeemaker.

Thunk.

Duffy's gaze cut to the kitchen window. There was movement. A blur of movement. And eyes. Bloodshot, beady eyes.

Later, Duffy couldn't recall if he'd released a primal yell or an unintelligible curse, but the kitchen reverberated with sound.

A face pressed to the bottom of the glass. Pale, wrinkled, with grayish-purple-tinged hair in pink curlers. It was his neighbor Eunice. No doubt on her tiptoes considering the house sat on a raised foundation.

Duffy charged toward the front door, grabbing a sweatshirt he'd left on the living room couch.

It was still dark outside. The sky above Parish Hill was tinged orange. Streetlights flickered off as an older woman in a white flowered housecoat and fuzzy pink slippers ran across his driveway.

"Eunice!"

She froze at the hedges marking the property boundary. Shoulders hunched, rollers trembling.

Duffy reminded himself that he was new to a town full of curious old folk. He reminded himself that Eunice was more than a bit of an odd duck. She'd brought him a brussels sprouts, chocolate and bacon casserole as a housewarming gift, and practically done inventory on his belongings. He reminded himself to be patient as he tried to modulate his tone, tried to ignore a voice in his head pointing out he slept in the buff in the hot summer months. "Can I help you with something, Eunice?"

"I was…" She turned around slowly. Her gaze dropped to the Hawaiian boxers his mother had given him last year and then flew back up to his face. "I was just looking for my cat."

"You don't have a cat." There was a man in town who rescued cats. He'd been by a couple of times already to see if Duffy was interested in adopting one, and he'd been vocal in his disappointment that Eunice wasn't a cat lover.

"I…uh…heard a cat."

"Eunice." Over the past few days, he'd been badgered about his past (met with dead silence), his love life (met with deadlier silence) and had his small sack of groceries inspected (met with near-dead patience). And now this.

His toes were frozen. The cold nipped at his restraint. It must be barely forty degrees. It wasn't good for either one of them to be out here half-dressed. "I'm not an interesting man. I make coffee in the morning. I go to work. I come home at night and make dinner. You know all that." He'd caught her looking out her window at him a few times.

She tried to laugh. It sounded as fake as he suspected it to be. "You think that I…" *Ha-ha-ha*. "It was the cat." That was her story and she was sticking to it.

"Whatever." He wasn't winning this battle. "Be careful looking for whatever it is you're looking for. If you fall in my yard while I'm in the shower…"

Her cheeks reddened, then she mumbled something he didn't catch and hurried into her dark house.

He'd checked out several homes before deciding on this one. Duffy was only renting with the option to buy the place. It'd suck to move again so soon, but he didn't relish living next door to Peeping Eunice.

LATER IN THE DAY, Duffy was managing a crew who were caning the vineyards across the road from the Mionetti sheep ranch. The Mionettis, an elderly couple born and raised in the valley, had sold the property they hadn't been using to the winery. Now it seemed as if they were selling tickets to watch Duffy and the other workers.

Cars crowded the Mionettis' long driveway. Several older residents clustered about. They squinted. They pointed. Eunice waved. Mr. Mionetti dragged out folding lawn chairs. Mrs. Mionetti brought out coffee and what looked like baked goods.

"Get used to it," Ryan, the assistant winemaker, who was recently out of graduate school, came up to explain. He held a pair of long loppers which he used to clip thicker vines. "We're entertainment."

"All we're doing is cutting the vines back and tying the remaining canes to the trellis system," Duffy grumbled. There had to be close to twenty people loitering on the Mionettis' lawn. It was another cold day. The sky was a crisp blue and the air bit at exposed skin. Surely at their ages, they shouldn't be outdoors.

Ryan shrugged his gangly shoulders. "Nothing much goes on in this town, so anything that does happen is watch-worthy. I'm told I'll understand it when I'm seventy. But for now, the combination of you and activity in the vineyards? It's like the Superbowl."

"More like Mardi Gras." Duffy turned his back on the spectators and snipped off a vine with his battery-powered pruning sheers. There were eleven men in the vineyard— some cutting, some tying, some throwing cuttings into bins. Usually that meant lots of talking or music being played, but today the audience seemed to have thrown the workers off.

A vehicle backfired.

Rutgar pulled into the vineyard's dirt driveway in his beat-up green truck, blocking Duffy's car in. Rutgar lumbered out, a pair of binoculars in hand. He propped his elbows on the hood, and surveyed Duffy and his crew. He was close enough, he could have whispered a question as to how it was going and Duffy would have heard him.

The old man's arrogance. The town's fandom. Eunice's peeping.

Duffy felt his anger rising. "You've got to be kidding me." He took a step toward Rutgar, only to be held back by Ryan.

"It's not worth it," the younger man said. "You want less attention, you hope someone more interesting comes to town. Or you make close friends with someone who lives here."

From what Duffy had heard, until the winery began selling wine, the chance of anyone new coming to town was slim. "What do you mean, 'make close friends'?"

"Pick someone in town. Tell them a few things about yourself. They'll become the conduit for town gossip and you get left alone."

Eunice in her pink curlers came to mind. Duffy suppressed a shudder. He'd rather recruit someone to move to town. "Hey, you don't live in Harmony Valley, do you?"

"I live in Cloverdale." The younger man's gaze slid away. "With my parents. Student loans, dude. They're killer." And then his trademark smile returned. "My moving here wouldn't make any difference. I have three fairy godmothers—Agnes, Mildred and Rose."

With effort, Duffy turned away from Rutgar and his binoculars. "Don't they feed you lunch?"

"Yep." Ryan gave a peace sign to the crowd. Appreciative shouts and laughter drifted back on a breeze. "And they do my laundry—which my mother refuses to do anymore."

Hello, mama's boy.

Duffy clipped a vine. "You're quite the chick magnet."

"I'll get there. I'd like to be debt-free first."

Having only recently had his financial burdens lifted, Duffy admired Ryan for that.

"Did you have fun in Vegas last weekend?" Ryan asked.

"Yep." It had been great to decide Friday afternoon to go somewhere on the spur of the moment. Another few weeks and he'd make another trip somewhere. Anywhere. "I can't wait to get away again." Duffy loved the lack of pressing family and financial obligations, embraced the idea of leaving just because he could.

What about Jessica's baby?

Duffy swept the thought aside. Jessica's baby wasn't his responsibility or any of his business.

He, on the other hand, was still at the center of these Harmony Valley residents' business. Increasingly so, much to his annoyance.

He couldn't wait for someone new to move to town.

CHAPTER FOUR

"WHAT'S A LITTLE RAIN?" Jessica asked herself sarcastically as she parked on Harmony Valley's Main Street on Saturday night. The rain had been coming down steadily for the entire drive. Now it was pouring.

She'd located the restaurant the other day before she left town. There'd been almost no one parked on the street then. Tonight, the diagonal spaces along Main were full. She'd had to find a spot a block away from El Rosal.

"Perfect." It wasn't. She hadn't brought an umbrella. With her baby bump, it was enough that she had to juggle her purse and walk. Adding an umbrella to the mix was a bit much for her equilibrium on a windy night. "So much for doing my hair." For the first time in months, she'd put her long hair in rollers. It tumbled about her shoulders in soft waves that made her feel more like her nonpregnant self.

She gathered her purse and raised the hood on her jacket. Her girth brushed against the steering wheel. Baby shimmied in a way that made her feel nauseous.

Jess counted to twenty, hoping the nausea would pass and the rain would let up. Her stomach settled. The rain intensified. It was nearly six. She couldn't sit here any longer.

She pushed open the door. Before her feet so much as swung out of the car, she was wet. Rain plastered her face and lap. She walked with lumbering steps toward El Rosal, feet splashing in barely seen puddles.

The wind practically blew her into the restaurant decorated in an overload of primary colors. Red, yellow, green, blue. Walls, tables, chairs. It looked as loud as it sounded. The place was full. The music was blaring. And so had the conversation been, until everyone turned her way and stopped talking.

Duffy stood at a table by the window, looking glad to see her.

People began whispering, and Duffy frowned, maybe not so glad to see her.

She'd never been good at making a graceful entrance, and tonight was no different. Her hair drooped and as usual she'd been unable to close her jacket. The red maternity sweater over her baby bump was wet and clinging. She met Duffy's gaze, and gestured toward the ladies' room.

The bathroom mirror revealed a drowned, pregnant raccoon. She wiped at the mascara beneath her eyes, used the hand dryer to blow most of her hair and the sweater over her belly dry and shook the rest of the water from her coat.

An elderly woman with teased, purplish hair and a kind smile entered the ladies' room as Jess was finishing. "Hello, sweets. Are you all right?"

"Just a little wet." Jessica stepped aside so the woman could wash her hands.

"I'm Eunice. Duffy's next-door neighbor." Jessica introduced herself.

Eunice took inventory of Jessica's clothes and belly, but not in a negative way. "Are you Duffy's girlfriend?"

"No!" The word burst forth with enough energy to heat Jessica's cheeks.

Someone knocked on the door. "Everything okay in there?" It was Duffy.

Eunice was still waiting for more of an answer.

"I'm, uh…not his, uh…"

"Jess?" Duffy again. Mr. Persistent.

Jess tried to smile. "I'm sorry... I...uh... I have pregnant brain."

Eunice's gray brows puckered together.

"Baby steals my brain cells."

When Eunice still looked confused, Jessica excused herself and hurried out.

Duffy led her across the dining room, looking small-town hip in work boots, jeans and a forest green Henley. "I saw Eunice follow you in." He pulled out a chair for Jess. "She can be a bit...overzealous."

She sat. "Eunice was fine." It was Jess who'd shouted like an angry cockatoo.

He'd ordered a bottle of beer, and had a glass of water for her. Chips and salsa served as the table's centerpiece.

"You missed a spot of mascara." He took a paper napkin and gently wiped at her cheek.

Greg ran the back of his hand across her cheekbone. "So beautiful."

That was love. That was definitely love.

Jess blinked, as Greg's face morphed into Duffy's. "Thank you."

While he sat, Jess took a moment to look around. The clientele was mostly in their seventies and eighties. They studied her with unabashed curiosity. "Is this seniors' night?"

"No. This is Harmony Valley, average age

seventy-five." He raised his beer bottle in salute.

"That must make for a swinging singles scene for you."

He almost smiled. She noted his lips twitching upward before he hid behind his beer.

"Why are they staring at me?" It was beginning to creep Jess out.

"They don't know you." He seemed half amused and half annoyed as he leaned closer to the woman at the table next to him, and practically shouted, "This is Jessica. She used to date my brother."

The woman nodded, smiled at Jess and then addressed the next table over and relayed the news.

Duffy righted himself and lowered his voice. "Sometimes you have to use your outside voice. They don't always wear their hearing aids."

Was he joking? "Have you been drinking?"

"This is my second." Of which he'd drank very little. "I've been in town less than a month. I'm still the new guy and a curiosity. Most people who've moved here recently are either related to someone or grew up here.

In a word, *known*." There was a sharpness to his voice that hinted at annoyance. "I'm a stranger. And I don't talk much."

He was talking just fine to her. Much better than he had the other day.

"They're still trying to figure me out." He raised a hand to acknowledge Eunice, who sat on the opposite side of the room with several other older women—all looking their way. "I caught Eunice peeping into my kitchen window the other morning."

Jess envisioned Eunice framed in her quaint kitchen window on the other side of a white picket fence. "So your houses are close?"

"Nope. Her nose was pressed against my glass."

He had to be pulling Jessica's leg. If so, she was glad. She enjoyed this man more than the one she'd first met. Baby must think so, too. Her little bundle of joy was still.

"And Felix over there." He tipped his bottle toward a barrel-chested man with what looked like cat hair sprinkled on his black polo shirt. "He'd like me better if I adopted a cat from him."

That didn't sound so bad.

Duffy nodded toward the huge man across

from Felix. "And Rutgar… I think Rutgar believes I'm the advance wave of a subversive group. I'm surprised he didn't bring his binoculars to keep a close eye on me tonight."

"Ouch."

"Yeah, it didn't really start until the day you showed up." He rubbed his hand back and forth over his hair, unintentionally spiking up the cowlick at his temple. "My coworkers at the winery tell me it'll pass, but after only a few days, it's starting to get to me. I don't share my life with strangers."

And yet, he'd essentially shared a lot with Jess in the past few minutes.

A fact he apparently realized, since he picked at the label of his beer and mumbled, "I told myself I wouldn't crack under the pressure."

Of Jessica's appearance? Or the town's nosiness?

The elderly woman at the table next to him reached over to touch his arm. "Duffy, we're all curious about Jessica's baby."

Duffy's eyebrows lowered to storm-warning levels.

"Due in two months," Jess said impulsively, adding a smile that felt as fake as the time the bakery circuit breakers had blown and Vera had filled her cookie case with store-bought goods.

Jessica's smile eased as she faced Duffy. His predicament—or more precisely, the serious import he gave it—was amusing. "So you don't like them prying."

"Exactly." He sank back into his seat. "Have you remembered anything else about Greg?" She could tell by his guarded tone that there were many more questions in the wings. For starters, whether she remembered if he'd swindled her or not.

"Not much."

Outside, the rain came down harder.

"Well, dinner tonight is my treat."

My treat.

Another rainy night. A flat tire. *Hot coffee. My treat.* An irresistible smile.

"Greg stopped to help me with a flat tire in the rain." Jessica's hopes floated high with the realization. "A random act of kindness." If that wasn't an indication that Duffy's brother wasn't a bad man, she didn't know what was.

"Saw you as an easy mark, no doubt." Duffy stared out at the rain. "A woman. Alone."

DUFFY COULD TELL Jessica didn't like his assessment of Greg.

Her dark eyes cooled, until they were as cold as the stormy night outside.

Oddly, when she'd come in, he'd felt they were in the same lifeboat in the midst of a graying sea. He'd lowered his guard. Not that it mattered much. After dinner, he and Jess probably wouldn't see each other again. He'd ask to be notified when the baby was born, but otherwise keep his distance.

"What do you do for a living?" Duffy asked after the waiter came by to take their order.

"I'm a baker."

Greg's target of choice had been more established, professional women. Jessica lacked the age and paycheck that Greg had preferred. The good news was that the baby wouldn't lack for birthday cakes.

Jessica's gaze had grown distant. "Greg liked things with cream filling. Éclairs. Cream-filled cupcakes. Danish."

"Yes." Duffy dipped a chip into the small bowl of salsa. "I don't doubt you didn't know him."

"I'm not trying to prove anything. I'm just happy to be remembering." She had steady, dark brown eyes. Trustworthy eyes. The kind a man could look into all night long while they discussed everything from the latest sports scores to the meaning of life. "I'll try not to share if it bothers you."

Her memories didn't bother him as much as the increasing empathy he felt toward her did. He had no idea if she was running a con or not. Until he knew for sure, he couldn't afford to feel anything but suspicion. Duffy pushed the small bowl across the table. "Salsa?"

"Baby doesn't like spicy food." Jess stared at the bowl, and sighed wistfully. "I miss it."

"Greg hated spicy food."

A smile curled slowly on her face. "He did, didn't he? He was a…meat-and-potatoes man. A griller. He had a barbecue!" This last was announced with as much fervor as a fan announcing a game-winning touchdown.

He compressed his lips to keep from smiling. "Top-of-the-line." Duffy had sold it. Why had Greg needed a grill that could cook forty burgers at a time? Because Greg only bought the best. "Do you remember the car he drove?"

Her slender brows drew down. "Blue. BMW. It had really stiff seats." She rubbed her forehead as if her head ached. "Don't ask me any more questions. Tell me something about Greg's childhood." She added quickly, "Something nice."

That gave Duffy pause. He hadn't thought about his brother in a kindly way for a long time. "He brought home a puppy once."

"How sweet. A rescue?" Jessica's eyes roved across his features and seemed to catalog his movements. She looked at him as if he were precious to her.

He suspected she was trying to see Greg in him. It should have been an intense intrusion. But her searching for Greg in Duffy's appearance and voice touched him. She believed she'd cared for Greg. Duffy was oddly grateful, because sometimes late at night when he couldn't sleep, he felt guilty for not mourning his brother more deeply.

"We thought the puppy was a rescue." Duffy cleared his throat, unexpectedly reluctant to destroy her good opinion of his brother even more. "Turns out Greg stole it from a pet store at the mall." And had tried to blame Duffy. That had been the beginning of the end of their twin bond.

"I wanted to hear something nice," Jess chastised softly.

It didn't escape his notice that she wasn't arguing the fact that Greg had stolen something.

"There must be some memory," she prompted in a voice so tender, so full of hope, that disappointing her would have been a crime. "One where you think of him fondly."

It should have taken longer to dredge up something positive. "We both received model airplanes one Christmas. Our cat knocked mine off a shelf and it broke. Greg gave me his." Duffy had to force the last words out. "Greg *used to be* generous like that."

"A plane." She beamed at him as if he'd given her an unexpected gift. Candy or flowers or something. "Greg took me to the airport once to…to…" Her smile wavered as she reached for the memory. "To watch the planes take off. He said one day he'd fly away and take me with him." Her smile wavered. "I bet you think that was a line."

It was hard to believe Jess was a con artist when she seemed so naive. Duffy hated to disillusion her, and so he chose his next words carefully. "Greg could be kind. And in that moment, he might have meant it."

Her small smile pleased him. It shouldn't have. If she wasn't who she said she was, he was making himself vulnerable, becoming a mark.

It's only dinner. Then she'll be gone.

Their food arrived as thunder clapped strong enough to shake El Rosal's foundation. The room echoed with gasps and expressions of surprise.

Shortly thereafter, the sheriff entered the restaurant, calling for quiet. He was one of the few residents Duffy's age. "The rain is coming down so fast the roads are beginning to flood, especially on the east side of town near the river and the highway. Cal-Trans has issued a warning about the highway being closed between here and Cloverdale."

People began asking for checks and reaching for their coats. Duffy exchanged a glance with Jessica.

Hers was worry-filled. "The highway's closed?"

Duffy shared her concern. He called Sheriff Nate over. "There's no way to get out of town and back to Santa Rosa?"

"Not tonight. And maybe not tomorrow." Nate's expression was grim.

But it wasn't as grim as Duffy felt. "There's still no hotel in town?"

Nate shook his head. "I hear the Lambridge sisters want to open a bed-and-breakfast, but they haven't moved back here yet. Are you looking for a place to stay, Miss…"

"She can stay at my place, Nate." Duffy'd spoken before he realized what he was saying. Had he been played?

"Oh, I couldn't," Jessica protested, all wide-eyed innocence.

"It's that or the jail," Nate said, glancing at her baby bump, with much the same bachelor wariness Duffy had felt the first time he'd seen Jess.

"I'll take her home," Duffy repeated, trying not to let regret seep into his voice. "Finish your dinner." Although he'd lost his appetite.

Nate moved on to other tables, making sure people had rides home. Given how hard it was coming down and the way some of the elderly residents were unsteady on their feet, walking in many cases was an accident waiting to happen. The sheriff quickly assigned people that had come on foot into car pools.

Eunice pulled up a chair at their table and smiled triumphantly, like the cat who'd eaten the unsuspecting blue bird of happiness. "The sheriff said you could see me home."

Thunder boomed above them again. The lights flickered.

It was going to be a long night.

CHAPTER FIVE

DUFFY WAS A GENTLEMAN.

Not only had he offered Jess a place to stay, but since he'd walked from his house, he'd asked for Jessica's keys and braved the rain to bring her car to the restaurant's front door. Jessica waited in the crowded lobby of El Rosal with Eunice and the rest for vehicles to be brought around, hopeful that being stranded meant Baby would have a positive relationship with Uncle Duffy someday.

The sheriff braved the downpour and as vehicles pulled up, he called out the names of waiting passengers. It wasn't long before he announced, "Eunice and Jessica."

Eunice held on to Jessica's arm as they picked their way through the puddles to Jessica's car. Rain pelted them in big, angry drops, bouncing off the pavement and back at them.

Duffy was scrunched in the driver's seat, shoulders hunched and knees bent on either side of the steering wheel. "I couldn't get the seat to go back any farther," he admitted when Jess noticed. "Good thing it's a short drive."

"The last time this happened was 1992," Eunice said from the backseat. "The roads were flooded for five days."

Jessica began to feel foolish for ignoring the flood warnings. She didn't want to be trapped with Duffy for five days. Not to mention, Vera would fire her.

The rain pounded on the roof and the windshield wipers could barely keep their view clear. Duffy drove slowly, but they still created a wake in the rising water.

"When we get rain, we really get rain," Eunice was saying over all the storm noise, as if she were their personal tour guide. "Sometimes the rain doesn't stop for days. The clouds can't seem to make it past the range that starts with Parish Hill."

Neither Jessica nor Duffy said a word. She could tell by Duffy's gripping and regripping the wheel that he was having second thoughts about inviting her to stay since it might be for more than one night.

A turn onto the town square, a turn off the

town square and they were at Eunice's house. Duffy pulled into her driveway.

"Thanks for the ride," Eunice sing-songed. "I'll see you in the morning, Jessica."

"Let's hope we don't see her while I'm making coffee," Duffy muttered after he'd escorted the old woman to her door. He waited until Eunice was safely inside her house with the lights on before backing out and parking Jessica's car next to his truck.

Duffy's house was a small, old home with gingerbread gables. Most of it was dark and in shadow. The porch light barely reached beyond the front steps.

He waited in the downpour for Jessica to come around the hood, and then took her arm and led her up the stairs to the door. He paused with his key in the lock, gazing down on her with an endearingly sweet smile she'd never have suspected he possessed. "I can't remember what state the house is in."

"I don't care, as long as it's dry." She was wet, and starting to shiver.

He opened the door and turned on a light in the foyer. "Stay here while I do a quick run-through."

"I'm not Eunice. I won't snoop to see

what's in your fridge or which magazines you keep in your bathroom."

"I meant…" His grin turned mischievous, making Baby do an equilibrium-busting tummy flip. "I have a tendency to shed my clothes as I come. I usually leave them on the floor like…um, bread crumbs leading to the shower."

"By all means, pick up your unmentionables." Jess removed her jacket, hanging it on a coatrack near the door. Next to go were her wet sneakers. She held the damp sweater away from her skin. Baby was hunkered on her bladder. As soon as Duffy gave the okay, she was restroom bound.

The living room had worn hardwood floors and a fireplace with built-in white bookshelves on either side. Beyond that, the main room was classic, out-of-date bachelor pad—a brown leather couch, a black lacquered coffee table and a television mounted over the mantel. The small oak dining room table beneath the kitchen pass-through was in worse shape than Jessica's. Nothing was hung on the walls, but photos of people were on a couple of shelves.

At the risk of seeming as nosy as Eunice, Jess moved closer.

There were several photos of an older couple with salt-and-pepper hair. The man was in a wheelchair, and had Duffy and Greg's dark coloring. The woman had their smile, so rarely seen on Duffy's face. Sometimes Duffy was in the pictures with them, but never Greg. There was only one picture of Greg. He stood with Duffy in front of a Christmas tree. They might have been eight or nine. Slender bodies, pants that were too short for their long legs and T-shirts they didn't fill out. They were both grinning and holding baseball mitts.

Duffy wasn't as heartless as he appeared, which meant neither was Greg. Warmth blossomed in Jessica's chest.

"All clear." Duffy returned and removed his boots. "The house is only eight hundred square feet." He began pointing. "Kitchen that way. The three doors over there are my bedroom, the bathroom and my home office. You can sleep in my room."

"I'll sleep on the couch." Jess sat on it, sinking-sinking-sinking, realizing too late she should have taken a bathroom break first. Otherwise, the sleeping-arrangement stand-off was going to be short-lived.

"Yeah. That's not happening." The mischievous Duffy had gone, replaced by the resolute man she'd first met. "You'll take my bed. I'll change the sheets."

"No. Really. I'll be fine right here." She grunted attractively—not—as she lifted her legs onto the couch. It proceeded to swallow her in the crack. "I couldn't get up if you asked me to." But she would if Baby bounced one more time on her bladder.

He leaned on the back of the couch and stared down at her with hauntingly familiar, caramel-colored eyes.

"You were sleeping," Greg said, leaning on the back of the couch. "I didn't want to wake you." She'd reached for him and he'd taken her hand...

"Did you remember something just now?"

"Not enough to be meaningful." Had she looked at Duffy the way she'd looked at Greg? Her body felt as overheated as an oven set to broil. She tried maneuvering into a more upright sitting position so that Duffy could sit, too. The couch almost won the battle. "Greg had a great couch." Cup holders and everything.

"Sold it." Duffy knelt by the fireplace, where there was split wood ready to be lit.

Again she noticed his economy of movement, even when he started a fire.

When Greg moved, there'd been bold statements and unleashed energy. There'd been excitement and noise. Drama and passion.

Tired and wet, Jess appreciated Duffy's calm. "So you went through Greg's stuff and there was nothing about me?"

"Nope." He stood, leaning on the mantel and regarding her. Steady. Oh, so steady.

She frowned as an image teased the corners of her mind. "Maybe I'm imagining it, but I think I gave him a picture of us at a… um…a local food festival?"

"Nope," he said again, not pulling any punches.

The image sharpened. "It might have been in a heart-shaped silver frame. On his mantel." Or was her memory influenced by the pictures in the room and Duffy next to the fireplace?

"I found a heart-shaped frame, but it was in his desk drawer." His gaze slid to the pictures on his right. He repositioned the Christmas photo. "The frame was empty."

Jess felt empty, too, as if someone had carved out her heart. "Why would Greg do that?" she whispered, rubbing her belly, where Baby's little knee or hip was protruding, creating a numb spot.

Duffy was back to studying her. He would have made a good trial lawyer. "Didn't you find pictures of you two on your phone or social media?"

"I shut off my social media accounts when I went to culinary school because I didn't want to be tagged in something that would haunt me later." The few friends she still had from foster care and high school could be irresponsible and post things that could cost Jess a job. "And since I've been on a budget, I've had a little cheap phone, nothing fancy."

"You made it easy for him." Duffy shook his head. "You said a week before the accident your bank account was drained. Greg probably destroyed everything that tied you two together."

"I don't want to believe Greg was like that." That she'd meant nothing more to him than the money he could take from her.

Duffy sank into the other couch corner, but he was tall and had long legs. He didn't sink as far as she did. "Why is it so important to you that you meant something to him?"

"Because of Baby. Every child deserves to

be loved." She shifted again, but Baby didn't like it. A round of kicking ensued, delaying her explanation. "Every baby deserves to be created from love." Jessica had no clue if she'd been created from love or not. Her mother had abandoned her in a homeless shelter when she was nine.

Duffy stared pensively into the growing flames.

Did he agree? Did he think she was a gullible fool? "Say something."

"I was just thinking that my parents tried for a long time to have a baby and then they had twins." His gaze landed on her belly. "Do you want the baby? Are you going to keep it?"

Give up Baby? If she could've launched herself out of the couch, she would have. "I'm excited to be a mother. I can't wait to swaddle this baby with love."

"But children are such a huge responsibility in terms of time and money." There was more than a note of caution in his voice. There was certainty. And rejection. But not of her.

"Are you saying you don't want kids because they're inconvenient and cost a lot?"

He hesitated, staring at her as if weighing how much he should admit to, and then he nodded.

Jess glanced from the pictures of his family, and then back to him. "You *never* want kids or a family?"

He didn't so much as flinch. "I might get married someday, but no. I don't want any additional responsibilities. I don't even have a dog."

"Or a cat," she murmured, inexplicably saddened. "Why not?"

BECAUSE DUFFY WANTED a break from responsibility. Permanently.

After fifteen years of struggling to make ends meet, the thought of having a child, of being responsible for another life for eighteen years plus, had Duffy's muscles drawn tighter than a guide wire strung from post to post in the vineyard.

He didn't have to answer Jessica, but he felt compelled to.

"When I was fifteen, my dad was in an accident at work. It put him in a wheelchair." Duffy gestured toward the photos on either side of the fireplace. "He qualified for worker's compensation. And he got a lawyer who sued the company for a long-term settlement. But it took years for that money to come in. Years." In the meantime, for a teenager there'd been uncertainty, fear and shame as little by little everything he'd taken for granted had been stripped away—nice clothes, dinners out, the promise of a car when he earned his license. "My mom had to hire someone to care for Dad so she could work. I got a job to help out. And Greg… Well, he always said he had a job, but he never contributed money to the household." The words stung. "He'd come home with things he'd found 'by the roadside'—a new television still in the box, a microwave when ours broke. You get the idea."

Jessica frowned, palms cradling her baby bump.

"When Dad's settlement finally came in, I was incredibly relieved. I'd been accepted to college and I was on the brink of not going because money was just too tight." Duffy had lost ten pounds worrying about his future and theirs. "But the check came in. Dad paid for my first semester of college and off I went, leaving my brother behind to take care of them." Or so he'd hoped.

Jessica bowed her head, as if steeling herself to hear the worst.

"Greg offered to help run the household by paying the bills. Dad gave him access to his accounts. Greg said he had a new job, and he bought a new car. Soon he had the latest cell phone and a new wardrobe." Duffy swallowed, wishing there was a different ending to the story. He hadn't been smart enough to protect his parents at eighteen, but he could protect Jess by being honest so she'd never get swindled again. "Greg told my parents he was being sent for training in San Francisco. He left the week before Thanksgiving, and then he disappeared, along with the money in my dad's bank account." Duffy couldn't look at Jess anymore. But he had to finish. She had to know. "We didn't have a lot to be thankful for that year."

Jessica sat very still. "He wouldn't."

"He did." Duffy forced himself to meet her gaze, to keep the emotion out of his voice, to pretend he was over Greg's betrayal. "Dad didn't believe it, either. He refused to file a police report. He thought it was all a big mistake." That went on for about a year, until his old man could no longer avoid the truth—Greg was a thief. And not even a principled thief like Robin Hood. "I found a job working at a vineyard and kept going to school.

I lived frugally—no cell phone, a car I was constantly working on to keep running, borrowing books from friends taking the same classes. Because my parents still needed financial help."

Outside, thunder rolled. Inside, a log popped. Between them, tension crackled.

It had to be done. If she continued to romanticize Greg, she'd be an easy mark for the next guy. She had to hear all of it.

"I tried to find Greg after I graduated from college. I never located him, but I learned he was quite the ladies' man, seducing women and taking their money." Most of the women had been married and didn't want to admit they'd been played. "I have no idea why Greg filled out next-of-kin papers on his bank accounts or created a living trust for his assets. That's the only way we found out he'd died."

"You really think he stole from me?" she asked in a small voice, staring at her baby bump.

"I know he did."

"So…" Those dark, trustworthy eyes lifted to his. "Some of the money you recovered could be mine."

CHAPTER SIX

"I'M NOT ASKING for money," Jess clarified, not only because she meant it, but because Duffy's face had pinched and paled. "That's not why I'm here."

His features hardened like an overcooked scone. She'd ruined scones, ruined pastry with promise, ruined the fragile fabric of friendships. She'd come to Harmony Valley for her memories. She'd found so much more—the possibility of a family for her little one. She didn't want to ruin this for Baby.

Jess tried again. "I was only pointing out that if Greg took the money—*which I'm sure he didn't*—it would have been in his bank account. I'm not asking for anything. I just want my memories back."

His cool gaze said he didn't believe her.

Baby decided her bladder made a lovely pillow, one that needed fluffing. Jess wasn't feeling fluffy or pillow-soft. She was feeling as cold and hard as a lump of stale brown sugar. "I've always made my own way. And I've owned up to my mistakes. If what you say is true about Greg…" She paused to adjust how she was sitting, so both she and the baby were comfortable, using the time to remove the note of hysteria from her voice. "It's a mistake I made."

"Most people would disagree," Duffy said, as if aware of the tightrope they were walking with army boots on. "How much money did he take from you?"

Enough to buy a no-frills new car or start a great college fund or allow her to spend several months home after the baby was born. "It doesn't matter." The door to resentment, the one filled with embarrassing, hurtful memories of a life with no alternative but charity, banged open. And with that bang came a biting rush of outrage at being thought of as destitute. "I spent nine years living in a foster-care barracks with seven other girls. The woman who asked we call her Mother received a good salary to take care of us." It hurt to swallow the indignity of being boarded like a dog. There'd been no love, no nurturing, just a head count. "She got a salary. To be called *Mother*."

"But how much—"

"I won't ask you for a cent!" She awkwardly pushed herself to her feet. She'd had enough of relationships measured by dollar signs. If she told Duffy a figure, that's all she'd be to him, that's all her child would be to him. "I won't take your money. I won't even sleep in your bed tonight. The sheriff mentioned I could sleep at the jail."

Thunder rolled across the valley. It might as well have been resentment rumbling in her veins.

"Somehow, I don't think the jail will be as comfortable as my bed."

"I don't care." She was shaking. Her hands, her legs, her voice. "I've slept in worse places." On air mattresses and park benches and concrete floors.

"I didn't mean to hurt your feelings." He got to his feet, arms out placatingly.

She didn't see Duffy. She saw Greg. Heard his voice. Wondered if he'd lied. *I need a little money to tide me over. You trust me, don't you?*

Suddenly, Jess didn't feel as if she'd trusted Greg. But she'd loved him. She just knew. She'd loved him.

"Duffy, I want to look after myself and my baby. And to do that, I can't blame my situation or my mistakes on someone else. I can't accept a handout." Her mother's face came to mind, thin and taut with worry as she stroked Jessica's hair that last night at the homeless shelter. *You're a strong girl, Jess. You can make it on your own.* Jessica had clung to her mother's words after she'd disappeared, locked them tight in her heart when times were tough. She stepped around the corner of the couch, nearer the door, nearer the bathroom.

"I never said…" Duffy moved to block her path, looking perplexed. "Can we back up the conversation? To somewhere around the time I invited you to spend the night because the road's flooded?"

"No." The bathroom was in her sights and Baby was fluffing the bladder pillow again. "I told myself I'd never be like my mother and walk away from a child because there wasn't enough money. I work hard so that won't happen."

But what if she couldn't make it work? Vera had already begun asking questions about maternity leave and schedules once she returned. She'd hired Jess out of culinary school, and Jess suspected she was the highest-paid baker of the bunch, the only one with formal training, the only one who didn't speak Spanish, the only one who didn't fit in.

The tremble in Jessica's limbs locked her shoulders back.

Duffy was frowning. His frown conveyed doubt. Not suspicious doubt, but a kind of self-doubt, as if he was questioning what he knew. "I don't know what went on between you and my brother. I don't know how he got your money. But one thing I do know. You're never giving up that baby."

His words touched her, soothed and comforted. She was no longer shaking, no longer on the defensive.

"So you'll stay."

She gave him the stiffest of nods, and then beelined to the bathroom.

HE'D SAID TOO much about Greg and the assets he'd liquidated after his brother's death. But other than pointing out the money in Greg's bank account was most likely hers, Jessica claimed not to want anything from him.

Doubt prickled his insides like a porcupine with raised hackles.

His brain whispered, *Don't believe her. She was in league with Greg.*

But there was his heart—the part of him Greg had called soft and sentimental more than once—smoothing the hackles of suspicion: *She's not like Greg.*

Duffy changed the sheets on his king-size bed. He used the flannel set his mother had given him for Christmas, the ones he didn't like because they were too warm. Jess needed something soft and warm tonight. Duffy needed something no one could give him—complete faith in Jessica. He wanted to trust her, but there was Greg and there was a history of lies upon lies, twist-tied with lies.

"I'll sleep on the couch." Jess stood in the doorway. Her hands pressed into the small of her back as if it ached. "May I have a pillow and a blanket?"

"No." Clearly, this woman had developed an independent streak nearly as strong as Duffy's distrust of Greg. "The pillows and blankets stay in this room."

"I'm pregnant. Baby can sleep anywhere." Her smile had a you-should-believe-me quality that Duffy found hard to believe. She hadn't looked comfortable sitting on the couch. How would she sleep on it?

"If my mother hears I let you sleep on the couch, I'll never hear the end of it."

Jess hesitated, and then asked in a soft voice, "You're going to tell her about me?"

"Yes." He hadn't thought about it until then, but his parents would want to know. Or at the very least, they should be told. He'd held up on telling them about Jess because he wasn't sure of her agenda in tracking him down. He was still hesitant about the money, but… "My mom's going to spoil that kid rotten."

"Do you think so?" Jessica's whisper was pockmarked with wonder, thready with hope.

Her reaction made him put on a show of confidence. *"Please."* Duffy rolled his eyes for effect. "She points out babies to me like other parents point out good job opportunities." That much was the truth.

Head bowed, Jess rested her palm on her stomach. "Did you hear that, Baby? Grandparents are in your future."

For the first time, Duffy understood Jess. She had no parents. She couldn't remember her baby's father. She didn't want to let her child down as her mother had done. What to him was a casual mention of his mother's involvement was the promise of a special gift to her: *family*.

He hoped he hadn't misspoken. He hoped his mother would be excited about the news.

"I'm taking this pillow from the bed for me," Duffy said carefully. "Don't get any ideas."

She blinked at him. But it wasn't the I'm-remembering-something dazed look he'd seen her get every once in a while. Jess stared at him as if seeing him for the first time. As Duffy, not Greg's mirror image.

That look registered something deep inside him, something that warmed and eased, something he'd kept locked away and refused to name. A feeling he immediately dismissed.

Because Duffy had sworn off taking on any more responsibility, be it community, friends or family.

CHAPTER SEVEN

As SHE PREDICTED, the rain rivaled the storm of 1992. All the roads out of town remained flooded.

Eunice cackled. She was thrilled. Jessica wasn't leaving today.

Eunice was only being neighborly taking over this warm dish for breakfast. It had nothing to do with uncovering what might or might not have gone on last night. The question burning in her elderly mind was: Whose baby was Jessica's?

"Eunice." Duffy opened the door wearing blue jeans, a maroon T-shirt and thick wool socks. He stared down on her with a look that would have chilled younger beings. "What a surprise."

Eunice blinked at him. *See my pretty eyes. Be mesmerized by my pretty eyes.* Blink-blink-blink. "I brought breakfast." She stopped blinking long enough to try to peer around him, but couldn't see a thing.

He hadn't opened the door very wide and his shoulders were so incredibly broad.

"We had breakfast already."

"Maybe you'd like this for lunch." She held the warm casserole dish close to her chest, not wanting to hand it to him and lose the opportunity to come inside. "Why don't I just put this in the kitchen for you?"

There was a coldness to Duffy's features this morning, as if he'd awoken from centuries of slumber in a block of ice to find everything around him wasn't as it once was. "You're not going to go away, are you?"

His direct question took her by surprise. "I live next door."

The rain beat steadily while he studied her.

"I mean..." He sighed, rubbing a palm over the dark whiskers covering his chin. "You want to come in. Right now."

"Thank you for the invitation." She bumped her arm against the door, causing it to swing open wider. Ducking past him, she headed toward the kitchen, raincoat, rain galoshes and all.

Inside, everything was clean. The kitchen. The stove. The living room. From the kitchen pass-through she could see a folded blanket on top of a pillow on the hearth. Cross out the suspicion that they were lovers. Someone had slept on the couch.

"Where's Jessica?"

"In the shower." Duffy raised an eyebrow. "Did you come to see if something was going on?"

"No." Eunice sniffed. Why did the man always seem to know what she was up to? He'd probably ask her to leave next. "I came to be neighborly."

"You're dripping all over my kitchen." He stared at the trail of water she'd made across his hardwood floor, sighed wearily, and pointed toward the door. "Boots and jacket go in the foyer."

He was letting her stay? A rush of excitement had Eunice scurrying over to shed her wet things.

Duffy dragged a towel across the hardwood floor with his foot. "How's that cat?"

"I don't have a…" Too late, Eunice realized she'd been caught.

"Ah, I got you." He chuckled, but it was a chilly chuckle. He finished cleaning, sat on his couch and picked up the remote.

Shoot-shoot-shoot. "I had a cat. Once."

His television was tuned to one of those sports news channels that didn't interest Eunice. The sound was muted, but by the way his thumb roved the remote, she could tell he wanted to turn it back on. Instead, he said, "Cats are independent creatures. Did it run away because it wanted privacy?"

Annoyance elbowed aside the embarrassment Eunice had been feeling. "That's not a very nice thing to say." Didn't he know how to be a good neighbor?

"I'm not in a very nice mood in the mornings, Eunice, not until I've had more than one cup of coffee." A mug rested on the black lacquered coffee table.

She considered his closed-off expression, weighing it against the grumpy texture of his mood. "How many cups have you had?"

"This is my second." He angled his head toward her, wrinkling his nose. "What's that smell? It came in with you."

Eunice squared her shoulders proudly and moved toward the kitchen. She so rarely had a chance to show off her cooking skills. "It's bananas wrapped in ham with hollandaise sauce." It had been one of her mother's favorite recipes. "Would you like some?"

Duffy opened his mouth to speak, but nothing came out.

Jessica emerged from the bathroom, wearing gray sweats that dragged on the floor and an army-green sweatshirt that stretched across her girth. She looked like a child who'd raided her father's closet. Or more likely, Duffy's. "What's that smell?"

Eunice widened her eyes and gave Jessica her sweetest smile, the one that always landed her modeling jobs. "Bananas wrapped in ham with hollandaise sauce."

"It's just as shocking the second time you say it," Duffy muttered.

Jessica placed a hand over her mouth and nose. "Baby is sensitive to smells, but it sounds...*lovely*. Is there a story behind it?"

"It's a Fletcher family favorite, born of the need to entice my younger sister to eat. She loved bananas and she loved hollandaise sauce." They both stared at Eunice. She stood in the kitchen doorway holding her smile and herself very still, because that's what beauties did. They held still for everyone's regard.

Jessica made a small mewling noise, which Eunice translated to *yum*.

Duffy was suddenly on the move and heading toward Eunice. She'd forgotten the magnetism of her pose, the allure of her smile, the power of her incredible eyes.

"Whoa, big fella." Eunice raised a hand.

Men in her day weren't as tall a specimen as Duffy. "I know I pack some powerful mojo." And it had been years since she'd wielded it toward a man. "I'll tone it down a notch or two." Turn her smile into a small, secretive one, take her peepers off her wide-and-innocent setting.

Duffy paused in front of her. All six-foot-plus of big, intense man. "I'm here for the dish."

Eunice felt a jolt of indignation. She was *not* that kind of woman. "I'm old enough to be your grandmother," she sputtered.

"I'm here for *that* dish." He pointed to her casserole.

"Oh." *Pity.* For a moment, she'd felt twenty-five again.

"Let's put it in the stove for now." Duffy slid her dish into the oven, and then opened a window. "Coffee?"

"Please. It's my one vice." Eunice didn't count chocolate as a vice. Or keeping up with the neighbors. Those were necessities.

"Cream and sugar?"

"Is there any other way?"

"No, ma'am." He opened a cupboard filled with coffee mugs.

Eunice rose up on tiptoe to see inside,

and then dropped back on her heels in disappointment. There were no university logos, no Playboy bunnies, no comic book characters. Nothing to say what kind of man Duffy was. There were business mugs. Sam's Auto. Mike's Tractor Repair. Hancock's Fertilizer. Boring.

Duffy opened an old canning jar that had sugar in it—not packets, not sugar substitute. Real granulated sugar. His refrigerator was loaded and looked as if a woman had stocked it with healthy food.

Eunice hadn't known what to expect, but it wasn't this...this...averageness.

Jessica entered the kitchen and filled a glass with water, easy as you please. She rolled up the sleeves of her oversize sweatshirt another turn. "Thanks for the loaners, Duffy. And for letting me do laundry." Her feet were bare except for the velvety-brown color on her toenails.

Eunice had never been pregnant. "When is that baby due?" Soon, by the look of her.

Jessica waddled out to the living room. "Two more months."

"That long?" Eunice accepted her coffee from Duffy and trailed after Jessica. "You look ready to…" She didn't think *pop* was a politically correct term. "Ready to *go*."

"Nice save," Duffy murmured.

He really had the most annoying way about him. Eunice almost felt as if he didn't take her seriously.

Eunice dragged a dining room chair with arms near the couch. "Whose baby is it?" She smiled expectantly at Duffy.

"Not mine," Duffy said flatly.

Jessica's brows met together. She had the most beautiful skin and her long dark hair wasn't bad, either, but she shouldn't frown. It caused wrinkles. "It's—"

"None of your business, Eunice." Duffy sat on the couch opposite Jessica and cradled his coffee cup in both hands.

"Well…" Eunice regrouped with what she knew. "Sadie told Agnes that Jessica used to date your dead cousin or uncle or something."

"My life is like a game of geriatric telephone." Duffy contemplated the ceiling. "She dated my deceased *brother*. But that doesn't mean—"

"I can't prove who the baby's father is," Jessica said, making Eunice's jaw drop and

Duffy's brows draw down. "I'm sure it was Duffy's brother, but I can't remember."

Eunice leaned forward. "Why not? Were you drugged? Were you kidnapped? Did you have some kind of psychotic episode?"

"It was immaculate," Duffy blurted, earning two feminine scowls for his impertinence.

Eunice could barely sit still. This was better than the time Chadwick Spencer had fallen off a ship off the coast of Africa and returned years later with a beard and a scar and a vendetta. Of course, that was on a soap opera. This was the real thing!

Eunice was going to be queen of the next meeting for Mae's Pretty Things. If only she could collect more details. If only she could wait until next Saturday to say anything. If only the rain continued all winter, trapping Jessica here for good.

DUFFY NEEDED THE kink in his back worked out. He needed a few hours of uninterrupted sleep in his own bed. He needed his normally quiet Sunday morning.

Nothing was quiet with Eunice around. "Long story short, Eunice, Jess has amnesia."

Eunice raised a hand to her cheek and

gasped dramatically, as if she were a star in a silent film. She blinked at Jessica in that owlish way of hers. "Do you know who you are? Who the president is? What year it is?"

"Yes." Jess explained about her condition, occasionally flashing Duffy looks that said his rudeness and sarcasm weren't appreciated.

Give Jess a week with Eunice stalking her and she'd change her tune.

A week?

He didn't want Jessica to be here another day. Every time he'd nodded off during the night, an odd thought would jolt him awake, until he was bleary-eyed and lay staring at the ceiling, waiting for a reasonable hour to get up and make coffee. Those thoughts terrified him.

Jess can't make it on her own with a baby to support.

That baby is Greg's and deserves his money.

Someone should check on her regularly to make sure she and the baby are okay.

He'd spent the past fifteen years trying to balance the needs of his future with the needs of his parents. Weekends spent making sure Mom got a break and Dad could get out in the world. Nights spent juggling figures, trying to make his salary stretch to support two households. Watching commercials for vacations on television knowing he could never afford to get away.

Was it too much to ask that he not have another family member come into this world that needed his help?

Jess doesn't want my help.

He should have been relieved. Instead, his brain rejected her independence. His brain worked out ways to help her without seeming to. Dropping packages of diapers on her doorstep. Setting up a college fund. Encouraging his parents to watch the kid an afternoon or two a week. His brain wasn't supposed to be on nurturer mode.

Outside, the rain kept up a steady downpour. If Duffy squinted, the continuous drops on his windows looked like thin bars.

"So all you need is stimulation of your mind to remember." Eunice popped out of her seat and eagerly hurried to the bookshelves with Duffy's family pictures. She picked up a photo of his parents standing in front of their old house, moving the frame in and out. She slid on a pair of black glasses, hunching over as if she didn't want anyone to see her wear corrective lenses. Tucking them away, she faced Jess. "Here. Look at this. Perhaps it will help. They're just average old people, but—"

"Those are my parents," Duffy grumbled. "She's never met them."

"How do you know?" Eunice glanced down at the picture, squinting, but her secret was out. She was blind as a bat. No wonder she'd had to press her face against his kitchen window.

"Maybe Greg had a picture like this at his apartment," Jessica said kindly, accepting the photo.

Duffy could tell by the blank look on Jessica's face that the image didn't jar any memories.

"Does your dad come here to visit?" Jess asked, studying the picture.

"Not yet." Did she recognize his parents? "See anyone you know?"

"No. I'm just…trying to remember if Greg had any family pictures in his apartment."

"He didn't." Nothing personal, either.

Jess nodded. "It was like walking into a high-end hotel room. Impersonal, but lavish."

Duffy hadn't thought of Greg's things that way before. He'd looked at the extravagance and thought about the number of utility bills or car insurance payments that might have been made. He hadn't taken in the apartment in total. Jess was right. There was remoteness to it.

Jessica spoke softly. "It makes me sad to think he'd live that way, distancing himself from his family."

Without having to take responsibility or care for others. For a moment, Duffy envied Greg.

The moment was short-lived. He'd never envy a thief, especially one who sounded like he'd been lonely. "Do you have pictures in your apartment, Jess?" Duffy tried to envision what her place would look like. Comfortable furniture, for sure. Maybe an afghan for when she napped on the couch.

"A few. My friends from culinary school. A picture of me at my high school graduation. None of family..."

Because she had none.

"I have pictures on display at my house." His neighbor was hunched in front of his bookshelves, trying to hide the fact that she had those Clark Kent glasses back on.

"Eunice, which bothers you more?" Duffy was in an ornery enough mood to smile as he asked, "Needing your glasses to snoop or the fact that you don't have free rein of my house?"

The old woman startled at his question and fumbled to take her cheaters off. "Glasses? I... I don't need glasses." She returned to her seat, spots of color on her cheeks that made Duffy regret teasing her. But only a little.

"You have very pretty eyes." Jessica made up for his bad manners with kindness.

Eunice angled her head and batted her eyes as if posing for a camera. "I do, don't I?"

Even Jess, tolerant as she was, struggled to hide a smile.

The older woman fluffed her purple-tinted hair. "I was a model, mostly for makeup and...eyeglasses. I was flown everywhere—New York, Paris, Japan. Until Daddy died and Mama said we didn't need to work anymore." This last part seemed laden with regret.

Jess made a sympathetic noise. "Your father was wealthy?"

"It was really Mama who came from money, but Daddy was convinced we had to save for a rainy day, which meant we all had jobs. Lucky for me, Mama knew that I could earn a living with my purple eyes."

Duffy may have been blind to reds and greens, but he saw nothing special in Eunice's eyes. They looked brown to him. And he couldn't imagine her as a model. She was short and age-rounded. Her hair was an unnatural color. He supposed if she didn't scuttle around bushes and spy on him—last week he'd found her behind his trash can—he might say she had a friendly smile.

His gaze drifted toward Jessica. She was beautiful. Her long hair was dark, almost black, the color of rich walnut wood. Her eyes were also dark, wide and expressive. Her face and body were filled out and curvy from the pregnancy, but there was something delicate about the way she moved her hands that gave the impression of grace. She considered her actions and words carefully. She'd never blink her eyes owlishly at him and overshare. She'd enter and be everyone's calm and reliable rock.

Sure, she'd shown up in Harmony Valley and asked if he was her husband. But she hadn't been hysterical. She may get upset when he touched on a nerve, like when he challenged that self-reliant streak of hers, but he doubted much rattled her. She was taking

Eunice's interrogation as calmly as if they were discussing the weather.

Jess was a surprise. Surely, she'd surprised Greg. Maybe he'd loved her. Maybe he'd regretted taking her money.

And maybe pigs could sprout wings and perform flybys at football games.

He didn't want to think about Greg.

Duffy sank deeper into the couch, letting his eyes close, listening to the women without hearing their words.

CHAPTER EIGHT

"WAS YOUR MOTHER a good cook?" Jess asked Eunice, trying hard not to think about how horrifying the smell of the hollandaise and banana dish had been.

In his corner of the couch, Duffy's eyes were shut. At rest, the distance and skepticism were in remission, the barely veiled pain and sarcasm only traces in the air. Everything about him gentled, became more approachable, more in line with her memories of Greg, which should have brought her dead lover's face to mind. But try as she might, Jess couldn't recall watching Greg doze, couldn't superimpose Greg's face over Duffy's.

"Mama was inventive," Eunice was saying. "Ahead of her time in the kitchen. She made the best grilled-cheese-and-jelly sandwiches." While Jess tried to wrap her head around those tastes, Eunice continued. "When Daddy was alive, butter was sometimes too expensive for his budget, and Mama didn't approve of margarine. First she tried frying cheese sandwiches on top of pickle slices. Then she experimented with frying them in tomato juice. But the big hit was slathering both sides of the bread with jelly and frying them up in the pan."

Jessica's stomach rumbled. Grilled cheese and jelly didn't sound half-bad.

"He's lonely," Eunice whispered in a voice that blended with the persistent rain. She inclined her head toward Duffy. "I'm so glad you're here. Is he like his brother?"

"I can't really say." Her gaze drifted toward the photo of Greg and Duffy as boys in front of the Christmas tree. At first glance, they were exactly alike. Closer inspection revealed Greg's smile had been wider, bigger, brighter. They were the same, but different.

Duffy's home felt like Greg's—not that she remembered Greg's apartment in detail. But there was a feeling that everything was in its place in both abodes. The difference was that where Greg's apartment had felt luxurious, Duffy's felt utilitarian. There was no real expression of who he was. Only a few pictures of family. No matter what Duffy said about not wanting to have children, his family was important to him. And that made Jess feel warmer than Eunice's bananas wrapped in ham.

"Were you ever married, Eunice?"

"I was engaged once. A long time ago." Wistfulness seemed to slow her words. She parceled them out like Scrooge did coins. "Darryl wanted to move to Texas. To work the oil fields. Mama wouldn't allow it."

Jess couldn't imagine walking away from love or family. Poor Eunice.

The older woman's voice became weak and wispy, the way voices sometimes did when traveling down a lane of memory often avoided. "I was only nineteen. I fancied myself in love. Darryl was tall and handsome, and laughed at my jokes." Eunice set her coffee on the table, and mustered something close to a smile. "But Mama said it was a silly infatuation. She told me I'd never model again if I married him. I was a model. Few people could say that." There was a false bravado in her tone, as if she wanted to believe she'd done the right thing.

Jess knew better than most that you couldn't change the past. "Do you regret letting him go?"

"I didn't. Not when I was younger." Eunice's wrinkled face, her slight body, even her teased hair, they all seemed to shrink. "But… sometimes…now…when I can't sleep… I think about him and wonder where he is. Did he find someone else? Or was I the one great love of his life?" She swallowed, her gaze landing on Jessica's stomach. "I bet that sounds foolish to you."

"Not at all." Foolish was holding on to love when there'd been none. She wasn't ready to give up on the idea of having loved Greg yet. "You could try to find Darryl. Everybody's on the internet nowadays."

"You're very kind, but I don't think I could stand to know the answer." Eunice reached for her cup. Just holding the ceramic mug seemed to give her strength. She squared her shoulders, and batted her eyes with sly, matchmaking intent. "Duffy keeps to himself too much. You should stay in touch with him. Maybe…go out?"

Date Duffy?

"That's ridiculous." Except there was Duffy's mischievous smile from the night before as he warned her about what she might see inside his home, the subtle humor she sensed behind his guard and how family was so important to him. All of which made her pulse pick up, her body come alive and her chest ache with longing. None of which mattered. She'd rather give her child an uncle and grandparents than explore the whispered inkling of attraction.

Someone knocked on the door.

Duffy startled awake, looking rumpled and grumpy, but it wasn't a stay-away grumpy. It was an I-need-a-soothing-touch grumpy and it gave Jess pause. In that moment, she imagined her fingers smoothing the curl at his temple, her arms circling his neck, her lips consoling him. Kissing him.

Kissing Duffy, not Greg.

Baby must have been doing somersaults, because Jessica's head felt as if it were switching places with her toes. She gripped the arm of the couch.

Kissing Duffy was a bad idea. One put in place by Eunice. Wasn't it?

"If Eunice is here, I don't know who that could be." Duffy stood with a steadfastness that Greg had lacked, taking steps that didn't rush for the sake of show.

I should have fallen in love with Duffy.

The unfaithful thought and the subsequent sickening feeling were interrupted by a chorus of greetings rising above the sound of the rain.

Jess fought with the couch. She needed to sit up, feeling frumpy in Duffy's sweats.

Instead of smiling cheerfully at his visitors, Duffy looked despondent.

Some of it bled onto Eunice. "Those three always steal my thunder," she muttered.

"Don't get up, dear." A diminutive woman with gray hair cut in a short pixie barreled in with the authority of a school principal. She used the remote to turn off Duffy's muted television. "Now that the rain's easing up, we've brought you a care package. I'm Agnes."

"I'm Rose." A woman with the slight body and regal bearing of a ballerina headed toward the kitchen with a thermos and a plate of chocolate chip cookies. Her snowy-white hair was in a tight bun at the nape of her neck. "Duffy, it's the perfect day for a fire. Why don't you start one?"

Duffy might not have heard. He was helping an old woman in a walker over the threshold.

"I'm Mildred." The walker woman squinted through thick trifocals in Jessica's direction. With an abundance of white curls beneath her red raincoat hood and her round, pink cheeks, she looked like Mrs. Claus come to visit. "The sheriff says we're cut off from civilization for another day."

"Maybe two." Agnes perched on the arm of Eunice's chair, blocking Jessica's view of Eunice.

Purplish curls quivered indignantly, barely visible above Agnes's shoulder.

Duffy closed the door and leaned against it, probably counting to ten since his bachelor domain had been invaded by not one, but five females.

"We're helping the sheriff make rounds," Rose called from the kitchen. "Making sure everyone is all right and doesn't need anything. Hot chocolate or chocolate chip cookie, anyone?"

Jessica raised her hand. "Baby wants a cookie." Baby was going to be one sugar-happy bundle of joy.

"That baby needs something more nutritious than sugar." Eunice leaned around Agnes. Her eyes narrowed. "I brought bananas wrapped in ham with hollandaise sauce. It's in the kitchen."

The room quieted.

"Hollandaise." Rose sniffed deeply, then sniffed again. "That explains the off note."

"Anyway, we can't stay long." Agnes's statement caused Eunice to brighten.

"Nope. Not staying." Despite her words, Mildred flipped the seat down on her walker and perched on it. "But it is drafty in here." She angled her head to look at Duffy. "A fire would be lovely."

"I said that already," Rose chimed in, still puttering in the kitchen.

Agnes asked Eunice, "How long have you been here?"

It was as chaotic as the bakery on Saturday mornings. Jessica found herself smiling. Her gaze searched out Duffy's. His grump seemed to have been punctured, but he looked away without smiling back. Jess was reading him so well their connection should have sparked more memories. But there was no Greg. There was only Duffy. And the guilt of that visualized kiss.

"What is it you do for a living, Jessica?" Agnes asked. The question brought everyone in the house to silence, almost as quickly as Eunice's banana dish.

Duffy muttered something that sounded like "Here we go."

Jess was a bit flummoxed as to why her profession would be a conversation stopper.

"I'm a master baker at Vera's Bakery in Santa Rosa."

The trio of ladies all oohed and aahed. Eunice leaned forward and gave Jess a thumbs-up.

"We don't have a bakery here anymore," Agnes explained.

"Used to be one on Main," Mildred added from her walker seat.

"Cherry Martin ran the place." Rose handed Jessica a cookie on a napkin and a mug of hot chocolate. "She made incredible scones. Learned it from her mother."

"Grandmother," Mildred said.

"Great-grandmother, I think." Agnes stared at Jess with a gaze that weighed and measured. Whatever she was looking for, Jess hoped she didn't take into account Duffy's baggy gray sweats. "Seems like their family had been bakers for a hundred years or more. The sign is still there. Martin's Bakery."

Jess broke off a piece of cookie, wondering what it would be like to come from such a family, one with roots and traditions and generations of recipes. Even Eunice had family recipes. Jess had none.

"No one here can make a decent scone anymore," Eunice piped up from behind

Agnes in that falsely sweet way women had of establishing territories.

Didn't faze Rose a bit. She added her appraisal of Jess to Agnes's. "Are you a successful scone maker, Jessica?"

Jess, whose mouth was full of rich, soft cookie, nodded. As if Baby knew she was eating sugar, it bounced eagerly in her belly.

"You'll have to teach me the trick of it." There was a casual quality to Rose's words, as if she were certain Jess had all the time in the world in Harmony Valley.

Jess glanced at Duffy, who was leaning against the door, staring at his feet. Probably hopeful that at any moment he'd be asked to make way for them to leave. "I won't be around as soon as the roads open."

"Nonsense," Mildred harrumphed from her walker. "The town needs a baker."

"I'll ask Flynn about the state of the bakery." Agnes tugged on a short lock of hair thoughtfully. "Why work for someone else when you can be your own boss?"

Jess wasn't sure what they were talking about. It was every baker's dream to own their own place, but she was in no position to start up a business.

"Mayor Larry owns the building." Rose

returned to the kitchen and via the pass-through Jess could see her packing up her things.

"Of course, he does." Agnes leaned back, blocking Eunice from view again. "He owns most of downtown."

The reins of Jessica's fate seemed to be slipping through her fingers. "I'm not looking to move here," she felt compelled to say. Not that anyone seemed to be listening.

"Cherry never did serve good coffee." Mildred slid her thick glasses higher on her nose. "Coffee's important to people nowadays."

"And Rose's chocolate chip cookies were better than hers," Eunice said unexpectedly from behind Agnes, switching allegiances.

"But the scones made up for the coffee and the cookies." Rose sealed up the thermos.

They all looked to Jess. Not knowing what else to do, she nodded.

"It would be nice to have a place to go in the morning besides El Rosal," Eunice allowed.

Agnes gave Jess a nod. It felt more like the Godfather's blessing. "Jessica's Bakery has a homey feel to it."

Wait. What?

"I'm quite happy where I am," Jess protested weakly.

"Let them carry on," Duffy advised. "They don't actually hear anyone under fifty anyway."

Jess took Duffy's advice and occupied herself with her cookie and hot chocolate, while the ladies debated hours of operation, what she should fill her bakery case with and whether or not she needed a fancy espresso machine. They made running a business sound easy to master, as if this were one of their favorite and frequently played games.

"Didn't you say something about needing to check on other people?" Duffy jiggled the doorknob.

"We did." Mildred stood, flipping her walker seat back in place. "We're just excited that Jessica's in town. A bakery. I can't wait for warm croissants."

Agnes stood, barely taller than she'd been when she'd sat on the arm of the dining room chair. "Would you like to come, Eunice?"

"Me?" Eunice looked as if she'd been picked first for the class softball team when she was used to being last.

"Yes." Agnes shook her car keys. "We'll stop at El Rosal for lunch."

"I'd love to." Eunice hurried to don her rain boots and slicker.

Within five minutes, the house was quiet and Jess was exhausted.

Duffy collapsed into his corner of the couch. "I used to think I had it bad around here, and then came you."

"You mean they don't try to rearrange *your* life?"

"Nope." The way he looked at her with a half smile, as if they shared a private joke, made her heart beat faster. "They watch me work in the fields. They ask me questions about my social life. But they've never planned out my career path as completely as they just did yours."

"As much as I'd love to own my own business…" Just saying it out loud gave her a tiny thrill. "I have other priorities right now." She patted her tummy. Baby was still, probably tired after that sugar rush.

"But you're curious, aren't you?" There was a gentleness to his voice, a tenderness to his smile. And those eyes. Somehow, Duffy's gaze cut through to the heart of the matter.

"I am." Could she put a deal together to make it happen? Could she handle the dual responsibilities of single mom and business owner? The obstacles and pitfalls? The risks and rewards? Her breath caught. She could barely speak. "They're infectious, those women." Jess hoped she kept the wistfulness from her tone. "I'd love to look at the place, but I don't have the capital to start a business."

Duffy's smile faded.

FIFTEEN YEARS OF lies and betrayal were hard to get past.

At least, that's what Duffy told himself so he'd stop projecting Greg's swindling ways onto Jess.

She hadn't asked the town council to drop by and suggest she stay. If that were the case, she wouldn't have been wearing his old sweats. She'd have presented herself accordingly as a business professional.

Greg's laughter echoed in his head as Duffy dialed his parents.

"Michael." Duffy's mom's voice was warm and welcoming. "I'm so glad you called. We were just thinking of you. The news showed heavy rain up your way last night."

His parents were the only people to call Duffy by his given name, one he never thought really fit him. "The road up here is under water, but most of the town sits above the floodplain. I'm fine."

"That makes me feel better. Let me get your father." Mom was in good spirits, and would hopefully remain so after his news. Her words became muffled. "Honey, Michael's on the phone."

"Mom, hold on. I…" Since Jess was napping, he lowered his voice and stepped out on the front porch, immediately serenaded by the steady beat of the rain. "A woman got in touch with me. She used to be Greg's girlfriend."

"Really?" How quickly suspicion came to Mom, thanks to Greg, who'd jaded them all. "What does she want?"

"Nothing. She's…uh…" He glanced up and down the street, but he was alone. No Eunice lurking behind a bush or staring through her window at him. "She's having Greg's baby."

There were comfortable silences, and then there were uncomfortable silences. This was not a comfortable silence.

"Mom, are you still there?"

"What does she want?" Mom's voice sounded as rusty as the day they'd held a private service for Greg.

They'd taken a boat out to sea, saying little until Greg's ashes were spread. At that point, Mom had pronounced, *It's done*.

"She must want something," Mom said, the rust beginning to sharpen.

"Nothing. She wants nothing." Despite the awning over his head and the door at his back, the cold and wet seeped into Duffy's bones. Pride may keep Jess from asking, but Greg's baby deserved a spot in the Dufraine family. Whatever that meant.

Thunder mocked him with deep, rolling claps.

"*Michael.* Do I need to remind you about the old proverb? Fool me once—"

"Greg is dead, Mom." Maybe he didn't think about his twin often enough with compassion. Or maybe it was having Jessica speak kindly of Greg in a way no one had in years that got to him. Duffy just wanted his mother to say something nice about Greg, to believe he hadn't been rotten to his core. Wasn't that what mothers were supposed to do?

"Greg's gone and his people are coming out of the woodwork. We can't afford to give her anything."

What was the use of wishing? "Mom, he took her money, too."

There was a clatter on the other end of the line. "Are you staying dry, son?"

"Yep." Duffy forced cheer into his voice.

There was another painful silence. Duffy hoped his mother would give Jess a chance, give her grandchild a chance, give Greg a chance.

"Did I miss something?" his father asked.

"I'll let you two talk." Mom's voice was as dead as Greg.

Duffy wasn't sure if his mom wanted him to tell his dad about Jess or not. He told him anyway.

"This is like God giving us a do-over." Dad, ever the optimist. "I'd like to meet this woman."

"When the weather clears," Duffy promised.

The thunder rolled.

CHAPTER NINE

"WHAT DO YOU normally do on a Sunday?" Jess asked Duffy after lunch. Her dark hair fell in tousled waves across her shoulders. Sleep still shadowed her eyes. She sat cross-legged on the couch in the corner across from him, her pregnant belly like a large beach ball in her lap. "I don't want to keep you from anything."

The rain outside was as steady as white noise when the cable went out. The day dark and dreary. Or had it merely become so since his phone call with his parents?

Duffy lowered the television volume on the do-it-yourself program. "It's the one day of the week that I collapse on the couch and watch TV."

Jess moved with deliberate care to the dining room chair Eunice had occupied earlier. "It's all yours." She was always deferring to him.

Duffy refrained from extending his legs

across the cushions. "That said, I can't sit still for long. I usually get bored, so I drive to the vineyards I manage." He wondered which plots were flooded. "Or I head down to Santa Rosa to see my folks." Not possible today. And in hindsight, he probably should have waited to tell Mom about Jess in person.

"I'm sorry you're stranded with me."

"Don't worry about it." He didn't mind having Jess around. She was easy to be with, which was weird considering why they'd met. It was Eunice, her spying and her funky casseroles that got under Duffy's skin. "And you? What do you usually do on a Sunday?"

"Sleep in. Nap. Go to bed early." She yawned.

"Exciting times."

Jess gazed out the window, presumably at the rain, the rain and more rain. "Is it safe to drive around town?"

"Some parts, I'm sure."

"It'd be nice to get out." She snuck a glance at him, the beginnings of a smile showing. "You could check on the vineyards. We could take your truck."

"We?"

She patted her stomach and grinned. "Baby's bored."

"I don't want to put you two in danger." But Duffy couldn't shake his curiosity. A vineyard manager needed to know how the properties under his care received the weather.

"I'd settle for a drive down Main Street and back."

Main Street? Where the bakery was located? She didn't have the money to open the bakery.

She must have sensed his knee-jerk reaction, because she backpedaled. "Oh, shoot. I don't need to see the bakery. I can't afford it, and I wouldn't take your money if you offered." She fixed him with an obey-me glare. "Don't you dare offer."

Duffy measured her words with the same yardstick he'd have used on Greg—the one that delved for secret agendas and next moves. But she wasn't Greg and where she was concerned there was nothing to measure but sincerity. "I gave everything Greg had to my parents."

"Don't sweat it. My time will come." But there was a resigned note in her voice. She didn't think her time would ever come.

Duffy knew exactly how she felt. Fifteen years of waiting and his time had finally come. "After we check on those vines, we can drive by the place." What was the harm in that? He was rewarded with a small smile. "But only if you promise to wear my coat. If I recall, Baby doesn't like the rain."

"Baby doesn't like the rain," she repeated, rising. "Give me a couple minutes to change."

"Don't bother. We're just going for a drive."

She glanced down at his clothes. Granted, with the pants bagging shapelessly at her ankles and the sleeves rolled up, she looked dumpy. But then she smiled and the clothes she wore didn't matter. "At least I'm comfortable."

They bundled up. Jessica practically disappeared in his yellow rain slicker. Only her loosely laced sneakers were showing.

As they were backing out in Duffy's truck, the sheriff pulled up.

Upon hearing their plan, Nate said, "Make sure you stay north and west." He hesitated, and then added, "If you head up Parish Hill, could you check on Rutgar? I haven't been able to make it up that way yet. He hasn't answered his phone, but maybe he lost power."

"Or maybe Rutgar just doesn't want to be disturbed," Duffy guessed, pulling away.

"Greg didn't like to be disturbed," Jessica

said in her memory-cradling voice. "I had to call first before I came over."

Duffy could imagine why, but he didn't want to say anything to upset Jess. He drove, leaving her to think as he marked time by the speed of his windshield wipers.

"You can say it." Jess didn't allow more than a few wiper swipes before confronting the issue head-on. "Whatever you think Greg was doing and didn't want me to know about." When he didn't rise to the bait, she added, "The knowing is better than not, trust me."

Duffy pulled into the main winery property, driving past the old farmhouse and around to the back. "When it came to Greg, the truth is kind of brutal. Remember, there were other women he took advantage of."

She drew a shuddering breath.

"Married women. Wealthy women. They… uh…"

"Wow." She cut him off. "That's a side of him I definitely don't remember and didn't suspect. Thankfully."

Enough said. Duffy drove along the edge of the property, down by the river.

"There's something peaceful about a vineyard." Jessica gazed out over the drenched rows. "What is it you're looking for exactly?"

"Fallen trees or limbs. Flooding. General storm damage so I can manage the crews scheduled to work this week." The property had weathered the leading edge of the storm well.

He took her to the Mionetti property next. It was one big puddle.

They drove past two other vineyards that had minimal damage. Cleanup could be taken care of with the caning crew. If he hadn't had Jess in the truck, he might have seen if he could drive to the properties on the eastern side of town. Instead, he headed toward the only other property left to visit. The one on Parish Hill located down the slope from Rutgar's house.

He navigated the switchbacks slowly. Water rushed down a ditch next to the hillside. The higher they climbed, the closer they came to the gray, low-hanging clouds. The rain seemed to hit the windshield harder. A tree was uprooted alongside the road, its hold to the earth weakened by years of drought and brush fires.

"Whew. Baby gets carsick." Jess cracked her window and breathed deeply.

"Here we are." Duffy turned into the vine-yard's drive, but didn't get far. Another large oak had lost its hold on the higher bank and tumbled across the lane.

Jess leaned forward. "Those roots are taller than I am."

"I should have brought my chain saw." It was tucked away in the small single-car garage.

"Isn't it dangerous to wield power tools in the middle of a thunderstorm?"

"I haven't heard thunder in a long time."

Of course, thunder took its cue and rumbled across the valley.

"A lightning storm wouldn't stop you, would it?" He didn't have to look at Jess to know she was smiling.

Her words created some chest-swelling pride. "Depends upon the severity of the storm." She was right. The elements called to Duffy as the wind whipped tree branches around them. If she hadn't been with him, he might have gone back to get his equipment.

"In your own way, you're living on the wild side, just like Greg used to."

A fatalistic feeling grabbed hold of his gut. "I'm nothing like Greg." He didn't lie or cheat or steal.

"I think you're more like him than you're comfortable admitting." She closed her eyes and stroked a hand over her belly. "You're both good at what you do. You keep to yourselves. You like everything, including people, in its place or their place."

Duffy felt wrung out, too wrung out to speak.

"Greg may have done bad things," Jess was saying, "but he wasn't all bad. Just like you and I aren't all good."

Duffy wasn't ready to think about Greg in those terms. And if Jess wasn't 100 percent good, shouldn't he take that as a warning?

He put the truck in Reverse. "We've got one more stop." Rutgar's. Now that he'd seen some trees down, he wondered if the old coot might really be in trouble. He drove higher up the mountain until they reached a driveway that was marked: Trespassers Will Be Shot.

"Is this winery property?" Jess stared at the sign as they passed it, worry ridging her brow.

"No." Duffy considered backing out. After all, he wasn't sure what their reception would be, and he had Jessica's safety to think about. But he could see a roof through the tree line, which meant that most likely they could be seen. Was that a good thing or a bad thing? He wasn't sure.

They rounded a bend and the house came into full view. The two-story home was built on stilts and painted a dreary brown. The front porch jutted out at an awkward angle, holding up a large pine tree that had come from the hillside above. It was amazing that the roofline hadn't given way.

Duffy parked a safe distance from the house. "Wait here." He ran though the rain and took the porch steps two at a time. "Rutgar!"

The front window was broken, the frame bowed inward, a breath away from falling free. The front door frame was similarly damaged. The door hung askew on one hinge and banged in the wind. Add some creepy music and it could be a location for a horror film.

"Rutgar!"

"I've got my gun," came a weak voice from inside, causing Duffy to slow.

"Well, don't use it. It's Duffy. The sheriff sent me."

The sound of a shotgun being cocked cut

through the heavy patter of rainfall. Adrenaline surged through Duffy's veins.

Where was the old man? Would he shoot? If he hadn't pulled the trigger by now, chances were slim he'd do so. Weren't they?

Thank heavens Jess was safe in the cab.

"Don't shoot." Duffy tossed his hood back so that the old man might more easily recognize him. He walked cautiously toward the doorway. "I've got a pregnant woman with me."

"Hiding behind a woman. Ha! I knew the kind of man you were the first day I saw you on the mountain." Rutgar's voice may have lacked the booming quality that had annoyed Duffy on previous occasions, but he was still in turf-defending mode.

Duffy gritted his teeth and stepped through the arch, refusing to hold his hands up like a hostage. "I need to make sure you're okay, and then I'll leave." He peered into the gloomy house. There were heads of snarling dead animals and beasts with antlers mounted on walls. Definitely slasher movie location potential. Duffy's pulse kicked up another few notches.

Despite his every sense advising him to

make a run for it, Duffy took a few more steps inside. "Did you lose power?"

"Don't come any closer." Rutgar sat on the brown shag carpet beneath the worst of the roof damage. Blood shadowed one side of his face and darkened his golden beard. He held the shotgun in his lap, barrel wavering in Duffy's direction.

"You're hurt." Duffy surveyed the ceiling above the old man, looking for studs poking through the wall, listening for tell-tale creaks that the place was about to crumble.

Nothing.

A river-rock fireplace was to Rutgar's right, the broken window to his left. The curtains and the rain blew in on the old man. Why hadn't he moved to a drier, safer place?

"You're a liar, Duffy. Where's that pregnant woman?" Rutgar raised the gun barrel with hands that shook.

"I'm right here." Jess stepped through the doorway, bundled up like a yellow-robed wizard in Duffy's rain slicker.

The gun barrel swung in her direction.

Duffy's pulse pounded an SOS at his temples. Translation: *Run!*

He stepped between Jess and the gun, and said as calmly as possible in what might be the last seconds of his life, "Could you wait outside, Jess? I don't know if this house is stable, but I know Rutgar isn't."

"I can hear you plotting against me." Rutgar's gun remained pointed at Duffy's chest, except when the old man's hand tremors sent the barrel pointing toward Duffy's head.

Duffy hoped Rutgar's trigger finger didn't convulse. "He's got a head wound, Jess. I don't think he knows what he's doing." Duffy glanced over his shoulder at her and mouthed, *Get out.*

Her arms cradled her belly. She drew a deep breath and took a step…in the wrong direction. "I'm Jess. You must be Rutgar."

"Jess," Duffy hissed, reaching for her.

Jess dodged, moving closer to the old man and his gun.

Had he thought her being with Greg an anomaly? She was strong and took risks, unlike any woman he'd ever known.

She did a quick survey of her surroundings. "And this is your home. Looks like you're a mighty hunter."

Time slowed. Duffy played out several scenarios in his mind—dragging Jess to safety, rushing Rutgar, holding his ground and calling the sheriff. None of his scenarios ended well. His breath became leaden. Blood rushed in his ears. Jess. He had to protect Jess, and Greg's baby.

He snagged her arm, drawing her behind him once more. Clasping her hand to hold her in place. "If anyone gets shot today, it'll be me."

"You got that right." Rutgar's voice rumbled through the house like an upset grizzly's.

"Men can be so annoying." Jess peeked around Duffy's shoulder, seemingly unconcerned, but there was a tremble in the hand he held that gave her away. "Can I get you a glass of water, Rutgar? And maybe a dry blanket?"

"Go," Duffy whispered.

"Not without you," she whispered back.

Duffy spared her a glance. "You're beautiful and brave." He spoke the truth, because he might not be alive to tell her so tomorrow.

Jessica's eyes widened. Her other hand slipped around his forearm.

He almost hated to add, "And stupid. Run."

"She stays." Rutgar licked his lips. This close, Duffy could see his eyes were dazed. Water had soaked him and the carpet beneath the broken window. When the wind blew the curtains in, rain splattered Rutgar. Wet, cold, bleeding, no wonder the old man was irrational. More irrational than normal, anyway.

"I'll get you that water." Jess disappeared around a corner. "And then we'll take a look at your forehead."

Duffy drew a relieved breath. She hadn't obeyed him. But for now, she was safe.

"You play dirty." Rutgar lowered his gun. "Bringing your woman here."

"She's not mine. And you shouldn't point guns at people." Duffy couldn't keep the anger out of his voice as he dialed the sheriff. After speaking to Nate, Duffy felt calmer and more sympathetic to Rutgar's plight. "When did the tree fall?"

"This morning." Rutgar gestured a few feet away to a sideways coffee mug and dark stain. "*Crack-boom*. No warning. Every time I try to get up, I fall down. So I've been sitting."

Duffy had taken basic first aid, but that meant he knew CPR and how to bandage cuts, not much else. Certainly nothing about concussions. "So nothing hurts other than your head?"

"Correct." Rutgar lifted bloodstained fingers and tentatively touched his temple, wincing. "That burl-wood clock fell off the wall onto my head." A thick round piece of wood lay near his hip.

"Ouch." Duffy dropped to his knees next to him. "How about you put the safety on that gun before Jess comes back?"

Rutgar scowled at him, but did as he asked, placing the shotgun on the stone hearth next to him.

Duffy hadn't realized how much he wanted that gun out of the equation until the old man set it aside. "Your house looks solid, but I'd like to get you out of here."

"I built this place. It's not coming down from just one tree. It'd take a dozen or more." There was annoyance in the old man's voice. And pride. And perhaps a slap of arrogance.

"A dozen?" Duffy took the quilt from the back of the couch across the room, covering the old man and the vomit next to him. "That's about how many trees are on the slope above this place."

Jess appeared with a glass of water and a wet dish towel. She handed Rutgar the glass and knelt beside him. She sniffed and glanced up at Duffy.

"Don't look under the quilt," he said.

Rutgar had either drifted into unconsciousness or was refusing to acknowledge he'd been sick to preserve his dignity.

She pressed the back of her hand against her nose, and then put on a falsely cheerful smile. "I'm going to clean you up a bit so you don't look so scary."

"I always look scary." Rutgar chuckled the way a man does when he's pleased with a woman's attention. "My looks keep everyone on their toes."

"How many fingers am I holding up?" Duffy held up two.

"At least make it hard." Rutgar raised the glass in a wavering toast before taking a sip that sent water dribbling onto his already wet flannel shirt. "The light is dim in here, but I can see all five of your digits. I'm shaken up, not delirious."

"I'll argue that last point," Duffy said, making sure Jess saw he only had two fingers on display. "You pointed a gun at me. And Jess and her baby." It was hard to keep the exasperation from his voice. The man was injured. But what if Rutgar had shot first and asked questions later?

Rutgar's cheeks finally showed some color. "Trespassers always get the gun."

"That's not very nice." Jess glanced up at

Duffy. "Can I help you get him out to the truck?"

"No." Duffy gestured to the very large, possibly concussed old man. "I can help Rutgar up, but if he pulls a drunken sailor on me, we'll all hit the floor. I won't risk you and the baby."

"A real man could hold me up." Rutgar's acerbic tone might have carried more weight if his head hadn't lolled to one side.

Jess plucked the glass from his hand before it spilled.

"You're not tiny, Rutgar," Duffy countered, working hard to soften the edge of his words. "It's going to take two real men to keep you upright. We'll wait for the sheriff."

"Oh, don't start with the melodrama." Rutgar continued listing to one side, until his shoulder met the edge of the fireplace. "I'm fine. Get me upstairs to bed and tomorrow I'll be running around, same as always." Jess touched his temple with the dishcloth and he winced. "I'll give you that I might need a stitch or two, but I won't be put on a stretcher and into an ambulance. If the sheriff can't stitch me up, I'll drive myself to the urgent care clinic in Cloverdale."

"You'd have better luck taking a boat down

the Harmony River," Duffy said. "The roads are still flooded and closed."

"Who needs a doctor? I bet your little woman could sew me up." Rutgar glanced up at Jess. His eyes rolled back and his head jerked as if he was fighting sleep. He gathered the quilt to his chest, exposing his puke.

"Don't take that bet." Jessica's mouth worked. She looked green. "Baby doesn't like blood."

CHAPTER TEN

"YOU PUT YOURSELF and the baby in danger back there." The steady notes in Duffy's voice were missing, replaced by a sharp tension that filled the cab. "I told you to stay in the truck. It was dangerous."

Duffy took a switchback too fast, sending Jessica's shoulder banging against the door. She grabbed the handle above the window, almost wishing she'd driven down the mountain with the sheriff and Rutgar.

"Dangerous? An old man bleeding in his home?" Jessica's derisive snort came out more like a choking cough. "My mom and I lived on the streets for two years. Rutgar didn't scare me." The lie didn't fall easily from her lips. She'd been shaky on her feet, hiding out in the kitchen until she was sure the safety was on the shotgun.

But living rough had taught her you always hid your fear. She refused to admit it now. "I was annoyed with both of you."

"So you said." So much sarcasm. And disbelief. It was clear Duffy wasn't buying any of her bravado.

She needed a comeback, but her brain was as empty as a candy dish after Halloween. She cracked her window and breathed deeply.

Duffy noticed. "You okay?"

"I'm tired," Jess admitted. "And lately, when I get tired in the afternoon, I get pregnant brain."

Duffy spared her a quick glance. "What does that mean?"

"I might not remember a word I want to use. Or I might gaze off in the distance like a space cadet. Or I might say something totally inappropriate." Like admitting she appreciated the way he'd opened up to her about his family and Greg, or that she'd thought about kissing him.

She snuck a glance at Duffy. He had a strong profile. A few days ago, she would have said it was a stern, unforgiving profile. But now she knew better. A man who put up with neighbors like he did didn't have a heart of ice.

He caught her looking, and gave her a tender smile. "Everything all right?"

Mouth suddenly dry, Jess snapped her attention ahead. The rain was relentless, the wipers on high. Everything was in frenzy mode, including her heart. "I need a drink."

"That's a joke, right?" Another switchback.

The baby protested the shift in inertia by stretching.

"I need…" Jess had just been thinking about what she wanted to drink. The word escaped her. And then the muscles in her stomach tensed in a wave that started near her hips and worked its way up to her lungs, locking down all coherent thought.

"A bathroom? A back rub? A martini?"

The practice contraction passed. "Water," she gasped. "The word of the day is *water*."

"So that's pregnant brain." There was a teasing note in Duffy's voice. It was reassuring after the gun and blood and bodily fluids at Rutgar's. "I can relate to afternoon shutdown. That's when I have another cup of coffee."

"Baby doesn't like coffee." Baby wanted another cup of Rose's hot chocolate.

He smiled that tender smile again. The one that made her want to reach over and take his hand. "Why do you talk about your child as if *Baby* is its given name?"

"I don't know if it's a boy or a girl." She wasn't going to tell him the entire truth: that she talked to her child because she'd been lonely. "And so instead of saying *he* or *she*, I call my little one Baby."

Baby was fully awake, flapping elbows in her belly.

Duffy turned onto a straight and level street, and Jess breathed easier.

"You're having a girl," Duffy said with certainty.

"How do you know?" People made guesses about the sex of her child all the time. She was carrying Baby high, so it was a girl. She was carrying Baby far forward, so it was a boy. What was Duffy's trick?

"If Greg was happy about becoming a father, it'd be because he could spoil his little princess." It had to be the sweetest thing Duffy had ever said to her about Greg.

A thought dropped into Jessica's brain. An awful thought. "I don't think Greg knew about the baby. I don't think I told him."

"You don't seem like the type to hold important information back."

"I know, right?" The reason for her secret

was there in front of her. Jess could feel the answer like a physical thing pulsing behind her eyes. And then another practice contraction hit and her brain went blank. "I don't know. I just... I'm not sure."

He spared her another glance, perhaps noticing her flushed cheeks. "Pregnant brain?"

"Pregnant brain, practice contraction, fatigue, dehydration." The contraction eased. Jess wanted to collapse on a bed. "Did I mention fatigue?"

"We'll get you some water in town."

Minutes later, they pulled up in front of the sheriff's office and got out in the rain. Jess sought shelter beneath a sidewalk awning, waiting for the men to help Rutgar out of the sheriff's truck.

"I can walk," Rutgar said, putting his boots on the ground before anyone was ready to help him. And then he startled, beefy arms tossing about for purchase. "Why is the ground spinning?"

"Look up," Duffy shouted, rushing over to keep the old man from falling.

As they'd done on the mountain, Duffy and Sheriff Nate grabbed each other's wrists and had Rutgar sit on their arms. They carried him into the sheriff's office.

"No one needs to know about this." Rutgar's voice boomed as loud as thunder. He looked up at a gray-haired woman holding the sheriff's door open. "Patti, what are you doing here?"

"I've got a doctor in Cloverdale ready to live chat on my phone." She carried a backpack and wore a green scrub blouse over her blue jeans. "And I'll be telling all my friends how far the mighty Norseman has fallen."

As they carried him inside, Rutgar's response was lost beneath the sound of the pelting rain.

Jess should go inside to find water, but she wasn't keen on seeing any more blood or vomit.

Instead, she called Vera to give her a heads-up that she might be stuck in Harmony Valley more than a night or two.

"I told you to watch the weather report." The bakery owner's voice snapped with unexpected sharpness.

"I'm sorry," Jess said. She knew missing work was Vera's hot button. That's why she'd wanted to give her advance warning.

Vera made a noise that was the equivalent of the verbal evil eye. "I told you when I hired you that I need reliable employees.

Not people who get into car accidents and can't work. Not people who need maternity leave." Vera was sucking in air like a clogged vacuum. "This is only the beginning. First there will be weather. Then there will be a sick child. Then there will be a wedding and a honeymoon and more children!"

Jess refrained from pointing out that it was Vera who'd encouraged her to find a baby daddy or a sugar daddy—either of which might want to make an honest woman out of her. But the venom in Vera's rant played into her pregnant brain's malaise.

"How can I run a business like this? Huh? Huh?"

Jess kept her response calm and respectful. "I hope to be back in time for my shift Tuesday morning."

"If you're not…" Vera huffed and collected herself. "Be here." She hung up.

Baby shuddered. Jess tended to agree.

Wanting to be alone, Jess walked away from the sheriff's office, passing beneath several awnings atop old buildings adorned with quaint, old-fashioned gas lamps.

The space next to the sheriff's office housed huge vats and wine barrels. Small block lettering on the large plate-glass window proclaimed it to be the Harmony Valley Vineyards wine cellar. The next space looked to have been an office of some kind. There was a lone metal desk. On the corner was a small bar, also abandoned. She turned and hurried along the side of the building and across the alley to the next corner on Main Street. The wind picked up its pace and sent Duffy's rain slicker flapping against her legs.

Main Street had more action. Across from her was an empty grocery store, but down the block a barbershop pole spun lazily. Mae's Pretty Things sat across from the barber pole with quilts and afghans in the window. Next to it was a small restaurant called Giordano's Mexican-Italian Café. El Rosal was at the far end of the block.

And then Jess reached the empty bakery. A hand-carved wooden sign hung above the door: Martin's Bakery. Inside, there was a window seat and a collection of round and oblong tables. The chairs were wood, mismatched and stacked in a corner. Three feet of dark brown paneling was capped with a chair railing on the side wall. Three bakery cases made an L-shape in the space. A large chalkboard hung on the wall behind the register. It looked like the last daily special had been pumpkin scones.

But what kept catching Jessica's gaze were the photos on the walls. She pressed her nose against the glass. Sepia or black-and-white, yellowed with age and dulled with dust. There were group photos and photos of women standing in front of the bakery in long dresses with aprons, holding parasols or babies or bread. The bakery had roots. Agnes had mentioned generations of bakers and here they were.

Jessica's heart wrenched. She would have loved to have been a part of a large family with a business like this one. She longed for such history. For family traditions and favorite recipes. For the simple state of belonging.

A large black truck parked in front of the bakery. A man about Jessica's age leaped out and ran through the rain to join her. His smile was as bright as his reddish-brown hair. "You must be Jessica. I've been looking for you. Give me a sec to text Slade." His thumb flew over a fancy phone, and then he tucked it in the pocket of his gray hooded sweatshirt. "I'm Flynn, part-owner in the winery Duffy works for."

Duffy's boss? What did he want her for?

Jess wrapped the ends of Duffy's yellow rain slicker around Baby, taking in the wet cuffs of Duffy's sweatpants bagging at her ankles. For hours she'd been comfortable in the nonbinding clothing. She should have changed into her own clothes for the drive. Now she felt not like herself, a fraud. Or worse, someone guilty by association with Greg. Why else would this man be searching for her?

Had Greg stolen money from someone Flynn cared for? Was someone putting two and two together and incorrectly coming up with Jess as four? She took a step back.

"I was just looking." She bit her lip to keep her mouth closed, determined not to say anything else lest she get Duffy in trouble.

"Nothing wrong with looking." Flynn peered in the window. His voice held no hint as to why it was important to find her. "I remember grabbing a chocolate milk and apple fritter in here before school."

"Breakfast of champions," Jess blurted. That was the trouble with pregnant brain. You could be determined *not* to say something one minute and blurt out embarrassing things the next.

Flynn didn't seem to mind. "My wife,

Becca, thinks I turned out okay." He grinned, giving her bulky midsection a sideways glance. "When Agnes called and told me about you, I didn't think you'd be so…" He pointed at the baby.

"Pregnant?" Oh, pregnant brain. She wished she could flip a switch and go silent.

"Yeah." His cheeks colored slightly. "I didn't think you'd be quite so…"

"Large?" There was a time to beat around the bush and play coy, but now wasn't it. If her being at the bakery put Duffy's job at risk, Jess had to put things to rights. No games. "Duffy has nothing to do with my being here." But she wished he were by her side. She could use his strength.

A silver Mercedes sedan parked next to Flynn's truck. A man in a dress shirt and teal tie ran through the rain to join them beneath the awning. He looked as if he were running errands during his lunch hour from Wall Street. His black pants were crisply pressed. Platinum cuff links flashed at his wrists, along with what looked like a Rolex. Even his loafers were high quality.

He dresses like Greg.

Jessica's stomach clenched. She put a hand

on the glass for support as her suspicions seemed to be coming true.

Greg, what have you done?

"Really?" Flynn flipped the newcomer's tie. "It's Sunday."

"This is a business meeting." The well-dressed man turned to Jess and took her in with one sweep of his dark gaze. *"Oh."*

Jess wanted to excuse herself and be sick. Instead, she swallowed back the sour taste of fear and said, "I don't know what Greg did, but Duffy had nothing to do with it. And neither did I." At least, not that she remembered. Jessica's gaze bounced from one man to the other.

A gust of wind sent raindrops dancing at their feet. The men exchanged glances and a message Jess couldn't decode.

"We don't know any Greg." Flynn produced a key. "Why don't we talk inside?"

Jessica's knees wobbled. "This isn't about Duffy?" She swallowed. "Or Greg?"

"No. I'm Slade." The man with the tie took her arm and led her inside. "Part-owner of the winery. We don't know Greg."

"He was Duffy's twin and my... Anyway, it seems Greg wasn't always on the up-

and-up, but he's gone now." Pregnant brain strikes again.

"Say no more," Slade murmured comfortingly. "We didn't mean to upset you."

They glanced around the bakery. It smelled musty, but also yeasty, confirming many loaves of bread had been made here. Despite the gray day outside, the bakery felt dry and cozy.

Jessica fought the urge to study the family portraits, to close her eyes and breathe in the smells and imagine she was part of it all, and that the place was hers. Instead, she squared her shoulders. "What does the winery have to do with me?"

"Have a seat." Flynn had been dusting off chairs with his hand. He brought three to a small round table. "We'll explain."

Jessica was grateful of the sturdy chair legs, because her own had a hard-to-hide wobble. She hung Duffy's rain slicker on the chair back. It dripped onto the wood floor.

Flynn straddled his chair, crossing his arms. His smile was more welcoming than a used-car salesman's, not a point in his favor. "You may have noticed there aren't many businesses in Harmony Valley. We're trying to change that."

"Bringing life back to the town." Slade nodded, sitting and straightening his tie, as stiff as Flynn was loose.

"And we heard that you're a baker." Smiling kindly, Flynn gestured at the room. "What do you think of the place?"

She loved it. But that didn't mean she'd forgotten about reality and what was practical. "I don't have the money to open my own bakery." For the first time, anger, not dismay, coursed through her veins at the thought of her lost savings.

"You don't need much." Slade leaned forward. Cosmopolitan guys like him were used to working with movers and shakers, not bakers. "The owner of this property, our mayor, is offering a special deal. Free rent and utilities for six months."

Charity. Jessica's anger danced through the doorway to resentment, strengthening her backbone. "I won't be the town's hard-luck case." Although in Duffy's sweats, she looked the part.

"If anyone's in need of luck," Slade said, smile fading, "it's the town, not you."

"There's also an apartment upstairs." Flynn's smile was unfazed. "A studio, but it's perfect for you and the baby. We're willing to make sure the place is livable and everything would be move-in ready. Also rent-free for six months."

Their smiles and kind words made Jess want to believe it was really happening to her, but who would invest in a pregnant woman wearing a man's sweats and loosely laced sneakers?

"I don't accept handouts. I was in the system too long." At their looks of confusion, she added crisply, "Foster care and government assistance. I make my own way now. I don't need your charity."

Flynn and Slade exchanged silent glances. Again, Jess wished she shared their codebook. So much was being spoken, yet she didn't understand.

And then Slade changed. He sat up tall, leaned his elbows on the table and clasped his hands. His face was no longer relaxed and welcoming, but intent. It may have been Sunday. They may have been sitting in a rundown bakery in remote Harmony Valley. She may look like she'd tumbled out of bed as she headed for the delivery room, but Slade looked as if he were taking a very important business meeting in New York with a very important person—*her*.

"We're not making a special offer to you because *you* need it," Slade said. "*We* need help here in town, not the other way around. For every business we get to open and every family we bring to Harmony Valley, it creates the need for another four jobs."

"In theory," Flynn said.

Slade waved off his business partner's caveat. "Let's say that you came to Harmony Valley and you thought, 'Hey, there's no bakery here, what a great opportunity.'"

Jessica's nod was so tentative, the two men probably didn't see it.

"You'd find out who owned this place and negotiate a lease," Slade continued, as smoothly as the patter of rain outside.

On the wall over his shoulder, three generations of bakers stood framed behind the counter. There was room in that photo for another generation, for a slight woman with a passion for scones and cakes and....

Slade shifted back into Jessica's line of vision. "You might negotiate a few months rent-free given the low demand for space in town."

A photo of several women in long skirts standing in front of the bakery hung on the wall above Flynn's head. One of the women held a baby. Jess nodded, firmly this time.

Slade leaned closer, spoke with more urgency. "You'd sign a lease. You might even apply for a small business loan or other government help."

Baby kicked at being thought of as needing government help, causing Jess to jerk upright in her chair.

"We're just talking hypotheticals," Flynn reassured her, looking as serious now as his business partner.

Jess patted her baby bulge, soothing both of their ruffled feathers.

"So you'd start with some help," Slade said. On the wall near the register was a carved sign: Baked with Love from Our Family to Yours. Longing for the bakery became an ache in her chest. "We've just done the legwork for you. We've handled the negotiations and cleared the path through the city council so that you can apply for a business permit today if you wanted."

"Well, not today." Flynn's blue eyes twinkled. "Today's Sunday."

Jessica was feeling overwhelmed. Hope braided with fear and wound around Baby.

"I'm flattered you think I can do this, but I'm about to give birth."

"Right now?" Flynn stood, looking panicked.

Slade drew back, studying her.

"No, not now." Jess tried to laugh, but failed. "Baby comes in two months. I want this. I do." She was being offered the chance of a lifetime. The family, Cherry Martin's family, seemed to be welcoming Jess with open arms. But—the baby squirmed—how could she handle a newborn business and a newborn baby? "I can't do this now."

Slade's business facade softened. "Why not? No time is the right time. You'll use the same excuse after the baby's born. And when your child turns one. And when your child starts school."

The walls seemed to be closing in around her. Voices murmured in her head.

Mom: *You're strong.*

Vera: *Once the baby comes, things will be harder.*

Greg: *Take a chance. With me. Right now.*

A contraction hit, making her arch in her chair and lose whatever memory of Greg the conversation evoked.

Jess wasn't the type to ever be offered

the glass slipper. She wanted it, though. She wanted this place.

As if sensing she was about to cave, Flynn helped her up. "Let's take a look around. See what you're getting into."

She stood, locking gazes with a woman holding a tray of steaming loaves of bread in another photo. There was a tilt to the woman's lips that invited the question.

This, her heart whispered.

Could she do this? Have a place of her own? Set down roots and pick up where this family of bakers had left off?

Almost immediately, Duffy's cynical expression came to mind, the one he wore any time the topic of money entered the conversation. What would he think if he knew she was considering their offer?

Jess followed the two men to the kitchen. It was huge with four wall ovens, an industrial-size refrigerator and a large island.

"We need to turn on the power and ensure the equipment still works." Slade opened the fridge. "Refrigerators don't do so well if they've been off too long."

Everything was coated with a thick layer of dust. Above the sink was another family photo. This one showed what looked to be three generations standing around a multi-tiered wedding cake. Each worker was placing flowers around the edges.

Among a shelf of cookbooks and hardbound ledgers was a binder. Jess plucked it out and flipped it open, sending puffs of dust into the air. It smelled of flour and was filled with yellowed paper, handwritten recipes with notes in the margins.

Charlotte Libby's wedding cake. Could use more lemon.

Mionetti baby shower cupcakes, 1951. Excellent.

Halloween school carnival cookies. Raised more money than the Lipscomb's booth. Kid-pleaser.

Jessica carefully closed the antique book. All that history. How would it feel to know so much about your family and your town? In Santa Rosa, she was just another woman in line for gas or groceries. Here, people knew you. They welcomed you to town with hot chocolate and cookies. They checked on you during a storm. They invited you to stay with business propositions that were too good to be true.

The men had already moved on, climbing the rear stairwell. She hurried after them, tracing their footprints on the dusty treads, silently chastising Baby for bouncing on her bladder.

Just a few more minutes, please.

A familiar refrain of mothers everywhere. She heard it often enough from Vera's customers. She hadn't imagined she'd use it on her own child, hadn't realized she was already using it. Her steps faltered. She was failing at motherhood before her baby was even born! Jess should turn around right now.

And then she saw it, a sepia picture of a family gracing the landing at the top of the stairs. The father sat in a chair, cradling a baby. The mother stood behind him, one hand on his shoulder. They were formally dressed—he in a suit with a crisp bow tie, her in a floor-length, shiny dark dress with lace across the bodice. At their feet was the wooden sign now hanging above the front door: Martin's Bakery.

They'd started the bakery with a baby in their arms. A sign, literally, that Jess and Baby would be welcome here.

Flynn was laughing when she reached the top floor. "I'm surprised it's in such fine shape."

Sturdy hardwood floors. Walls smoothly plastered and painted a pale pink. A small kitchenette with plain white cabinets and small glass knobs. The countertop and sink were both stainless steel. It was a working family's apartment. Cozy and serviceable. *Home.*

"This is what a good roof does for a place." Slade opened the refrigerator in the small kitchen. "No mice, either."

The two men high-fived, taking credit for something they seemed to have no part in, but were happy about.

Jess moved past them to check out the bathroom. The tub, toilet and porcelain pedestal sink were pink. The walls had been tiled with ceramic pink squares. The floor had been done with round white tiles interspersed with pink ones set in a flowery pattern.

"Well." Slade sounded like the deal was a sure thing. "What do you think?"

If she'd learned anything from Duffy, it was not to take things at face value. "What's the catch?"

"There is no catch." But Slade crossed

his arms when he spoke, going into business mode.

Was he getting annoyed with her? Was she missing something? Or was she ruining everything? There were no photographs on the walls up here. No reassurance from the past. She was on her own.

Jess mirrored Slade, crossing her arms. She upped the ante by arching a brow.

"Hang on." Flynn stepped between them. "Full-disclosure time." He smiled, but it wasn't a smarmy smile. It was a guy-next-door, nothing-to-hide smile. "I promised my grandfather before he died that I'd continue his work—in bringing people back to Harmony Valley. We brought in the sheriff—"

"Nope. Your grandfather invited him," Slade pointed out drily.

"We got the vet to—"

"Nope," Slade interrupted again. "Doc recruited him."

"Okay. How about the Lambert twins?" Frustration frosted Flynn's voice.

Slade chuckled, and that chuckle loosened him up. His arms uncrossed. His lips curled upward. His voice brimmed with guy-ribbing humor. "I'll give you the twins, but only when they finally do more than talk about moving here."

"Uh…guys?" For the second time that day, Jessica broke up a man-fest.

Flynn was immediately on-call intense. "Are you in labor? Do we need to go to the hospital?"

"No. Two more months, remember?" She'd like to think it was Duffy's ill-fitting clothing that gave the impression childbirth was imminent, but she was afraid she was just plain large.

"Then we'll get to the heart of things." Slade had on his deal-making face. Eyes that noted everything. Lips curled in a crocodile smile. If she chose poorly, he'd eat her in one bite and destroy her dreams in another. *Chomp. Chomp.* "We want you to move to Harmony Valley. Without people willing to make their futures here, the town will die."

"That's your closing line?" Flynn rolled his eyes with schoolboy levity. "Here's mine. We're pushing this year to bring in more people than ever. El Rosal offers breakfast, but it's egg-and-potato fare. You'd have very little competition for coffee and pastry. I'd love to order my wife a birthday cake here. I'd love to stop by in the morning for espresso and a doughnut. I'm sure others would, as well."

The pressure to say yes was nearly overwhelming. But was it the right choice for Baby? She couldn't simply walk in one day and be open for business the next. She'd need things. And right now she needed to spend on Baby, not bakery.

"There's no espresso machine. And…" She felt her cheeks heat. "Espresso machines are expensive."

Flynn looked to Slade.

Slade sighed. "Good coffee is hard to come by in this town. I suppose we could—"

"You'll do no such thing." Jess cut him off, the door to resentment banging back open. "If I take you up on your offer, I won't be nickel-and-diming you. I'll pay for things myself." *How* was another question. Her savings were a meager five months old. "But I can't see moving here. What about day care? What about the school system? What about a medical clinic?" All the things that should be more important to a new mom than inheriting a bunch of recipes or photos of strangers on the wall.

"What's going on up here?" Duffy appeared at the top of the stairs, looking wet and stormy, drowning the promise in the place.

"We're trying to convince Jessica to start a bakery in town," Flynn said. "All she needs is a little backing. You'd like hot pastry and great coffee every morning, wouldn't you?"

Duffy didn't answer. He moved into the room, a bottle of water in his hand. He studied Jess with wintery caramel eyes. She knew caramel could cool and harden, but she preferred it warm and soft.

"She's a tough negotiator." Slade nodded to Jess. "And just so you know, Jessica, we're working on your concerns. We've been trying to recruit a doctor. We recently had a nurse practitioner named Patti retire here. For now, the nearest schools are thirty minutes away. Our schools should reopen by the time your child is ready for kindergarten. And there are dozens of retirees in town who would love to take care of a baby."

Duffy's expression turned as dark as the thunderous skies were last night. "Did she ask—?"

"No!" Jessica cradled her baby bump, feeling chilled, and not from her wet clothes. "I was standing on the street looking in the window when these two pulled up."

Flynn gave Duffy a questioning look that went unanswered.

"No, she didn't ask, Duffy. Agnes told us about her." Slade shed his business persona and took both of Jessica's hands in his. "You could be your own boss here. As a master baker, you've probably dreamed of having your own place. All we ask is that you think about it."

The two men led her and Duffy downstairs. Jessica wanted to pause in the kitchen and soak it all in one last time, but Duffy was telling them about the fallen tree in the Parish Hill vineyard and was already moving toward the door. The family watching over the apartment above, the women who'd filled the bakery with love and pastry. She should have known she couldn't belong here.

Outside, she took a final glance at the plate-glass window, but before she could say a word, a helicopter landed over in the town square. Flynn locked up.

"Rutgar's wound was that bad?" Jess huddled deeper into Duffy's rain slicker. Her wet clothes were starting to bother her. Or perhaps it was that she was going to walk away from this opportunity.

"He's got a concussion and needs to be

under a doctor's care." Duffy's tight response made Jess want to leave Harmony Valley and never return.

Baby deserves this chance.

But not if it meant alienating Baby's uncle. Providing a family for her child was more important than Jessica's dreams.

CHAPTER ELEVEN

DOUBT ATE AT Duffy's insides like a famished man at a Chinese buffet.

Doubts created by the specter of Greg. Doubts he didn't think he should have about Jess. Doubts that feasted and hollowed him out until the only thing he could trust was the fact that Greg was dead.

Had Jessica's entire visit been a setup for this?

Stranger things had happened. The only reliable part of Duffy's life right now was the continuous rain.

Flynn and Slade went to see how Rutgar was doing before he was airlifted out, leaving Duffy and Jess beneath the bakery's awning.

Duffy handed Jess a bottle of water. "Should I have gotten you something more celebratory?"

"You think I'm scamming them?" Her voice rose above the helicopter rotors, high and tight. "Like Greg would do?"

"This has nothing to do with Greg." Or cons. Or lies. Or... Duffy stared into Jessica's dark eyes, sparking with indignation. She wasn't Greg. So why was he upset with her?

"It has to do with Greg and something." A bit of the flame in her eyes died. He had to strain to hear her words. "But it has nothing to do with Greg and me. I won't take money from you or your family."

"You seemed more than ready to take theirs." The hurt and accusation clung bitterly in his mouth. What was he doing? He liked Jess. "We'll talk about this later." When he'd had time to think, to be more rational and less reactive. He hurried toward the helicopter at a pace she couldn't match.

"I'm taking Nate up on his offer to sleep at the jail tonight. Or over at Eunice's. They don't think I'm a swindler." Jess breathed heavily behind him. "Wait up, dang you. I want to say goodbye to Rutgar, too. Baby doesn't run like that."

He slowed down. Stopped. Faced her and his jumbled emotions.

Her cheeks were flushed. Her hair damp at the temples where her hood had slipped back. There was pain in her eyes.

That pain. It lanced the hold he had on his anger. "I'm trying not to let years of experience with my brother, of his lies and betrayal, reflect on you. But it's hard."

"I understand," she puffed, still trying to catch her breath. "I'd rather provide Baby with family than a bakery. If it makes you feel better, I'll sign a document releasing all claims to Greg's money."

It would erase his concerns. It would allay his mother's fears. But it wouldn't be the right thing to do. "If you want to be part of this family, we shouldn't need a document."

"But it would prove you could trust me." She glanced over her shoulder at the bakery, and then back at him. "Do you know what I thought when I looked in that window? I wished I could have been part of their family. While Flynn and Slade were talking about rents and fixing things up, all I could think about were the generations of bakers that had brought that place to life. I wanted to be one of them." She wiped at her nose. "I have no idea who my grandparents are or what they did for a living. My father is a blank space on my birth certificate. And my mother...is gone. I have no heritage. Not even a brother who was a sneak and a thief."

Her voice had become a ribbon of hurt, one that curled around Duffy's heart and tugged, ever so gently. "I'm like one of those trees up on the hill we saw today. Alone. Upturned. Unwanted."

The helicopter took off. The decibel level dropped to a guilty ringing in Duffy's ears.

He'd never encountered such raw emotion so innocently tossed out into the air. His family tended to deal with things quietly, privately, buttoning emotion into a back pocket where no one could see it. He wanted to tell her she wasn't unwanted, but someone must have stuffed cotton down his throat. He couldn't say anything.

"I would love to have a business like that." Her words were stitched hoarse with longing. "Somewhere to call my own." She stared at the bakery a few doors back. "But you'd always believe that I'd come here to milk you of cash. And you might look at my child and see that brother you hate so much." She walked past him toward his truck.

He was the one hurrying to catch up this time, because the sincerity of her words smothered the suspicion he'd been trained to feel when it came to money and unexpected financial deals.

She was muttering to herself. "I need… I really need…"

"A drink?" Duffy said. "I gave you the water."

She stopped and stared at him, cheeks flushed, eyes watery. "I really need to bake. It calms me." She kept staring at him, her gaze delving deep, peeling back layers of suspicion and betrayal, until she came to the place inside him that understood her, that took notice every time he learned something new about her. And in that stare, he heard her unvoiced question: *Can I bake at your house?*

He nodded. "You bake. I'll cook dinner."

The tension in her evaporated, from the lines around her eyes to the set of her shoulders. "You make it very hard to stay mad at you."

Duffy opened the truck door for her and held on to Jessica's hand as she climbed in. It was a warm hand, a strong hand. He was reluctant to let her go.

"WHY DO YOU want to own a bakery?" Duffy's words filled his galley kitchen and Jessica's head.

She'd been blending oats with flour and

sugar. Her wooden spoon fell into the bowl as memories assailed her.

This is a perfect opportunity for you, Jess. You'll be your own boss. Greg's voice tinged with a hint of I-know-best.

Duffy was browning pork chops in a pan. He turned to face Jess, concern in the slant of his eyes. "What is it? What do you remember?"

She held up a shaky hand, trying not to stop the flow of memories.

Isn't that what life savings are for? Creating a life? Greg's voice, loud and annoyed.

She reacted now as she had then, with gut-clenching dismay. Her hand sought Duffy's. "Greg asked me for money to start a bakery. He and I were going to be business partners." She'd worked in bakeries until she'd entered culinary school and had worked nights at the same time, preserving a sizable chunk of her savings.

Duffy's touch soothed. His voice calmed. "And then…"

"I didn't want to. I was afraid of…" It was gone, the hint of memory. Only the unease remained. "I don't know what I was afraid of." She studied their joined hands, knowing she should let him go.

"I don't like the idea of Greg scaring you." He threaded the fingers of his other hand through her hair, brushing it behind her ear.

She leaned into him and his arms came around her.

This, her heart whispered, more vocal than it had been in the bakery.

"It wasn't a physical fear."

"But you were scared." Duffy released her, bending his knees until he was eye to eye with her. "That's why you didn't tell Greg. On some level, you knew things would change if he found out about Baby. Greg wasn't father material."

"Do you always have to be so negative?" Her words were barbed. She couldn't help it.

"Just when it comes to my brother." So matter-of-fact. He sprinkled mushrooms in the pan. They sizzled in the combination of oil and meat juices. "Admit it. You had an inkling of what he was up to."

The warm smells pulled Jess further into the present, into the warm kitchen with the now familiar beat of rain on the roof. "It doesn't seem like that's where my fear was coming from."

"Let's talk about something else." He stirred the mushrooms, and then met her gaze without the doubt he'd had at the bakery. "Do you want a bakery of your own?"

"I do… I did…before Baby." She didn't feel fear when she thought of owning Martin's Bakery in Harmony Valley. Not the fear she'd recalled with going into partnership with Greg. Why had she felt such gut-shaking anxiousness with him?

A new feeling, one of shoulder-bending betrayal, took hold. Maybe she hadn't loved Greg. At least, not the way she should have.

Oh, how she wished she could remember everything.

"What do you love about the idea of having your own bakery?" Duffy's voice. Grounded. Supportive.

Jess swallowed. "I'll be able to bake what I want. To try things I want to try. To…" The Martin family recipe book came to mind. "To pass on the things that I love to Baby."

Baby elbowed her lovingly.

"I don't have much of a connection to my mother," Jess continued, rubbing the spot where Baby moved. "But passing on recipes—sharing a kitchen together—it creates a bond that lasts long after people are gone from your life." She glanced up at him, hoping her words reached him. "Don't you agree?"

It was then she realized they were sharing the kitchen. She and Duffy. Creating a bond.

Her gaze dropped to his lips and then skittered away.

I do not want to kiss this man.

Baby elbowed her again.

It's just echoes of Greg.

Baby elbowed her harder. Why was it so difficult to lie to her child?

Her attention ping-ponged around the kitchen. The cookie dough needed something. Brown sugar? Cinnamon? She couldn't remember. Her face began to heat. Duffy somehow managed to capture her gaze again. And there it was—awareness. Of her. As a woman.

Her pulse pounded and her body felt lighter than it had in months.

And then he chuckled in a way that destroyed the impression.

As it should have. She didn't want his male appreciation. She didn't feel like a woman. She felt like an overinflated beach ball with legs. Darn pregnancy brain couldn't be trusted to read anything right.

"You and I will always have a bond in Baby." He spoke gently, from the heart. It was the truth. "You mentioned you don't know who your father is. What happened to your mother? When did she give you over to foster care?"

Admitting the details of her past would only make her feel closer to him. She told him anyway. "My earliest memories are of living in a small room in a big house. My mother took care of the children. Later, we moved to another big house and another small room where Mom did the cooking." Those were the good memories—of warm kitchens and warm beds. But there were other recollections she wished she could erase. "And then we were homeless. For a long time. I didn't figure it out until I was about nine. I hated the days I wasn't in school." She picked up the wooden spoon and gave the dough a halfhearted stir. "We'd had a couple of rough weeks where Mom had fought off men. I didn't understand back then, but I realize now they had intentions…"

Duffy cursed under his breath.

"I like to think she left me at the shelter because she knew the system would take care of me better than she could on her own." Jess also liked to think her mother was watching over her, waiting for a time when she'd be back on her feet and able to care for her daughter again. It had made leaving the Los Angeles area difficult. But chances were that her mother had started a new life without Jess as a burden.

Duffy cradled her chin in his big hand. His touch was no doubt meant to be friendly and supportive, but all she felt was his compassion and the need to touch him. "It took guts for her to leave you."

"Do you think so?" Jessica's voice shrunk to a small, fragile thread. "Sometimes I think she took the cowardly way out."

His hand dropped away, but his gaze remained. Rock-steady. Certain. "Doing nothing is the coward's way out."

Jess repeated the words to herself for the rest of the evening: *Doing nothing is the coward's way out*.

She could continue to work for Vera and do nothing to create a future for herself and Baby. Or she could adopt the family who'd started the bakery and risk ruining everything.

Twenty-four hours.

Duffy had only really known Jess for twenty-four hours. Their first meeting didn't count.

In twenty-four hours, he'd learned more about her than he knew about his boss or any of his coworkers.

Her lost memory was a fragile thing that rolled in as quickly as the tide and receded almost as swiftly. He could tell by the distance in her eyes if she was regaining a memory. He could recognize a memory's impact on her by the crinkle in her brow—unpleasant—or the smile at the corner of her lips—pleasing. He could sense her mood by the shifting tempo of her voice.

He felt a friendship forming. Something comfortable. Except while they'd been in the kitchen earlier discussing her fears and her past. A tug of attraction had passed between them, so tentative he wasn't convinced she'd felt it. But he had. And he'd moved quickly to reestablish their boundaries.

The dinner dishes had been cleared. Some oatmeal raisin cookies eaten. Jessica sat curled in one corner of the couch and Duffy in the other. He'd called the hospital to check on Rutgar and his concussion, receiving a verbal thrashing from the old man for bothering him.

It still rained. The television was tuned to a do-it-yourself program about small houses, those less than four hundred square feet. They didn't talk. He and Jess seemed to have run out of things to say.

"I bet your house qualifies as a tiny house." Jess yawned.

"That apartment over the bakery would, too."

Her body convulsed. "Ouch." She rubbed the curve of her stomach.

"Was that a kick?"

She extended her upper body. "No. It's an, um…*contraction*."

"What!" Duffy shot to his feet. "I'll call the sheriff. He'll get Patti."

"No… I…" She put her feet on the ground with a groan. "These are Braxton Hicks contractions. Practice contractions. Although… I've never had them so strong before." Her face was turning red, features contorting with pain.

"What do we do? What can I do? What do you need?" *Darn you, Greg.*

"Walk it out." Jess extended a hand for him to help her up. "Remind me to breathe."

Duffy backed up a step. "Shouldn't you relax?"

She waved her hand impatiently. "Help. Me. Up." She was as far from relaxed as relaxed could be. Her words sounded more like choppy groans. "Need. To. Walk."

He got her to her feet and led her around the room. "Better?"

Her cheeks were flushed. Her breath came in rapid pants. Even her hair seemed unsettled. It was as mussed as if he'd been kissing her.

Duffy ground to a halt.

Jess stumbled against him. "What's wrong?"

"Nothing. Nothing is wrong." He was just being a guy. A dumb, insensitive guy. Duffy began walking again, tugging her along, tugging his defenses back in place.

"Whew. It stopped." She drew him to a halt this time. "Thank you for not panicking when I did."

Duffy had to look at her because she was talking to him.

He gazed down into her dark brown eyes. It seemed natural to smooth her silky hair behind her ears. It seemed natural to allow his gaze to brush over her lips. It would seem natural to close the distance between them and kiss her.

Her grateful smile faded under his scrutiny. *Idiot.*

Duffy forced himself to release her arm

and think about something else. Football or his vineyard to-do list or the sweet way her cookies tasted fresh out of the oven. He would not think about her independent streak or how she defended Greg or her desire to be part of a family. And he certainly would never, ever, not in a million years, dwell on how her lips might feel beneath his.

And then she was in his arms, lips pressing to his. She was warm. Soft. Curvy. And sweet. She tasted so sweet. Unbearably sweet.

Her hands were in his hair, fingers circling the cowlick at his temple. His arms drew her closer.

And they kissed.

It was like surrendering to a craving for nachos and finding everything in that one first bite made the world seem right.

There was a sound at the front door.

Eunice. He was going to kill her.

He and Jess drew apart slowly. She looked dazed and ready to be kissed again. He wanted to oblige. He wanted to hold her hand and tell her to reach for her dreams. He'd be there to help, come rain or shine, good times or bad. He'd help her. He'd help...

Help!

His arms dropped to his sides. His gaze dropped to her belly. He liked Jess, but he would not take on more responsibility. And that's where more kisses would lead. Not to being a sounding board if she took over the bakery. Not to having a date to go to the movies with. Jess and Baby. They were a package deal.

Duffy felt sick for his selfishness. But she had to know. He couldn't lie to her. And he couldn't be—

There it was again. The sound on the porch.

He practically ran to the door. "Eunice, it's too late for visitors." Or one of her off-the-wall food dishes. She'd probably brought over pickles and ice cream for Jess.

No one was there. The wind blew the rain in his face.

Duffy stepped onto the porch. "Hello?"

"Who is it?" Jessica stood in the doorway behind him. "Oh, hey." She knelt and held out her hand. "You're all wet."

There was a clack-clack-clacking noise from the far end of the porch. A cream-colored dog the size of a football trotted forward with dainty steps. Its long fur was drenched and matted. It shivered pitifully.

"Poor baby," Jess cooed. "Come inside. We'll get you dry."

Duffy searched the street for the dog's owner. But the street was empty.

Jess picked up the little beast and cuddled it on top of her baby bulge. Big brown eyes stared up at him.

"Poor thing. Get me a towel, will you, Duff?"

Duff? No one called him that. He was Michael to his parents and Duffy to his friends. Not Duff.

They needed to talk about that kiss and what it didn't mean.

But Jess was already sitting near the fire, talking baby talk to the wet pup.

He got the dog a towel. And a bowl of water. And some leftover chicken from a few days ago, which he shredded. "I bet someone's looking for that dog." He thought no such thing. No collar. No tags. Matted hair. Thin as a rail. That pup was a stray.

Duffy took up his position in the couch corner.

"We'll find your doggy parents in the morning," Jess promised, setting the tiny, fluffy beast in Duffy's lap.

The dog stretched across Duffy's legs and closed its eyes.

"You can call someone, right?" Jess asked in a whisper, as if she didn't want to wake the dog. She sat next to him instead of in her corner. "To find its home?"

"There's a vet in town. And I can ask the sheriff." Now was the time to broach the topic of that kiss.

The dog snuggled closer.

"And Eunice. She'd know whose dog this is." Jess stroked the dog's fur.

She sat close enough that he felt the warmth of her thigh near his. She'd been warm in his arms, too.

Here came the silence. There was something they needed to discuss. Pregnant brain must be contagious. Duffy couldn't remember what it was.

"Such a sweet little thing," Jess murmured. "She'd be a good dog for you, Duff."

"Oh, no." Dogs were like kids. You couldn't just take off on a whim. They needed to be fed and walked and loved. Duffy wasn't in that stage of life. He was a carefree bachelor. Ah, yes. The topic of conversation returned. His gaze managed to find Jessica's

lips. They'd talk about that kiss just as soon as
he tackled the dog issue. "You can have her."

"My apartment has a no-pet policy." Jess
sounded wistful. No doubt, she considered
animals part of that family she'd never had.

"I can't keep her." The words couldn't
tumble out fast enough.

"Why not?" Jess scooted a seat cushion
away, nearer the opposite corner. "Ah, your
rule about no responsibility."

"Yes." He was relieved she understood.
This would make the kissing conversation
that much easier.

But Jess wasn't understanding. "Eunice
wouldn't be able to sneak up on you if you
had a dog."

"I'm not keeping this dog." The dog's ears
slanted back. Without realizing it, Duffy
softened his tone. "It doesn't like me anyway."

Jessica's smile refuted his words.

And when Duffy woke up the next morning, the dog was spooning him on the couch.

CHAPTER TWELVE

"AM I TOO LATE?" Eunice stood outside Duffy's door holding a plate, eyes blinking at Jess at an unnerving pace. Eunice's purplish hair was flat on the left, as if she'd rushed to get ready and forgotten to tease it out on one side. "Have you had breakfast?"

"No." Jess sniffed cautiously, not sure if she wanted to let Eunice in with something that would make her nauseous.

The rain had finally diminished to a drizzle. The little stray sniffed Eunice's feet. Duffy was in the shower. To date, they'd avoided discussing their kiss.

Jess didn't want to dissect it. Not who had initiated it—her. Not whether she'd thought of Greg before, during, or after—definitely no. Not the escape-from-responsibility lecture she was sure Duffy wanted to give her—ugh.

The old woman put her purple blinkers on

pause and squinted at the pup. "How could I miss Duffy getting a dog?"

"She showed up late last night." The cutie definitely preferred Duffy to Jess. She'd even attempted to join him in the bathroom. Jess tried not to take it personally, but at this rate when Baby came she hoped it didn't prefer Duffy to her. "Did you bring something for breakfast, Eunice? You shouldn't have."

Really, Eunice, you shouldn't have.

"It's fried cornmeal mash." Eunice shuffled closer, crowding Jess at the door.

Jess smelled corn bread and something fruity. Baby approved. She stepped back and let Eunice inside.

"I made it the way Mama used to." Eunice handed the plate to Jess and removed her shoes. "Flavored with strawberry Jell-O and jalapeños."

Baby did not approve. Baby shuddered as if Jess had eaten five-alarm chili.

"Eunice." Duffy stood in the doorway to his bedroom in jeans and a gray T-shirt. He rubbed his hair with a black towel. "You shouldn't have."

"That's what Jess said." Eunice was oblivious to his sarcasm as she headed toward the kitchen.

The dog trotted to his side. Jess stopped herself from doing the same. Stopped herself from grinning at him stupidly. Stopped herself from staring at his strong shoulders.

"What is it?" Duffy tossed the towel over one shoulder and followed Eunice, the stray trailing happily at his heels. "Broiled Spam with chipotle and celery topping? Rum cake with tequila icing? Pigs' feet with Alfredo sauce?"

"Duffy." Jess closed the door, trying not to imagine any of the tastes he'd suggested.

"Such imagination for a man who shows none when it comes to his own diet." Eunice smirked. "Bacon and eggs, sausage and eggs, toast and eggs. Where's the fun in that?"

Duffy flashed Jess a look of disbelief before turning back to his neighbor. "You've been spying on me." Not a question.

"Of course not." Eunice sniffed, but stared at the floor. "Your garbage tells a better story."

"Did you put on your glasses to Dumpster dive?" Duffy retorted.

"*I* do *not* need glasses." Eunice's words shook as indignantly as half of her purplish curls—the teased-out ones.

"Eu-nice." Duffy wound out her name like

a pitcher about to deliver the game-winning fastball.

"I don't think we need to go there." Jess raised her voice to an octave she imagined mothers used to keep kids in line. "In fact, we're not going there. Get some coffee. Cut up the mash and let's eat."

They both blinked at her. Even the dog stared at her with wide eyes.

"You heard me. Both of you. Eat." She'd eat mash if it meant there'd be peace.

Baby squirmed, but then stilled, perhaps realizing Jess wasn't to be messed with on this point.

The two neighbors exchanged sullen glances, and then did as they'd been told.

Just as they sat down to eat, there was another knock on the door.

It was the sheriff. He wore his familiar rain slicker and ball cap. He surveyed the group, making note of the dog with a raised brow. "Cal-Trans says they're opening the road in a few hours."

Duffy looked at Jess. Jess looked at Duffy.

She wanted to say, *I'm not ready to leave.*

She liked it here with Eunice barging in, Duffy pretending he wanted to be a bachelor, one who didn't care for his brother, and a town that was equal parts nosy and nurturing. She liked his grumpy front, the one that hid his considerate side. And she especially liked the way he kissed.

Seeing as how the people in the room seemed to be waiting for Jess to respond, her pregnant brain made an intelligent response. "Oh."

Duffy opened his mouth, then closed it, possibly to save himself from the embarrassment of a similarly astute remark.

Nate nodded, as if understanding everything that hadn't been said. "Whose dog?"

"We don't know." Duffy stared at his four-legged companion, the one perched on his toe. "It showed up last night."

"No one's reported a dog missing." As usual, Nate was a step ahead of everyone. "You might take it to the vet to see if it's been microchipped." His gaze landed on their plates. "Fried cornmeal mash. Tastes better with Eunice's marshmallow glaze and lots of milk."

Baby squirmed doubtfully.

"Now there's a man with good taste *and* imagination." Eunice blessed the sheriff with a big smile and several wide-eyed blinks.

Nate promised to call when the roads were open, and then left.

"Dig in," Eunice said. "There's plenty more."

"That's what I'm afraid of," Duffy said under his breath.

Jess poked his arm. "Behave."

Duffy sighed the sigh of the defeated and took a bite of the red corn-bread-ish meal. He chewed slowly, made a pleased sound, swallowed and then gave Jess the fakest smile she'd ever seen. "Yum. You've got to try it."

"And you doubted me," Eunice said before taking a dainty bite. "There's hope for you yet."

Jess narrowed her eyes at Duffy, deciding she wouldn't tell him how the mush looked on his teeth. "Is it spicy? Baby doesn't like spicy."

Eunice swallowed. "I remove the jalapeño seeds and then soak them in pineapple juice. Tones down the heat."

Jess's curiosity got the better of her. "Do you use the juice to make the mush?"

"Certainly. Sweetens up the batter."

Corn bread was already sweet. Jess took a nibble. It was almost too sweet. And then there was a mild hit of heat as she swallowed, but it wasn't an overwhelming heat. "How interesting."

"I told you. Mama was ahead of her time." Eunice bent her head and got to eating.

The dog whined, a genteel reminder that she had yet to be fed.

"It's chicken for you, girl." Duffy reached down and ruffled her hair, perhaps without even realizing it.

There was one less thing for Jess to worry about. That dog had found a home, for sure.

"What's the dog's name?" Eunice asked, wiping red crumbs from her lips.

"Only her owners know. She doesn't have tags." Duffy. Always intent upon distancing himself from others.

"She needs a name," Eunice insisted.

"*Dog* works." Duffy moved to the kitchen and prepared her a breakfast of shredded chicken mixed with cottage cheese.

The pup gobbled it up, licked the bowl clean, belched and gave him the soulful-eye treatment until he fed her more.

"You can't call her Dog," Eunice said when he returned to the table. "That's like calling Jessica 'Pregnant Lady.'"

Duffy grinned mischievously, showing the

effects of eating red mash by his now not-so-bright smile.

"Don't you dare," Jess warned, liking that grin far too much.

Could she kiss him again? Just once without ruining things for Baby?

Sadly not.

"When it comes to that beast, *Dog* will do." Duffy stared at his plate. "Did I really eat the whole thing?"

"Yep," Eunice gloated. "There's enough for seconds."

He pressed a fist to his chest as if removing an air bubble; more likely it was to tease Eunice. "Let's see if it tastes as good in an hour as it did going down."

"Ignoramus."

"Snoop."

They were both smiling, although not at each other.

Jess took a sip of milk, swishing it around her mouth. "Her hair is the color of golden champagne."

Duffy rolled his eyes. "Dog has more of a beer appetite."

"You can't call her Dog." Jess reached down to pat the pup's little head. "You should call her Goldie."

The sweetheart swept her fanned tail across the floor.

"I'm not keeping her." Duffy's voice firmed up harder than overdone shortbread. "If I can't find her owners, I'm sure a shelter can find her a good home."

"You wouldn't." Eunice stared at him in near horror, forgetting to blink.

Jess was afraid he would do exactly that. He was the most infuriating man, thinking he could go on with this solo act. He needed friends. But not her. She'd be family. She couldn't pretend that not talking about the kiss would make it slip through the cracks. The big-girl panties would need to be put on after Eunice left.

"I'm sure she's microchipped," Duffy continued with the hard-hearted dog-rejecter routine. "As soon as the veterinary clinic opens, we'll take her in."

"All of us?" Eunice perked up.

"Jess and me," Duffy said firmly. "Don't press your luck."

"I feel compelled to tell you," Jess said, wanting to knock Duffy off his very tall pedestal, "the cornmeal mash made our teeth red." She smiled, baring every molar, which she was sure were as red as Eunice's and Duffy's.

Eunice gasped. "Maybe that was why Mama stopped putting food coloring in the mash."

"Did you put food coloring in this? In addition to the red gelatin?" There was resignation in Duffy's voice.

Eunice didn't answer. She didn't have to.

They all knew she had.

IT TOOK DUFFY an hour to get rid of Eunice, during which time his dad called and asked if he could meet Jessica. "I'll call you back." Duffy had no idea how long Jess would stay after they opened up the road.

Sunlight broke through the clouds and the kitchen window, bathing Jess in dust-moted rays. Her skin glowed. She hummed happy notes that filled his small house. How easy it was to picture her here permanently. His gut clenched at the thought.

I don't want to be tied down.

Duffy leaned in the kitchen doorway, the golden pup at his feet. "You don't have to leave right away, do you?"

Jess faced him. Instead of her soft smile, there was a crease to her brow. "Staying is a bad idea." She wiped her hands dry on a dish towel, unaware her words had clenched his gut another notch. "You don't really want me to stay. Just like you don't want Eunice hanging around, or a dog or cat."

He'd expected her to look like Goldie, big eyes that silently begged to stay with the promise of more kisses. Her reaction threw him. He forgot for a moment that he was working his way up to asking her to stay later today, not stay forever, and went into defensive mode. "I have my reasons for wanting to be alone."

She gestured as if indicating he should share those reasons with her.

"After fifteen years of scrimping and sacrificing, I want a life of my own."

She should have looked away, should have looked sad, or heartsick. They'd kissed, after all. And it'd been a knee-quaking kiss. Instead, she crossed her arms and stared at him like a traffic cop stares down a speeder. "If you won't say it, I will. We kissed. It was an interesting experiment—"

"Experiment?" he sputtered, gut knotting near the base of his spine now.

"—but I'm like you. I'm not looking for a

wedding date or a baby daddy. I'm happy to have you in my life as Baby's uncle."

Relief. He waited for it to unknot the knots in his gut. It didn't come.

"You have this foolish idea," she continued, "that life owes you a responsibility-free period because you've had some struggles."

The word *foolish* bounced around Duffy's head like a ricocheting bullet seeking a target.

"But by virtue of having a job and renting a house, you have responsibilities." Jess rubbed the side of her stomach. The sun slipped behind a cloud and the kitchen fell to shadow. "As someone who came from nothing and has no one, you don't know how lucky you are. You have the luxury of sitting down for coffee with your neighbors, of helping out a friend after a storm, of having a loyal dog who loves you."

Duffy rubbed his forehead.

"So, no. I won't stay. I like you, Duff. But the next man I let into my personal life is going to be interested in having a family." Her composure slipped. The hurt he'd expected bled into her words. "And that's not you."

The bullet struck home, unknotting knots. Duffy rubbed his forehead once more. There was still no sense of relief, no feeling that the freedom from financial woes was protected. There was only a sense of disappointment.

His gaze drifted to her stomach, her lips and then the no-holds-barred honesty in her eyes. Fifteen years. He'd wanted fifteen burden-free years in exchange. This feeling that he was missing something was only a by-product of their kiss. Once Jess left, once his memory of the kiss faded, once they limited contact to birthdays and holidays, he'd be fine. "My parents want to drive out as soon as the roads are open. They want to meet you."

"Today?" Jess curled an arm around her belly.

"Why not today? The vineyards are too muddy to work in. My mom's off and you don't have to be at work until tomorrow."

"Okay." But it was a reluctant agreement. "I'll leave after we visit."

"Thank you." He should shake her hand or pat her shoulder, establish some distance, although not the awkward one they'd just achieved. There was one other olive branch to extend. "Do you want to come with me to the vet's office?"

Her eyes narrowed. "You're only inviting me because you think I'll adopt her."

"Dog loves you." He had to remind himself not to use the name Eunice and Jessica had given her.

"Goldie loves you more. And once you realize that, you'll keep her."

They drove to the vet's office. Goldie rode on the truck's center console as if she'd been riding in trucks all her life. For such a frou-frou-looking dog, she had chutzpah.

The vet's office was small. There were cats in carriers, slanted eyes peering out suspiciously. Someone had a guinea pig in a large shoe box. A man with an overweight dachshund sat in the corner reading a magazine.

Despite not having a leash or a collar, Goldie sat quietly between Duffy's feet. She didn't growl or shake. She looked as if she were used to being around other animals every day. *Ho-hum*. Someone had done an excellent job training her and was probably heartbroken that they'd lost her.

An old man with wild white hair, bushy white eyebrows and thick glasses sat behind the counter. After about thirty minutes, he called their names. Duffy carried Goldie forward.

After Duffy explained they'd found her, the old man took her from his arms. "We'll see if she's microchipped. I've never seen this dog before. And I've been a vet here for decades."

After a few more minutes' wait, a much younger man returned with Goldie and introduced himself. "I'm Dr. Jamero. She's not microchipped. I checked reports of lost animals with the shelters in Cloverdale and Santa Rosa. No dog fitting her description has been reported missing."

"What does that mean?" Duffy asked, although the sinking feeling in his gut knew what it meant.

"The last stray that turned up here was reclaimed within two weeks." Dr. Jamero transferred Goldie into Duffy's arms. "If she wasn't abandoned, someone will claim her soon. You can keep her until then, can't you?"

He'd been wanting to take off next weekend and drive up the coast. Just him and his truck, with no schedule. A dog changed all that. Even a temporary dog.

"He can keep her until her owners show up," Jess answered for him.

Duffy didn't argue.

Jess was wearing her own clothes today. Jeans and a red sweater. She looked like a woman with her act together. No one would suspect she'd grown up on the streets, or been romanced out of her savings, or that she'd lost a chunk of her memories. She was a strong woman. Again, Duffy wondered why Greg had chosen her.

Lacking answers, Duffy turned away from her. "How much do I owe you?" he asked the old man behind the desk.

"Nothing. It's on the house." When Duffy arched a brow because nothing was free, the old man added, "We do, however, sell dog food, collars and leashes."

Duffy bought a bag of dog food, a leather leash and a gold rhinestone-studded collar that Jess couldn't stop admiring. His purchases would go with the dog, of course. As soon as her owners showed up.

CHAPTER THIRTEEN

THE CLOUDS WERE SPARSE, but large, and blocked the sun for several minutes as they walked out of the vet's.

The most recent cloud to pass overhead made everything in the clinic's parking lot seem gloomy. Jess shivered and shoved her hands in her jacket pockets. Duffy hadn't argued with anything Jess had said about who he was or what he wanted from life. She hadn't realized how much she'd wanted him to want her until he'd stood there as distant as the clouds. Sadness sat like a lump in her throat. She should have been excited that Duffy's parents wanted to meet her. Today. Without delay. But she couldn't shake the sense that she'd already lost something, something she wouldn't gain by meeting them.

"What now?" Duffy asked, sounding irritated, as he pulled into his driveway.

Agnes stood in front of a dated green

Buick parked at the curb. Rose and Mildred waved from behind foggy windows. Eunice stood on Duffy's front steps, a rain-slickered guard who still had a lopsided hairdo.

"We came to show Jessica the town." Agnes was wearing the welcome-mat smile.

Jess took it at face value and smiled back.

"Why are you going to show her around?" Duffy the killjoy was back, ignoring the little dog bounding happily across the grass to greet Agnes.

"So she can grow to love it and open the bakery, of course." If there was something that unsettled Agnes, Jess had yet to see it. She certainly wasn't fazed by grumpy vineyard managers. "Wouldn't it be lovely to have your niece or nephew close by? You could really help Jessica out with babysitting and running errands."

"Maybe this isn't such a good idea." Jessica came around the front of the truck in time to see Duffy's lips compress, his arms cross.

Icicles gave off more warmth than Duffy did. "Don't let me stop you." But he looked at Goldie, not at Jess. He scowled at the well-behaved, sweet-tempered dog in need of a home. It didn't matter that Goldie wouldn't be much trouble. Duffy didn't want any ties. He would have seen a caged bird in the same light.

It hit Jess then. The reality. In Duffy's eyes, she was like a cat. Independent, but still in need of care and feeding. If she stayed in town she'd be a burden to him. Not financially. She thought they were past that. But he'd feel a need to check up on her, just as he did Rutgar. He'd see her as part of the excess baggage he had to carry.

The icicle that was Duffy prickled Jessica's skin. It made her feel ornery and ready for a fight. Since she'd come to Harmony Valley, she'd tried to respect Duffy's wishes, but that was useless. He wouldn't feel better if she moved to Siberia. She couldn't live her life trying to please him. Why not take a look around town?

"Okay. I'll go," Jess said.

That drew Duffy's full attention, like a cold wind from the top of Parish Hill.

"You're afraid." She poked him in the chest. "And what you're afraid of is that you can't stop us, any of us, from needing something from you. I might need babysitting. Eunice might need help starting her car. And Flynn? He might need help bringing people to town. He might need you to smile at a stranger and say hello." She poked him in the chest again. "They call old men like you curmudgeons." Jess marched to Agnes's car.

"What do they call young men like me?" he asked.

"Sticks-in-the-mud," Eunice hollered at him.

"Did someone paint a target on my back?" Duffy feigned trying to look over his shoulder.

"You did." As Jess was getting in, she looked over at Eunice. "Aren't you coming?"

Eunice brightened like a purple glow worm. "I'd love to." She hustled across the lawn.

The sun came out. Car doors slammed. Goldie hesitated on the lawn between the Buick and Duffy.

"Come on, Dog," Duffy said in a gruff voice. "You should know when you're not wanted."

Jess rolled down the window as fast as she could turn the crank. "*Goldie* is wanted." Jess spoke to Eunice as Agnes pulled away from the curb. "You'd take her, wouldn't you?"

"I'm not an animal person," Eunice hedged.

Drat. "Ladies?" Goldie deserved a good home.

"Jessica." Rose had rejection in her tone before the rejection ever came. "We're so old, we don't even buy green bananas. Taking in a pet at this point in our lives wouldn't be wise."

"I'm afraid she's right." Agnes idled at the corner. "Which way should we go?"

Jess longed to turn back. How could anyone reject such a wonderful dog? Baby gave Jess's bladder a good kick, as if to say if things were different, Baby would want Goldie. How Jess wished things were different. She rolled up the window and leaned her head against the glass.

"You should take her by the schools first," Mildred said from the front seat.

"Parish Hill," Rose said from her side of the car. "The view is spectacular."

"The town square is right here." Eunice adjusted herself on the hump. "It's the most romantic. And we are coming up on Valentine's Day."

"I believe Eunice has a good point." Agnes made the turn to drive around the town square.

Jess glanced back. Duffy and Goldie stood on the lawn, looking like woebegone castoffs.

I won't feel sorry for him.

But she did. He looked as if he'd just realized he didn't want to be alone. Jess knew all about being alone.

Baby gave her bladder another thump. Jess patted her belly. She was lucky. She wasn't alone anymore.

"Look around, Jessica." Agnes could barely see over the dashboard, but that didn't stop her from pointing out the sites. "This is where so many good things happen."

The town square was a large, grassy space presided over by a large, spreading oak tree.

"We hold the spring festival here," Mildred piped up.

"And pumpkin bowling for the Harvest Queen." The way Eunice said it, she'd been chosen Harvest Queen a time or two.

"Marriage proposals." Rose pointed toward the lone bench under the oak tree. "Will asked my granddaughter to marry him right there. It's a town tradition."

They drove Jess around the block for a complete view, and then headed toward the schools, chattering all the way. When they passed Duffy's house again, he'd gone inside.

"It looks sad," Eunice said when they parked in the elementary school parking lot. The high school was right next to it. She craned her neck to see past Mildred's teased white curls.

Agnes shushed her. "It needs children, Eunice. Excuse me." She stepped out of the car to make a call.

The playground equipment was rusty. The stucco walls were a dingy gray. Even the lines in the parking lot were faded. Eunice was right. It was sad. And then the sun disappeared behind a cloud and it became even sadder.

They moved on to an empty plot of land at the southern edge of town. The ribbon of two-lane highway that Jess had taken to get here curled around the far side of the property.

Agnes turned in her seat, smiling like a real estate agent on the scent of a sale. "Mayor Larry says there's a small grocery store chain interested in building out here."

"They'd open a pharmacy," Mildred added. "With a drive-through, I hear."

"And have one of those movie-rental machines." Rose wiped the fogged window with her sleeve. "Do you think they'll have musicals? I love musicals."

Agnes and Mildred reassured her they would.

"Flynn mentioned last night that he's got another lead on a doctor," Agnes reported. "We could have used one with Rutgar on Sunday."

"We could use a doctor who isn't as old as dirt and about to rest in some." Mildred's comment received shushes from everyone in the car but Jess.

"But we don't want someone wet behind the ears, either," Rose allowed. She tapped Agnes's seat back. "Where are we going next?"

"The bakery." Agnes put the car in gear and headed back.

A few minutes more and they were driving down Main Street, which was filled with cars.

"What's going on?" Jess asked. But no one answered her.

Agnes pulled into the one empty space on the street, right in front of the bakery. "We wanted to show you how many people are interested in you having a business here."

Chairs had been placed on the sidewalk. They were all filled. More people were gathered inside. And they weren't all elderly, gray-haired people.

Flynn had his arm around a woman with a long dark braid down her back.

Slade was there, holding hands with Christine, the winemaker Jessica had met the first day she'd come to Harmony Valley.

There was the young vet, Dr. Jamero, with his hand on the hip of a petite blonde woman who looked to be a few months pregnant.

There was a tall blond man with his arms around a smiling brunette with a streak of what looked like blue paint on her cheek.

And then there was Duffy, standing on the outskirts of the crowd with Goldie at his feet. He still had that lost and rejected look about him.

It took them a few minutes to get out of the car. Mildred with her walker. Eunice because she'd seen her reflection in the rearview mirror and worked like mad to fluff up her hair on one side.

A weed-thin Asian man sat in a walker and reached for Jessica's hand as she approached. "We're supposed to tell you what type of baked goods we'd buy from you. I got stuck with bran muffins." He peered over his shoulder to make sure the woman with Flynn wasn't within hearing distance, and whispered, "Don't tell Becca, but I'd much prefer a chocolate doughnut."

"Thanks for the honesty." Jess moved on up the receiving line.

People wanted cookies and scones and cupcakes and brownies and all sorts of breads and muffins. They all seemed so happy to see her, ready to become her customers, and perhaps, her friends.

"This is my wife, Shelby." Dr. Jamero looked like he was moonstruck in love with the petite blonde.

"I wanted to introduce myself because I'm pregnant, too." Shelby's belly was a molehill compared to Jessica's mountain. "And reassure you. The hospital in Cloverdale is very close. Just thirty minutes. And Patti just retired here with her sister. She's a nurse practitioner." She leaned in to whisper, "I'd love to have someone else in town with a baby."

Jessica's cell phone rang. She stepped between two parked cars for privacy.

"Will you be in tomorrow?" Vera asked sullenly. "I had people asking for your blueberry scones this morning."

Jessica refused to feel guilty. She didn't normally work Sunday and Monday. Tomorrow, Tuesday, was her regularly scheduled shift. "I'll be there." But her gaze drifted to the bakery and the people who seemed to appreciate her more than her boss.

"Good. Your scones have become our bestselling item." Vera was in a much calmer mood today. "Where are you? It sounds like you're in a crowd. You didn't lie to me and go to the Bahamas with a man you just met, did you?"

"No." Jessica choked the word out. Her gaze collided with Duffy's. Immediately, she felt steadier. "I'm at a bakery in Harmony Valley."

"Your bakery," Eunice said unhelpfully, having been eavesdropping. "We want you to stay."

"What?" Vera shouted. "What was it that woman said?"

"She said have a nice day." The lie dropped from Jessica's lips easier than too-thin frosting from a teaspoon. Jess hung up.

She'd most likely have to deal with an upset Vera in the morning. But there was too much noise, too many people drawing her inside and wanting her attention for Jess to dwell on her boss's mercurial moods for long. Besides, the Martin photographs were there at every turn.

Jess let herself get lost in the crowd and believe, if only for a few minutes, that she could have it all.

"DOES YOUR DOG need a playmate? My Bailey is free on Thursdays and Sundays."

"So well behaved. Do you train dogs? My Sparky could use a little obedience work."

"Which vineyard will you be working on next?"

"Are you and the baker having a baby?"

Each comment snipped at the cord tethering Duffy's patience in place. And with each snip, Duffy took Ryan's advice about misdirection and pointed toward Jess. "Have you talked to Jess? She's a great baker."

Residents turned away from him too easily. He'd come here because Agnes had given him a call after she'd taken Jess on a tour of the town. But now that he was here, he felt like an outsider. He was no longer the newest addition to Harmony Valley. It was Jess they flocked to. Not that she'd agreed to move here, but he had to face facts: it was only a matter of time before she did. He should be happy for her. Life didn't always put dreams within reach.

Goldie whined softly, crowding his feet.

She looked as if she were afraid she might be stepped on by an orthopedic shoe.

Duffy picked her up. "Don't get used to this."

She promptly licked his chin.

People were starting to leave, shuffling and limping and laughing as they headed toward cars or made their way down the block. Jess stood talking to Flynn and Slade. Duffy joined them.

"We've got trucks. We can move your things up here," Flynn was saying. "Pick a day."

A tic took root in Duffy's cheek.

"I…uh…" Jess pressed her hands into the small of her back, gaze sweeping the sidewalk.

"You haven't said no. To us that means yes." Slade gave her his business card. "When you're ready, we'll be here."

Jess opened her mouth to say something, but nothing came out. It was past lunchtime. She and Baby hadn't eaten anything since Eunice's teeth-staining mush. She didn't have a bottle of water with her, either. Looked like pregnant brain was settling in.

"You guys forget how overwhelming Harmony Valley can be to newbies." Duffy took her arm. "Baby needs to be fed." He led her toward El Rosal.

"I'm still mad at you." Jess tugged her arm free.

"I know." He set Goldie on the ground. She trotted on the sidewalk next to him. "I'm not so happy with you, either."

Jess walked in silence.

He should have left it at that. He couldn't. "I earned it, you know."

She kept walking, but wouldn't look at him. A very un-Jess-like move. "I don't know what you mean."

"When Greg took the money, he left me to help Mom and Dad. I wasn't the kind of guy who could just let them fend for themselves. Not only did I help them financially, but I was the good son. I showed up every weekend. I took my dad to watch Little League games, because he used to coach."

"*And* they were free."

"That, too," he admitted. There was pride in his voice, shoulder to shoulder with the resentment. "I was there for my mom when she went through a cancer scare. I was there through my dad's depression when he was rejected for experimental spinal treatment that might have restored the use of his legs.

For fifteen years, I came second to them. Is it too much to ask that I take some time to worry about me for once?"

"I'm not asking you to take me under your wing." She stopped. "I'm not asking to date you. I came here for answers and was over-joyed at the chance for Baby to have family."

He stopped with her. Goldie trotted ahead to El Rosal's patio, where a few bakery sup-porters had stopped for lunch. Several pairs of eyes turned their way.

It was Jessica's gaze that caught him, along with her pique. "We can be friends, right?"

Her exasperation was clear, but being friends with Jess was impossible. Because he'd kissed her. Duffy's nonanswer only seemed to frustrate Jess more.

"I haven't asked a thing of you. I don't plan on asking anything of you. And if your aversion to making friends annoys me, that's my problem."

He believed Jess. He knew her well enough now that he could tell the determined set to her mouth meant he had to explain or she'd keep at him about having a friendship.

Duffy tapped his temple. "Up here, I get that you aren't going to ask for money. Up here, I get that you don't want me on call for babysitting." And then he placed a hand over his stomach. "But here. Here's where all that worry sits. All the gone-wrong, what-if scenarios. This is where my memory of Greg lives. And I don't think it's ever going to move."

But it was times like these, when he looked into Jessica's dark eyes, when he wished it would.

A familiar white car turned onto Main Street and honked.

Duffy's parents had arrived.

CHAPTER FOURTEEN

THEY HAD LUNCH on the patio of El Rosal, where Goldie was welcome to join them.

More clouds were gathering. The combination of the propane heaters lining the patio and Baby, plus the opportunity to be part of Greg's family, should have warmed her. But she'd taken one look at Duffy's mother and felt a chill in her bones.

Duffy's father sat across from Jess in his wheelchair. His hair was a rumpled gray-brown. His face was creased with lines. Knowing some of his story, Jess could've assumed the lines came from stress and disappointment, but his caramel-colored eyes had too much twinkle and his smile too much joy.

"You knew my boy." Thomas Dufraine reached across the table for Jessica's hands. His legs may have been boney, but his hands clasped Jessica's with strength and vitality. "And this—" he pointed to the belly crowding her ribs "—must be my grandchild."

Jessica smiled tentatively.

Sitting kitty-corner from her, Duffy's mother, Linda, hugged herself with bony arms and glacier-like disapproval. Her shoulder-length hair was too-dark brown, as if she'd just had it done and had used the wrong shade for her pale and pointed features.

"How did you make it up here so quickly?" Duffy asked.

"Your father saw on the internet when the road was scheduled to open." Linda's voice was sour, as was the downward slant to her lips. "We parked on the road for thirty minutes. Waiting."

"We don't know much about the last few years of Greg's life," Thomas said, brushing aside his wife's bitterness. "Could you... would you...share?"

He wanted her memories. Beneath the table, Jessica's knee started to bounce. Goldie had been lying on the patio between their chairs. She sat up and looked at Jess.

"I told you she had amnesia, Dad." Duffy's hand drifted from his lap to Jessica's knee. His hand was big and reassuring. He may not want to nurture anyone, but he knew how to give comfort when needed.

Jess moved her smaller hand over his. "I remember only a few things."

Linda cleared her throat and hugged herself tighter.

"The times I do remember were spent simply. He liked to go to the airport and watch the planes take off."

The smile on Thomas's face broadened. "I used to take you boys to the airport when you were young, remember, Michael?"

Duffy nodded.

"We went to the farmers' market a few times. He…um…liked fresh vegetables." She had the vague impression that Greg enjoyed talking to farmers.

"Linda's quite the gardener. The boys used to help." Thomas seemed delighted with Jessica's vague recollections.

Linda's face was pinched as tight as a dried prune.

"I'm sorry that I don't remember more," Jess said.

"You remembered who the father was." There was no mistaking the venom in Linda's tone. "And somehow you found Michael."

Duffy gave Jessica's knee a gentle squeeze. "She saw my picture in the paper. Otherwise, she'd never have found us."

"It's a blessing." Thomas rubbed his wife's stiff arm. "You don't question blessings."

Linda wanted to. It was there in her unwelcoming eyes. But she sat as still as a statue immortalized in an unflattering pose. Only the flare of her nostrils gave away that she was actually breathing.

Linda was quiet all through the ordering process, quiet through the wait for their food and all through their meal, which she barely touched. Jess had considered Duffy a hard case when they'd first met, but Linda was a hard case times eleven thousand.

When they were done, Duffy took his father inside to use the restroom and pay.

As soon as the restaurant doors closed behind them, Linda uncoiled like a snake preparing for a strike. Her arms extended along the length of the table. Her hands gripped its edges. "Can you describe my son's tattoos?"

The chill in the air became a brittle cold that needled Jessica's bones. Baby pressed against her lungs. She managed to gasp out, "I don't think he had tattoos."

Linda didn't acknowledge if Jess was right or wrong. "And his habits? Was he a morning person? Did he drive too fast? Did he slurp his spaghetti noodles?"

Jess didn't remember. Baby squeezed her lungs some more. Her gaze darted to the restaurant windows, but she couldn't see Duffy. And she couldn't breathe. "Don't you know?"

"Of course, *I* know."

Jess couldn't picture Linda holding Baby and singing sweet lullabies. She couldn't picture Linda taking dozens of pictures at Baby's first birthday. She couldn't picture Linda shooing her out the door so she could babysit her grandchild. Which was exactly what Linda wanted, she realized.

"You want to make sure I'm not lying." Jess tried to fill her lungs with air. Failed. Shifted. Wheezed, "I can't prove anything."

Linda's gaze glittered with hate and suspicion. "Then we'll want a DNA test."

"To prove the baby is Greg's?" Duffy had never asked for proof. "Do you have Greg's DNA?" A strand of hair? A baby tooth?

A glint of movement showed Duffy pushing his father's wheelchair closer to the door. Goldie was waiting just outside for him to return.

"I have Michael. They have the same DNA." Linda followed the direction of Jessica's gaze. She leaned over the table, her chest nearly sitting in her untouched beans and rice. "How much do you want to disappear?"

"Nothing." Jess wanted to be part of a family. She pushed herself to her feet, her cold and clumsy feet.

"What are you two talking about?" Thomas asked, smiling as Duffy wheeled him to their table.

"It was a pleasure meeting you." Jess tried to smile. It felt as if she were lifting her lips when they'd been tied to hundred-pound weights. "I need to get back." To her life. To a place where her heart and her baby would be safe.

"Mom." Duffy's voice was a quiet reprimand. There was no surprise in his expression. He'd anticipated this from his mother all along.

Linda had sat back in her chair, arms crossed again. "She's lying about everything. That's not even Greg's baby."

"I didn't come here to get something from you. Any of you." Jess found Duffy's gaze. He hadn't warned her. He'd said his mother would want to spoil the baby. "I came here to learn about the father of my baby. I don't put conditions on love."

Linda scoffed. "Who said anything about *love*?"

"Mom," Duffy warned, more sternly this time.

"No," Jess said. "Let her cling to her fear. Even if I shared my memories of Greg with her, she wouldn't be happy."

"You said you couldn't remember." Linda was spiraling out of control. "She said she couldn't remember. She lied. It's Greg all over again."

"Linda, please." Thomas wheeled himself closer to his wife. He reached for her. "This is our grandchild."

Linda shook her head back and forth, as if she could erase the situation if she denied it vehemently enough.

Duffy moved to Jessica's side. "I'm sorry. I was hopeful she'd believe you the way I did."

"What made you believe her, Michael?" Thomas asked.

This was so wrong. Love wasn't supposed to be like this. There was supposed to be trust, not proof. Jess turned to go. Baby thumped her bladder.

Duffy reached for her hand, holding her in place. "I believe Jess. That should be enough."

Linda made a derogatory sound.

It didn't matter. Duffy's hand was warm around Jessica's cold fingers. He trusted her. He believed her.

He just didn't want anything to do with her.

Jess found her voice, as thin and fragile as a silken thread. "I can remember Greg being kind to me, stopping to help me change a flat tire. I can remember him bringing me flowers and sharing a dessert in a restaurant. But those vague memories will never satisfy you. You'll always doubt me and my child." She stayed when she should have left it at that. Her gaze fell on Duffy's father. "Thomas, you refuse to see the bad in your son. I loved him, but he wasn't a saint. I may not remember enough to prove it, but I feel it in my heart." Duffy's mother looked aghast. "And Linda, you only see the bad in him. I couldn't love a man who was more bad than good. Why would you resent anyone who could see the good in him?"

Duffy's grip on her fingers tightened.

"And Duff…" Here, Jess hesitated, because she didn't want to hurt him, but the words—*the words!*—they pressed forward. "Duffy, you don't want to see your brother at all. I don't even know why you carry that picture in your wallet or why you framed that photo in your living room. I may not remember Greg, but I want to. Not only do you not want to recall anything positive about your brother, you don't want to make good memories with the people around you today." She'd run out of air, but somehow managed to get out this last: "You all need to forgive Greg and each other."

The Dufraines were speechless. The lunch crowd at El Rosal was speechless. Even Baby was still.

"I have to go. I really have to go." Jess managed to work her way past the wheelchair, the bitter woman and the man whom her heart felt she could love.

"DON'T SAY A WORD, Mom," Duffy rasped after Jess crossed the street heading for his house.

Jessica's shoulders were hunched and her head hung low. Duffy could relate. He felt defeated, too. It was one thing to think about Greg poorly, to feel relief when he was gone, but another to have his lack of love for his brother be spoken out loud.

I loved him, his heart protested weakly.

Around them, the other customers had fallen silent, enjoying the show.

His mother looked as if she were about to launch into a repetitive chorus of *I told you so*. At his glare, she pressed her thin lips together.

"I like Jess." Dad was altogether too chipper. "She hit all the points on the bull's-eye."

That unhinged Mom. "What does it matter what that woman thinks?" She gathered her purse. "She knows now that we won't be easy marks. We'll need proof before she gets a dime."

"She doesn't care about money." All she'd ever wanted was family. Even if it was only a make-believe one in an abandoned bakery.

"She cared about Greg," Dad said gruffly. "And she seemed to care about you, Michael."

He'd done a good job of squelching anything in that direction. "I'm not looking for a relationship." And what she'd said about forgiving Greg? He wouldn't know where to begin.

"Exactly what Jess said." Dad reached for Duffy's hand. "We've talked in circles about Greg for so long, kept our wounds and defenses on lockdown. It's refreshing to hear someone give it to us straight. I loved Greg, despite what he did. The loss of a son is worse than the loss of money."

"You're a fool," Mom said, moving to take the handles of his wheelchair.

"I'm a fool with a big heart. I've got room in it for you and Duffy and Greg and my grandchild. And maybe even for Jessica."

Another maternal head shake. "You'll be broke in a month if you let her come around."

"I don't think so." Dad gazed up at Duffy. "Michael doesn't believe it, either."

"I can't have any part of this." Mom looped her purse over a wheelchair handle. "Not without proof."

"What if she signed a document saying she had no claim to Greg's money?" Ah, the price of peace. Although it had been Jess who originally suggested it, Duffy felt it would take a global summit to get Jess to agree now.

"Talk to her before she leaves, son. Give your mother some time to get used to the idea of being a grandmother."

He didn't say anything about Linda forgiving Greg. They both knew that was impossible.

ALL TOO SOON, Jess was at Duffy's house, digging through her purse, setting a ten on the table to cover her lunch bill. When she reached her car, Duffy appeared at the hedge.

As if sensing she was leaving, Goldie ran up to her, most likely because she didn't want to miss out on a car ride.

"Not today, girl." Jess bent to pet her. When she straightened, Duffy stood before her, his face as hard-edged as the first day they'd met. "Thanks again for putting up with me. I…uh… I'm not going to apologize for lunch."

"I'm not asking you to." Classic Duffy. "But about that—"

"I'll let you know when the baby comes." Best not rehash the negative.

He'd given her his cell phone number earlier, but hadn't asked for hers in return. She imagined it was his way of keeping his distance. He couldn't call to check up on her, as he had with Rutgar, if he didn't have her number.

Duffy's attention drifted toward Main Street and the bakery, but he didn't bring up her moving to town. "Are you sure I can't talk you into a dog?" Goldie had taken her usual position at his feet, one of her small paws on the top of his boot.

"No." Impulsively, she reached up and hugged him, pressing a kiss to his cheek. Without meaning to, her belly bumped him and she wobbled.

His arms came around her. "Careful."

Careful, darling. That china cost more than you make in a week.

Jess gasped.

"Are you okay?" Duffy asked, lips close to her ear.

She gripped him tighter.

I hope you're okay, because I'm not. I missed an important business meeting to have dinner with you.

Memories drenched her. Each one a hit from Greg's ugly-boyfriend playlist.

"No," she whispered. "No."

Greg's laughter. Not joyous. Not friendly. Not warm.

It was a gamble. We pooled our money for the franchise application and it was turned down. If you can't build another nest egg soon, we're done.

She'd left him. She'd left him. She'd left him.

With her pride in tatters and her heart bro-

ken and her bank account empty. Because
she was afraid if he knew about the baby,
she'd be tied to him and his lies forever.

Or worse. That he'd consider her and her
child nothing but a financial obligation.

"Greg didn't steal from me." Jess stepped
from Duffy's embrace. "I gave him the
money. I loved him. He said we were apply-
ing for a bakery franchise. The application
money was nonrefundable."

"And you believed him?"

"I…" A feeling set its grappling hook
on her insides. A feeling, not a memory. "I
think I gave him the money because I was
pregnant. I think I wanted him to stay and I
thought… I believed the only reason he'd stay
with me was if I gave him what he wanted."
She was pathetic. Money didn't make people
stay. Love did. She'd known that before the
accident and had fled…into the path of an
oncoming car.

"How much? How much did he take?"

If she told him, Duffy would feel responsible. She knew him well now. He may claim
he wanted no part of being responsible for
anyone, but that was only a lie he told himself. He cared. He'd try to make things right.

Goldie sat at his heels. She knew a good man when she saw one.

"It doesn't matter. I gave him the money. He didn't steal it from me. I might just as well have gone to Vegas."

"You remember it all?"

"Snatches. Answers." An ugly side to Greg she didn't want to think about.

"My mother…"

"She'd eat that for breakfast and demand more at lunch."

His hesitation indicated he agreed. "My parents want to see you again."

That wasn't happening. "I'm not going to answer twenty questions for your mother." Not because she wouldn't, but because she couldn't.

"She might be the grandmother you want if we drew up a contract."

Jess placed her hand on his cheek. There was stubble there. And warmth. And strength. None of it hers long-term. "I meant what I said. I don't want your money. I don't want to prove who I am. If I sign a paper, it won't make us family." That had to be earned. "Baby deserves a positive, happy environment."

"Baby deserves family." His eyes were

caramel-soft. His voice honey-smooth. "And a contract is the best way to compromise with my mother and solidify family. Isn't that what you came here looking for?"

"Some families you're born into. And some you wrap yourself up in along the way." She could feel the Martin Bakery calling from here. Jess pulled her hand free. "I want to be wrapped up. Or else I'll take nothing at all."

CHAPTER FIFTEEN

JESS WAS GONE. It felt like for good.

He should have been relieved. Instead, he was shamed. She'd loved Greg. His brother had taken her money. And she'd forgiven him. Why couldn't Duffy do the same?

Because he didn't want to. Along with the money, Greg had stolen some of the best years of Duffy's life. Dad's accident fifteen years ago had changed things forever, but it was Greg's greed three years later that had started a slow press that threatened to squeeze the life out of Duffy. Just thinking about it made him sick.

In bed that night, Goldie snuggled closer to his shoulder with a gentle sigh. He stroked her thin, curved spine, resting his palm on the silky fur over her haunches. She rubbed her nose on his hand and then relaxed with another contented sigh.

Duffy relaxed, too. Goldie didn't put any conditions on affection. If you treated her with respect and care, she'd love you in return. Duffy couldn't understand how Jess and Dad could love and get past the hurt and betrayal.

Sleep was elusive. In the wee hours of the morning, he took Goldie outside, staring up at the cloud-darkened night sky. More rain was coming.

He brewed coffee, half listening for the snap of a branch, half looking out the window for the tremble of pink curlers. He ended up on the couch, his limbs cramped and coiled as he stared at the picture of him and Greg in front of a Christmas tree. That photo was one of the few his mother hadn't torn up when Greg had left them.

He had fond memories of his brother, didn't he? Why couldn't he remember?

How did Jess stay so calm in the face of lost memories?

It began to rain again. The wind blew drops against the living room window, like a series of spats in his face. More rain. The vineyards would be too wet to work. After taking a "rain day," there'd be a team meeting at the winery first thing. He should probably call Rutgar and see how those nurses he'd complained about were treating him.

He'd check the internet to see how the roads were looking and give Ryan a heads-up. He continued reviewing his mental to-do list.

Unexpectedly, his otherwise occupied brain dredged up a memory: Greg stealing his Halloween candy. His brother had been wearing a superhero cape and it had snagged on the corner of Duffy's dresser after he'd fallen asleep, waking him. He'd chased Greg around the house until they'd both collapsed on the couch, exhausted and laughing.

There'd been backseat slug-bug fights. They couldn't ride anywhere without one. Greg had given a good charley horse. But there'd been plenty of laughter, too.

And those arguments over who'd open their birthday presents first. They'd resulted in odd years being Greg's turn. Evens, Duffy's.

Once the gates had opened, the memories kept coming, like planes on a tight landing schedule.

They'd played on the same Little League teams with Dad as their coach. Duffy at shortstop. Greg in center field. Spring afternoons spent warming up with a game of catch, always paired up. But competitive. If Duffy got a hit, Greg tried for a home run.

They'd ridden scooters and skateboards, outgrown cleats and sneakers, mowed lawns and clipped hedges. There was nothing out of the ordinary about the fights they'd had as siblings. Nothing indicative of Greg's potential to derail them all. Nothing one had done much differently than the other.

They'd been in the same classes together through the sixth grade. Shared the same circle of friends. Liked the same girls.

The same girls.

As if they shared the same DNA and heart, wanting the same thing.

Jess.

He'd kissed her. Was it because Greg had dated her? Had the old competitive streak been reignited?

Jess would spit fire at the idea he'd wanted to kiss her to put Greg in his place.

That kiss had nothing to do with Greg and everything to do with the empty spot in Duffy's chest, the one he hadn't realized was empty, the one Jess seemed to fill.

Not that he needed her here or needed to kiss her to fill that void. Not that he needed the void filled at all. He liked his life. He could acknowledge his biases and follow the path he'd taken after Greg's death without remorse. No attachments. No outside responsibilities. He was free and happy.

Goldie rested her chin on Duffy's hand and stared at him with those I-don't-care-if-you-lie-to-me eyes.

"Don't get comfortable. Your owners will most likely turn up in the morning."

Unconcerned, she closed her eyes.

On a sigh, Duffy did likewise.

He dozed off only to be awoken by a knock. The sun was up and the rain was gone. Goldie ran to the door, wagging her tail. Duffy shuffled after her, yawning and working the kinks out of his neck.

"Good morning." Eunice held a plate of deviled eggs. "I thought I'd bring breakfast over early today."

Duffy rubbed a hand over his face and peered at her eggs. "Are those anchovies?"

"Yes. And chopped green olives. I used curry powder instead of paprika." She beamed at him. "Old family recipe."

Duffy's stomach rolled in on itself. "Jess isn't here."

"I know." Eunice's smile dimmed. "I saw her leave yesterday. She was gone before I could get my shoes on to say goodbye."

More likely Eunice's face had been glued

to the window during their farewell. The old woman was nosier than a bloodhound on a fresh fox trail. It was too much to hope for that she'd go away.

Duffy opened the door wider. "Don't you eat normal food for breakfast? Pancakes? Sausage?"

"No." She headed toward the kitchen. Purplish hair, red jacket, matching slacks and neon green sneakers.

Duffy needed sunglasses. Or at the very least, another cup of coffee. He followed her.

Eunice put the plate down and turned, hand on hip. "You should have kissed her."

"You should mind your own business." Duffy poured her some coffee, and then got down the pancake griddle. "I'm not eating your eggs. And you're not feeding them to the dog, either."

Slumping her shoulders, Eunice put the egg in her hand back on the plate. "I suppose I can take them around town. Most people enjoy my cooking."

"People are too kind to tell you they throw it in the trash when you leave." Duffy took the mixing bowl Jess had used to make cookies out of the cupboard. It was just a bowl. And yet holding it brought a smile to his face.

"You're not nice," Eunice said, doctoring her coffee.

"I must have something going for me." He felt a smile spreading on his face like the weeds he'd no doubt find in the vineyard after all this rain. "You keep coming back."

"It's the coffee." She'd put on red lipstick today. It marked the lip of her mug. "Women put up with a lot for a good cup of coffee."

"This I did not know." He went back to staring at the bowl. It was as empty as the void in his chest.

"That just goes to show how little you know about women."

Duffy opened his mouth to comment, but nothing came out. In an odd way, Eunice was right.

JESS WAS LONELY.

Oh, she had Baby. But there was no Goldie with her conversational whines, no Eunice with her off-the-wall recipes, no Duffy. Really, that was it. There was no Duffy. She'd gotten used to his steady presence, his straightforward questions, his shoulder to lean on if she needed it.

And the bakery. She missed Harmony Valley's bakery. She felt welcome there, not a misfit like she did at Vera's Bakery. Why had Vera thought she'd fit in there?

Jess walked into Vera's Bakery on Tuesday morning. There were polite greetings exchanged, but everyone was soon busy. Jess assembled ingredients for scones at her workstation.

Vera stopped by. "Don't scare me like that, *chica*. I wasn't sure you'd come in today."

"I told you I'd be here." *Leave it at that. Leave it...* Jess couldn't. "Why did you hire me?"

Her boss waved her hand as if the question was inconsequential. "I run a bakery. You were needing a six-month apprenticeship."

"But why me?" Jess had a feeling she knew.

Vera frowned. "Are you asking for a raise since your apprenticeship is over? Because I'm not giving you one." Before Jess could refute her assumption, Vera barreled on with the feistiness of the guilty. "Yes, you've been an asset. You make the flakiest croissants in town. And maybe our cakes are lighter now, too."

"Don't forget the scones. They're your best-seller." Jess crossed her arms and looped the conversation back to the beginning. "You made me a job offer without interviewing me."

"And you accepted without coming to interview," Vera countered.

Because she'd been flattered. "You hired me because I have a Spanish last name. You assumed I'd speak fluent Spanish like the rest of the girls."

Vera nodded. "True enough. But I wouldn't have hired you if you also didn't come with the proper credentials."

She'd gotten her answers. Jess looked at the eggs, at the butter, looked at her life in a whole new light. "I don't fit in here." She wouldn't have questioned anything if she hadn't seen Martin's Bakery in Harmony Valley.

"You do just fine, *chica.*" The cupcake earrings swung over the rose tattoo on her neck. "You come, you bake, you get paid. Why do you need to fit in? What more do you want?"

She wanted what she'd had in Harmony Valley. To belong, to have people interested in her as a person, not Jess the baker. But there was Baby to consider. And Duffy. The last thing she needed on her conscience was to take on a bakery she couldn't handle and be put on Duffy's to-take-care-of list.

"You young people." Vera shook her head. "Never satisfied with what they have."

"That's because we know there's something better waiting for us," Jess murmured.

"THE VINEYARDS ARE still mostly puddles." Duffy leaned against the kitchen counter in the winery offices where they were holding their staff meeting. "I've got my chain saw in the truck. Ryan and I can clear the tree from Parish Hill."

At the mention of power tools, Ryan's eyes lit up as if he were a child counting down to an Easter Egg hunt.

Goldie rolled onto her back and thrust her delicate legs into the air. Duffy doubted she'd like the roar of power tools as much as his coworker did.

"If you're headed up that way…" Christine topped off her coffee and returned the pot to the warmer. "Would you mind helping Slade and Flynn remove the tree from Rutgar's porch, as well? I saw a picture of it and I think the job might need skills outside their wheelhouse."

Working on Rutgar's house was not in his

job description. Removing the old man's tree fell under the heading of community involvement. And community involvement led to other favors, and other favors led to expectations, and pretty soon there went his weekends again. "Well, I…"

"I wouldn't ask, except I know Slade has never operated a chain saw and the tree is huge." Christine's eyes held a worried plea. She'd never tell Duffy to do it. "Plus my grandmother said you've been calling to check up on Rutgar in the hospital."

Ryan gave Duffy a double take. "You've been checking up on the big man?"

"I carried him out of his house." Duffy tried not to remember how Jess had looked down on him for not wanting to create ties to the community. "I'm allowed one phone call." Or three.

"You're brilliant." Ryan grinned as if his school loans had been paid off. "Rutgar will never get in our way again."

Duffy seriously doubted that, but he let the kid think he'd done it just to create some winery goodwill.

"So you'll help clear the tree?" Christine wasn't letting him off the hook.

"Aren't there contractors for that?" Duffy

scuffed his work boots on the wood floor. "Insurance agents and the like?"

Christine shook her head. "Because most residents are older, they either can't fix things themselves or they can't afford to pay for the work. A five-hundred-dollar deductible can be devastating." She smiled the smile of a woman unwilling to take no for an answer.

"So you've cleared this with Rutgar?" Duffy asked. The tug to volunteer was stronger now, as if Jess were behind him urging him to accept. "He asked for help?"

"Well...no..." Christine's smile faded. "My grandmother had a feeling that he'd want to tackle it himself."

"Old fool would probably kill himself." Part of the reason they hadn't released Rutgar from the hospital was that he continued to have severe headaches and vertigo, side effects from his concussion.

"My sentiments exactly," Christine said. "Flynn and Slade are headed up to his house soon."

"Millionaire repair," Duffy said half-under his breath. "That's what they should call it." When Christine raised a brow, he said louder, "I've seen them around town." Slade, Flynn and their wives and buddies roped into cleaning out rain gutters and replacing missing roof shingles.

"It's not as if they don't have real work to do themselves. They go through weeks where Flynn's writing code and Slade's on the road networking with potential buyers." There was a note of pride in Christine's voice. "They won't admit it, but they enjoy the physical work, and taking care of others brings them satisfaction."

Of course, they would. They were millionaires.

"Anyway." Christine picked up her mug. "I know as a vineyard manager, you've probably supervised the removal of trees, fallen or upright. For my own peace of mind, could you head out there?"

"Pretty please," Ryan added. "I'll help."

Goldie jumped on the bandwagon, sitting up and cocking her head.

Jess would have approved.

Which had nothing to do with him saying yes.

"WHAT'S THAT?" VERA CROWDED next to Jess to see what a courier had delivered. "A lease? What do you need a lease for? Are you moving?"

The kitchen at Vera's bakery was nearly empty. Only Jess, Vera and Rocio remained. The morning baking had been done. They were working at a slower pace now, filling orders for pies and special-occasion cakes to be picked up later in the afternoon.

Jess lowered the sheaf of papers. "It's nothing." But her heart was pounding. Everything she'd been promised in Harmony Valley was outlined in the first few paragraphs. Rent free. Utilities free. Facilities up to code. Appliances provided. "They don't have a bakery in Harmony Valley and they made me an offer to move there."

"What?" Vera shrieked. "After all I've done for you?"

"I'm not leaving."

"Lies," she scoffed. "You tried to leave me before."

"Before…" Jess clutched the edge of the table.

I paid the institute for the right to hire a master baker. And now—mere months after you arrive—you tell me you're starting your own place? This had been followed by a string of words Jess hadn't recognized. But the tone was clear—she'd turned her back on the woman who'd given her a chance.

"You knew about Greg?"

"Well…uh…" The heat left Vera's expression. "I never knew your baby daddy's name." She waved her arm as if wiping a slate clean. "I knew he wanted you to go into business together. And then you had that accident and he disappeared. It all disappeared."

"You came to the hospital." Minutes earlier, Jess had been trying to convince herself she was content. Now she was anything but. "When I told you I couldn't remember being pregnant, you held me when I cried. You never mentioned anything about the details I didn't remember."

"I was happy you were staying." Vera's gaze switched to calculating. "You are staying, no?"

She doesn't care about me. She never cared about me.

Jess had been in a cage without ever knowing it. Her fingers had a moist hold on the lease. On freedom. "I thought we were friends." Worse. She'd thought they'd formed a family of sorts. She'd put up with Vera's outbursts and pendulum temper, because there was security in the kitchen.

"I like you, *chica*. I want you to be happy

here. Why do you think I encouraged you to find someone?"

Jess shrugged, but it felt like an act of surrender.

All those months. The fear of the unknown. Vera said nothing.

"I figured if you found someone, you'd stay." Vera sharpened her stance and her voice. "You're a hard worker. I can rely on you. Tell me I can rely on you."

In the corner of the kitchen, Rocio had stopped sweeping and was staring at Jess. She wasn't as skilled a baker as Jess, but Rocio had talent. The bakery would go on if Jess left. Their scones wouldn't be as good, but the bakery would continue.

Jess couldn't lie to herself. There was a part of her that wanted to remain here. And in that regard she was no better than Duffy, drawing into a shell because life had been hard before.

But she couldn't quit, not mere weeks before Baby was due. She had no real savings to speak of and no one would hire a pregnant woman, not to mention, Vera might not give her a reference.

"I'm trapped here." The papers shook in her hand as if they were trying to catch her attention, pointing to a means of escape, one that was too difficult to reach. "I don't think I can stay."

Vera was shouting, but Jess couldn't hear above the rushing noise in her ears.

She couldn't stay. And she couldn't go to Harmony Valley. What was she going to do?

CHAPTER SIXTEEN

DUFFY ARRIVED AT Rutgar's with Ryan, Goldie and a fair amount of reluctance.

"Did my fiancée send you?" Slade's question would have been off-putting if not for the trace of humor. He came over to the truck. His blue jeans were new. His jacket was new. Most likely his experience with big fallen trees was new, as well. "Christine thinks we're going to kill ourselves."

Duffy noted where they'd placed a ladder—leaning on the fallen tree that was balanced on the porch—took in their lack of rope either on the ground or tied to the tree with something to stabilize it, and the small size of their chain saw, and sighed. "Christine was right."

Ryan turned to Duffy and whispered so only he could hear, "I so worship you right now."

"I was just about to search online for a fallen-tree-removal how-to video." Flynn raised his phone. At least his clothes looked like they'd seen a hard day's work. "We'd have figured it out."

"Probably after one of you was flattened by that tree." Duffy didn't relish putting the men who signed his paycheck in their place. But he did want them to live so they could continue to sign his paychecks. He reached in the truck for the necessities—safety goggles, gloves, Goldie.

Ryan hurriedly produced his own goggles and gloves.

The little dog began a perimeter search, nose to the ground. Duffy hoped she didn't rile something that would eat her. It wasn't unheard of out here to come across foxes, bears or mountain lions.

"You two can go back to work." Slade pulled the boss card, too late in Duffy's opinion. "We'll be fine."

"Trouble is…" Duffy bit back his annoyance as he tugged the goggles over his head, leaving them looped around his neck. "We don't report to you. Christine sent us to do a job."

Other than a woodpecker hard at work, there was no sound on the mountain.

"We're not going to win this fight," Slade

said to his business partner. "If we send them away, Christine will show up next."

"With my wife." Flynn shrugged in defeat.

Duffy opened the tailgate, grateful the two men were open to reason. "Why is it I only ever see you two working around town? Where's Will?" The third business owner.

"He's buried deep in some code he's trying to crack for a new app we're creating." Flynn earned points by slipping on a pair of work gloves. "Once he gets his part done, I'll be wrestling with the graphics."

"And once it looks semisuccessful…" Slade also had gloves. His were unmarked tan suede. "I'll be setting up meetings to see where we can sell it."

Duffy dragged the chain saw case closer and flipped open the lid.

Ryan hung over the side of the truck bed, practically salivating. Flynn and Slade started to laugh.

"That thing is huge." Flynn punched Slade's shoulder. "Makes the saw we bought look like a starter set."

"Have you used that thing before?" Slade eyed it, and then took stock of Duffy with newfound respect.

"This isn't my first rodeo, boys." Duffy

took in the wear and tear on the saw and smiled. He was as bad as Ryan, excited to use his equipment. Jess was right. He did have a wild side.

It took several hours to clear the tree and cut it into chunks that dropped safely to the ground. Once Duffy had the tree clear, the winery owners were more in their element. They shored up the porch with support beams, and removed the cracked and damaged wood.

Flynn's father stopped by at one point. He was a grayer, wirier version of Flynn. His truck wasn't new or shiny. He had a lockbox filled with tools in his truck bed and wore work boots that looked as if he'd had them for twenty years. The older man surveyed their progress, nodded at Duffy and said, "You'll do." He left them a box of shingles, roofing nails and a new rain gutter.

Duffy and Ryan packed up their tools, preparing to make the short trip to the Parish Hill vineyards and clear the driveway of the fallen tree. Goldie wasn't so gold anymore. Her coat was mud-darkened and wet. But the look on her face was dog nirvana. She'd barely flinched when they ran the chain saw. She must have been a Labrador in another life.

"Thanks for all your help." Flynn shook Duffy's hand.

Slade was next in line to thank him. "What are you doing later? There are more trees and branches around town that need removal. And we can always use a helping hand when things come up."

Warning bells rang in Duffy's head. *Ding-dong, freedom is dead.* "Like a regular thing?"

"Yeah." Slade wasn't picking up on Duffy's hesitation. "What are you doing this weekend? We were thinking the reason we aren't successfully luring any doctors here is that the old clinic is…well, old."

"Needs some work," Flynn agreed.

A gust of wind worked its way past Duffy's jacket, tensing his shoulders. "Sorry, guys. I was planning on driving up the coast this weekend."

Flynn and Slade regarded him as if he were one of their unsolved strings of code. Ryan shook his head as he retreated to the truck. Duffy could only imagine what Jess might have said had she been here. But he couldn't say yes. He just couldn't.

"Well," Flynn said, filling the awkward silence, "if you change your mind, you won't have to look far to find us."

The two men walked toward the house.

Guilt gripped the back of Duffy's neck. Or maybe it was muscle fatigue from hours of wielding a chain saw.

"Hey," Flynn said to Slade. "When we're done, let's stop by the bakery and see if they got the power turned on."

"Why?" Duffy asked. "Did Jess accept?" He didn't like the eager way he'd asked, as if he cared if she accepted or not. His life would be easier if she turned them down.

"She hasn't said yes. Not yet." Slade turned around. "But I have a good feeling about Jessica. The mayor sent her the lease today so she'd have the offer in writing."

"YOU WERE TRAPPED in a moat-flooded town for three days, and your life changed." Ryan dragged a branch off to the side of the vineyard's drive.

Duffy looked up from lubricating the chain saw. "What are you talking about?"

"You got a dog and a girlfriend."

The wind seemed to swirl at Duffy's ankles, circling, shackling him to obligations he hadn't asked for. Duffy chose his next words carefully. "I'm fostering a dog, and my *brother's* girlfriend came to visit." Duffy saw again Jessica's soft smile, heard her gentle laughter, could almost feel the strength of her hand in his. He planted his feet firmly on the ground and glared at Ryan. "You gossip like an old lady."

"That's because I hear all the news from old ladies." Grinning, Ryan didn't flinch under Duffy's angry reaction. He tugged another branch free of the tangled, downed mess. "I get it. None of my business."

"Exactly."

"It's just that—"

"Ryan." Duffy rocked back on his heels, unable to keep the irritation from his voice. "It's a long walk back to the winery from here."

The younger man considered that for a moment and then nodded, dragging the tree limb out of the way.

Duffy's phone rang.

Christine thanked him for helping at Rutgar's. "Ask Ryan when we're getting results from the lab on the Parish Hill samples we sent in."

Duffy did. "He says by Friday." At least one loose end would be tied up by then.

He hung up and finished lubricating the

bar and chain. He was about to start the chain saw when his phone rang again.

It was Nate. "They're sending Rutgar home on Friday."

Duffy had a ship-sinking feeling he knew where this conversation was going.

"I'm due in court that day, otherwise I'd pick him up." It was hard to get a bead on the sheriff. Was he annoyed? Stressed? He had one tone of voice: unflappable. "I'm not comfortable with one of the elderly residents bringing him home in case he's still unsteady on his feet. So I talked to Christine and she said she could spare you to go get him."

Duffy's lower back twinged, the way it used to when his debts became too heavy.

THE WOMEN IN Harmony Valley talked about two things—their men and their grandchildren.

Lacking both, Eunice usually kept quiet when they gathered. But a strange thing happened after Jessica left town. Women asked Eunice about Jessica and Duffy. Two days after Jessica left, Eunice was running out of things to say.

She ignored the quilt she should have been

redoing, and knocked on Duffy's door before he left for work.

The little stray he'd adopted barked.

When he opened the door, she handed him a casserole dish.

"Is that for me?" He looked down on it with a turn of his nose. "What is it?"

Eunice didn't want to say before she was invited in. And when he didn't invite her in, she squeezed past him. His house looked the same, but without Jessica it seemed lifeless. "Last Minute Casserole."

He closed his eyes briefly. For a man, he seemed to have the most delicate constitution and the most limited experience with food. "Which means what?"

"Tater tots, Spam, cream of mushroom soup, broccoli and cheese." Lots and lots of cheese.

"It sounds more like dinner."

"The Spam makes it a breakfast food." Eunice bent to pet Goldie, who wagged her tail. At least someone was happy to see her. "And the tater tots. Also breakfast food."

"I suppose you want to join me for *breakfast*." He sounded incredibly weary for first thing in the morning. He was probably missing Jessica.

A MEMORY AWAY

"It tastes better on top of toasted English muffins." And she knew where he kept them. Eunice charged ahead.

"This is becoming a thing," Duffy said.

Eunice turned from the cupboard, holding the muffins. "What is?"

"You bringing food over every day." He crossed his arms. "I'm capable of feeding myself."

"I'm sure you are." She decided offense was the best defense. She put two English muffins in the toaster, and then asked casually, "Have you heard from Jessica?"

"Ah, I should have known. You're the conduit to the town grapevine."

"I'm not following," Eunice fibbed. The trouble with Duffy was that he was too smart.

"I know how things work in this town." He had the most annoying way of looking at a person, as if he could see inside their brain and tell exactly what they were thinking. "One person gets the goods and tells everyone else."

"You say that like it's a bad thing." She sniffed. "I wouldn't stop by if I didn't care." No one else seemed to. Not even Agnes had visited him. "Oh, look. Your dog has filled out. I can't see her ribs anymore."

"She isn't my dog." Duffy frowned. It was a deep, deep frown. "She's only staying here until her owners turn up."

Eunice might have believed him if not for one thing—Goldie was a dainty little dog, the kind of dog single men didn't usually own. If Duffy didn't love her, he'd have gotten rid of her days ago. "Last fall, Shelby, the vet's wife, found a Saint Bernard and the family came to claim him a few weeks afterward." She tsked, watching Duffy closely for any sign he might fear losing the dog. "Letting go nearly broke Shelby's heart."

"She's not mine." He sounded adamant and looked just as determined not to show her he cared.

Goldie sat next to Duffy with her paw on top of his foot. Anyone could see that dog was here to stay. It was typical of Duffy to overlook the good things that passed through his life.

Why, the man needed a good pair of glasses!

JESS WAS IN TROUBLE.

No job. No job prospects. No job paycheck.

No one wanted to hire a master baker who'd be needing time off in a few weeks.

Not that they told her that specifically. She'd dropped by every bakery she could find in town, résumé in hand, bun in the oven. Surprise, surprise. No one had an opening.

She wanted to phone a friend. Too bad she'd fallen out of touch with her foster-home sisters. And she was too embarrassed to call her fellow culinary school students. That left Duffy or Eunice or…

Instead of calling, Jess paced the living room of her small apartment Friday morning. The lease, Slade's business card, the newspaper clipping with Duffy's photo and her cell phone sat on her secondhand dining table. Each time she completed a circuit around the table, Baby kicked.

Okay. That was an exaggeration. But it certainly seemed that Baby wanted to go to Harmony Valley. Jess wanted to go, too.

If only she could be sure it was the best choice for her child.

Unfortunately, it seemed like the only choice left for her. *Doing nothing is the coward's way out.*

Jess picked up the phone and called Slade.

"How's Jessica?"

Everywhere Duffy went, people asked him about Jess.

On the one hand, it was starting to annoy

him. He wasn't sure how Jess was doing. On the other hand, the town had stopped watching him as if he were a veteran quarterback trying to make a comeback.

Goldie rode shotgun with him everywhere. She loved exploring the vineyards. She loved people. Duffy kept trying to find her a new home, but everyone kept telling him that it was too late. Goldie was his dog.

Picking up Rutgar on Friday got Duffy out of town and gave him an excuse to see his parents before taking the old man home. He hadn't counted on his dad insisting Duffy take them to see Jess. He hadn't imagined his mother would have drawn up legal paperwork for Jess to sign, forgoing any claim she might have had to Greg's money. Didn't contracts like that take time? He'd been hoping she'd forget he ever mentioned it.

Duffy drove them to Vera's Bakery. The weather was still blustery, but most of the clouds had cleared away. The ride over was mostly silent. Goldie sat in Dad's lap.

"I like your dog," Dad said.

Duffy felt the beginnings of a headache. "I don't think that contract is the best way to approach Jess."

"I need it," Mom said.

"It's a compromise," Dad said.

Duffy was afraid it was a deal breaker.

It took a few minutes to get the wheelchair out and set up, and push Dad inside the building. Mom stood near the door, clutching her contract and a ticket with a number on it. Her hands were shaking.

"It's going to be okay." Duffy put his arm around her shoulders. "Why don't we leave the papers for another day?"

"No." She was stiff and unyielding in the crook of his arm. "You'll thank me later."

Duffy doubted it.

The bakery was high-end. Planters and umbrella-covered tables outside. Inside, slate floors. Mosaic-topped tables. A new-construction smell. Glass display cases that were filled and ran the length of the place. Two fancy espresso machines. And customers. Lots of paying customers.

They waited silently for their number to be called. It was a long wait. There was only one woman working the counter—Rocio, by her name tag.

Duffy ordered three coffees and three blueberry scones. "Is Jessica working today?"

The clerk stared at Duffy as if he'd sprouted fangs and asked to suck her blood.

"Uno momento." She practically ran to the back room.

"You didn't have to scare her," Dad said.

Duffy spread his hands. "I didn't do anything."

But others in line shot him with sharp, dark looks.

An older woman with a white hairnet covering her too-bright red hair appeared. She smiled the way vendors did with customers when they suspected there was a problem. "I'm Vera, the bakery owner." She spoke with a heavy Spanish accent. "May I help you?"

"We're looking for Jessica." Duffy felt like Prince Charming had come calling for Cinderella. All he needed was a glass slipper and singing mice.

"She doesn't work here anymore." There was no longer welcome-and-I'm-ready-to-please in her tone. Vera had her guard up. "Are you her lawyers?"

"I knew it," Mom burst out in scalding tones. "We need this." She raised the contract to the ceiling.

"Linda, please." Dad reached for Mom's free hand, but she snatched it away.

"Is Jess okay?" Duffy asked. "Did she

have the baby?" And why would she need a lawyer?

Vera narrowed her eyes. "Oh. But it's you." Her tone softened. She squeezed Duffy's forearm, and then picked up the plated scones. "I recognize you from the newspaper. Come. Sit." She led them through the crowded dining area to a table near the window. "So you're the baby daddy's family." She looked them over as if she were trying to determine which apples to include in a tart and which to toss out.

"She stole from you, didn't she?" Mom blurted, dropping into a chair. "This…this… *Jessica*. If that's even her real name."

Jess deserved none of his mother's scorn. Shame and anger burned through Duffy like a gas-ignited fire. At any moment, he'd explode. "If you can't behave, Mom, you'll have to wait in the car."

Surprisingly, Mom sealed her lips.

Vera frowned. "Jessica would never steal."

Duffy seconded that. "Then why did she leave?"

"Because…" There was a trapped look in the older woman's eyes. It took her too long to answer. "Because she has a…a…*benefactor*."

His mother huffed. Duffy felt like huffing, too. How could she afford to leave her job right before Baby came? The truth was she couldn't. She should have called him. Hopefully, she would soon.

"Someone offered to help her start a business," the bakery owner chattered warmly, except it was the false warmth of a snake before it struck. "She left. Without giving her two weeks' notice." The woman's tone and gaze dropped, and she muttered, "Without sharing her recipe book. I'll be ruined."

Mom shook her pages, but otherwise remained silent.

That didn't sound at all like Jess. "Did you argue?"

"No, no." Vera drew back in mock denial. "She wasn't going to work out anyway once the baby came. She couldn't put in the hours. No matter how many times I told her this, she wouldn't believe me."

Duffy didn't believe the bakery owner, either.

"Sounds like discrimination," Dad said. "On your part."

"I would never fire her. Her skills have made my bakery trendy." Vera waved to Rocio and said something in Spanish, then gave them that fake smile again. "Take a dozen cookies. On the house."

"She's bribing us." Mom crossed her arms, content to direct her bitterness at a new target.

"Dos docenas. Dos!" Vera called to Rocio. *"Rápido."*

"Two dozen?" Now Dad looked as uptight as Mom. He leaned forward. "What have you done?" he asked.

"I can give you three dozen," Vera offered. "Final offer."

"We'd rather have *her*." A sense of urgency snapped Duffy's shoulder blades back. They were wasting time. Something had happened, something that wasn't right if Vera thought they were Jessica's legal team. "We need Jessica's address or phone number."

"It would be inappropriate for me to give that to you." Vera stood and backed away. "Enjoy your cookies."

"I'm going to choke on them and then sue this place," Mom declared loudly, causing several patrons to stare. "Michael, why don't you have Jessica's phone number?"

He had trouble admitting it. "Because—"

"Because you didn't want anything to tie yourself to her," Dad said with a disappointed shake of his head. "A phone number would mean you'd feel responsible to call."

The three of them looked at each other. The father with unshakable love. The mother with a broken heart. And the brother who boxed up his relationships and stored them out of reach.

Duffy couldn't speak for his parents, but he was afraid of what he might lose if he opened up. Not fear for his bank account. Not fear for his free time.

This was a fear that hit harder, had the potential to devastate. He feared for his heart.

CHAPTER SEVENTEEN

"THIS IS ALL your stuff?" Flynn scanned the suitcases, few boxes and furniture in Jessica's apartment Friday afternoon. Once Jess had accepted, the young entrepreneurs had wasted no time coming to get her.

"I don't have much." Jess had more boxes marked Kitchen than she did clothing in her two suitcases. It had been too easy to pick up empty boxes from a local grocery and pack them. Was she moving too fast?

She still had doubts about moving at all. What Harmony Valley was offering felt like a handout. And then there were the unknowns…starting with how she'd sustain her energy level through to the end of her pregnancy, to what Duffy's reaction to her showing up would be, ending with how much time she'd need off when Baby came. And what had they said about day care? The unknowns. They sat on her chest, squashing her lungs, making it hard to breathe.

Slade's broad shoulders filled the doorway. He took inventory quickly. "We didn't need two trucks for this."

"You don't have a dining room set?" Flynn seemed stuck in a state of disbelief.

"I have a kitchen table. No chairs." Jess tried not to agonize over her lack of possessions.

"What about a crib?" Slade glanced into her bedroom. "Or a rocking chair?"

"I haven't bought any furniture for Baby yet." And she'd have to balance that need with the cost of buying supplies for the bakery. She desperately wanted an espresso machine. "Do you really want me to come?"

"Of course, we do." Flynn shed his doubts as easily as he adopted a fresh smile. "Let's take out the couch first."

In no time, Jess was back in Harmony Valley.

"WHERE'S YOUR WOMAN?" Rutgar asked, petting Goldie, who sat next to him on the center console in Duffy's truck. "Did you trade her in for this poor excuse of a dog?"

Duffy resisted the urge to defend Goldie. She had a quiet way of winning people over.

"Jess went home." Duffy's voice was louder

than necessary, but he was worried, his ego bruised by her lack of contact. He couldn't wait to get back to Harmony Valley and track down Slade. Surely he had Jessica's contact information. Why hadn't she called him when things went sour with her job?

Because I made it clear I'm not interested in taking on more responsibility. Even friendship.

"In my day—" Rutgar's voice was sandpaper-coarse, pumicing Duffy's jangled nerves "—if you wanted a woman, you asked her to stay and made the offer attractive with a ring, a big juicy steak and the promise to remodel the house."

"I don't need your advice," Duffy said through gritted teeth. "She's not… We're not… She *dated* my brother." He carefully avoided using the word *love*. The more he dwelled on Jess loving and forgiving Greg, the more his own unresolved feelings tumbled about his gut.

"I wouldn't hold a grudge against her for that." Rutgar's chuckle was as rough as his voice. "Heard your brother's dead. That baby's gonna need a father."

They passed vineyards owned by the winery, flanking the two-lane highway. Overgrown vines undulated in the breeze, calling to Duffy to transform them into neat, tidy vineyards.

A change of subject was in order. "Flynn and Slade fixed your porch."

Rutgar ignored him, drawing Goldie into his lap. *Ha!*

"You young bucks nowadays need a masculine influence. If you aren't going to be there for the girl, I will."

"What?" Duffy nearly choked.

"You heard me. I'll need her address, so I can write her."

Forget for the moment that Duffy didn't have Jessica's address. "There's a new invention you might not have heard of—a telephone."

"I read in *The Wall Street Journal* or somewhere that no one calls anyone anymore."

Rutgar read *The Wall Street Journal*? Duffy's head hurt. "They were right. People don't call, they text." He could text Jess. If he had her cell phone number.

"Well, I type," Rutgar said firmly. "I have a perfectly good electric typewriter. And I trust the US Mail to deliver messages for me."

Duffy made the turn toward Harmony

Valley. "Do you need to pick up anything downtown before I take you home?" El Rosal had a mini-mart in their lobby area that sold the essentials.

"I do." He pointed to the road ahead. "Now, what you'll want to do is take this road for three miles, then turn right on Kennedy, then right on Main Street."

"You do realize I *live* in Harmony Valley." And had for nearly a month. Duffy knew the way.

"That doesn't mean you know how to get there the right way."

There were only two roads into town from the highway—one to the east, one to the west. They'd taken the latter. "That tree hit you harder than I thought," Duffy deadpanned.

"I didn't ask for a comedian," Rutgar spat, splaying his fingers through his massive beard. "I asked for a ride."

JESSICA PARKED ON Main Street. Flynn and Slade had driven into the back alley with her things.

Martin's Bakery. The sun made the front windows sparkle with blinding intensity. She didn't care. She was steps away from it being hers. Jess could barely breathe for fear she'd wake up and this would all be a dream.

"This is it, Baby." Pregnancy brain or not, she was doing this. "We're home."

When she got out, the glare off the windows diminished, revealing a legion of elderly women inside.

Jess opened the door and the women surrounded her until she felt like a fat sardine in a too-small can.

There was still a musty odor, but now there was also the strong smell of disinfectant.

It didn't matter what the place smelled like. The photos were there. Familiar sepia faces that welcomed her, reassuring her that this was where she belonged.

"We've been cleaning." Eunice's purplish curls were trembling with excitement. "Upstairs and down."

"Oh…" Pity alert. It shuddered through her system and threatened to put a snap in Jessica's tone. "Thank you, but I can't afford to pay anyone."

"My dear." Agnes laughed, a reassuring sound. "We don't expect you to pay us."

Sweet curls, sweet smile, sweet pink cheeks. Mildred bumped a woman out of the way with her walker, and patted Jessica's arm. "You're family now."

Family. The word blanketed Jess with warmth, eased her breath, settled her nerves.

"What do you want done with all the pictures on the wall?" Rose asked, pointing to the faded photo of three generations of bakers behind the counter. "We saved dusting them until last in case you want them taken down."

"I *love* them. They stay. They're a part of the bakery's history." And they gave her a much-needed confidence boost.

The mayor, an older man with a tie-dyed T-shirt and ratty blue jeans, stepped forward. His gray hair fell in a long braid down his back. "Did you bring your lease? Signed, I hope."

Jess fumbled in her purse for the paperwork and handed it over.

After a cursory check to be sure she'd signed everywhere, Mayor Larry grinned. "I'd like to present you with keys to the building, and wish you good luck." He handed her a small key ring.

Jessica pressed the keys firmly into her palm in the hopes that the sharp edges would prove she wasn't dreaming, that this feeling of euphoria was real and right.

And then the door behind her opened. It was Duffy. Not frowning, not scowling, not looking as if the world was about to end. That didn't stop her chest from cinching with worry. His acceptance was important to her. For Baby's sake.

Rutgar stood behind him, a bandage on his forehead. Goldie danced on her hind legs at the window, peering inside.

Duffy had told her to do what she felt was right. But that didn't mean he could set aside his fears and embrace her moving to town.

Embrace. His arms. His kiss. Her heart. Not the appropriate word.

"Baby needs to sit down," Jess said, sinking into a chair.

The crowd parted to let Duffy through, but didn't back away to give them privacy.

Not that they needed privacy. Anything Duffy had to say, he could say in front of the entire town. She hoped.

"I was looking for you." Duffy's hand hovered in midair as if he wanted to touch her but was undecided about where. Finally, he rested it gently on her shoulder. "My parents and I went to Vera's this morning. Why didn't you call me about what happened?"

"I'm sorry… I…" And then to her horror

she felt the weight of the week—of quitting, of an unfruitful job search, of the unknowns of starting a business—it all fell on her. The weight crushed her composure like walnuts beneath a meat mallet. She started to cry.

The women pushed Duffy aside, quick to offer tissues and hankies and consoling hugs.

Rutgar sat heavily in a chair next to Jess, knees bumping table legs. He claimed one of her hands. "I could clear this place out in thirty seconds if I had my gun."

A dozen women let Rutgar know exactly how welcome that suggestion was. Unfortunately, they did so all at once.

"I was joking," Rutgar roared, silencing the room.

"I'm so embarrassed." Jessica wiped away her tears. "Baby likes a good cry at all the wrong moments. I'm fine. I swear." Mortified, but fine.

A small bundle of fur was placed into her arms. Goldie licked her chin.

"She missed you," Duffy said.

"Hey," Flynn yelled from the back door. "What's going on in here?"

"Nothing," Duffy called out. He was head-and-shoulders taller than anyone else standing since Rutgar was sitting.

"Duffy's so sweet," Mildred whispered loudly.

"A keeper," Eunice added.

"I'm sweet. I'm a keeper," Rutgar announced, flicking his long hair over his shoulders like a fashion model.

Duffy's jaw hardened, but he kept his eyes on the rear of the bakery.

"Here's the paperwork for your licenses and permits." Agnes dropped a thick stack of papers on the table. "If you fill them out this weekend, we'll take you to get them submitted at the city, county and state levels on Monday. As soon as you pass a health inspection, you'll be officially in business."

The feeling of being overwhelmed returned. Jess was about to reach for Duffy's hand when Flynn said, "Hey, Duffy, we could use some help back here."

Duffy gazed down at Jess, his expression unreadable. "You okay?"

Jess nodded, glad she hadn't reached for him. She knew the last thing Duffy wanted was for her to rely on him in any way.

"WHERE'S THE REST of it?" Duffy asked after they set the love seat down in Jessica's pink apartment.

A twin bed. A dresser. A love seat. An end table. A small kitchen table. A couple of suitcases. And less than a dozen boxes, most of them labeled Kitchen. Jess had fewer possessions than he did. There were so few items, Goldie was almost done inspecting them all.

"This is it," Flynn confirmed with a sad shake of his head.

"This is it?" Eunice joined them. "All Jessica's things?"

Nodding, Slade kept his voice low. "She doesn't even have a crib. I'm sure someone in town has one she could borrow that's been stored away in an attic or garage."

Duffy didn't like the idea. "Safety standards on cribs have changed a lot since anyone here had kids."

"Maybe the town could throw her a baby shower." Flynn bent to pet Goldie.

Anger at Greg was usually a bitter, hollowed-out feeling in Duffy's stomach. Not this time. This anger pounded in his veins, demanding action. Greg should have done better by Jess. He should have realized she was different than his normal mark. "Jess has known people here less than a week and she has an aversion to charity. She'll have kittens if we throw her a baby shower."

"She'd accept a baby shower if you and your family threw her one." Eunice eyed Duffy speculatively. "*Family* are expected to throw baby showers."

His mother's attitude toward Jess and Baby was still a work in progress, contingent upon a document Jess might never sign. "We could wait until after Baby comes." Hopefully by then his mother and Jess would have found neutral territory.

Runaway train that she was, Eunice ignored him. "We're not waiting. We can have it downstairs. I'll take care of everything. The invites, the cake, the food…" Her purplish hair was the last thing Duffy saw as she hurried downstairs.

"This is going to be a disaster." Duffy looked down at Goldie.

She returned his regard with a cock of her head that seemed to say, *What's the big deal?* Despite his rules, the traitorous little beast had been the recipient of some of Eunice's creations slipped to her under the table by the cook herself. Goldie may like Eunice's goods. Duffy did not.

"Come on." Flynn smiled as if the problem had been solved. "Women love this stuff. Let Eunice take over."

The problems were just beginning. "The food," Duffy said, hoping his words could convey the horror. "She'll serve something like pickled raviolis with peanut butter on the side."

"You just made my stomach turn." Slade put a hand above his belt.

"Exactly." Heaven forbid Eunice make that teeth-dying fried mush. She'd be the laughingstock of the town.

"Agnes will know what to do." Flynn proceeded downstairs. "But if not, you'll need to fix it."

"Me?" This wasn't a vine that had to be pruned or a downed tree that had to be removed. This was a baby shower. And Jess.

Slade slung his arm over Duffy's shoulders. "Imagine for a moment that Jessica learns you knew what Eunice was planning and did nothing."

Duffy imagined. Duffy felt sick. Duffy caved.

"BUT I WANTED to do this," Eunice said when Duffy stopped by her place after dinner.

From what he could see, the inside of her house looked like it had been preserved from the 1950s. Wingback chairs with doilies on the backs and arms. Mod wooden coffee tables. Lamps with shades as large as small children.

"It's a big job." Duffy tried to sound as kindly as he could. But this was Eunice and kind words didn't always sink in. "I'm not trying to take over. I'm simply offering to help with the food."

"You're being sweet." Eunice gave him a suspicion-filled once-over. "That's not like you."

Duffy worked hard to keep his mouth shut. This was for Jess, after all.

It was hard to take Eunice seriously. She was wearing lavender polyester pants, a black sweater with a sequined heart on it and slippers with heels and pink fuzzy pom-poms. "You won't give me any trouble?"

"No trouble." It might kill him, but he wouldn't even pick on her ridiculous footwear.

"I accept your help." She smiled and batted her eyes at him like a red light at a busy railroad crossing. "You're now officially the assistant baby shower coordinator."

"Goody." Mission accomplished.

A few minutes later, Duffy sat on the couch

with Goldie in his lap. The do-it-yourself show on television couldn't hold his attention.

Jessica had moved here. She was pregnant. Who would check on her every morning? Eunice? He shuddered, thinking of her bananas-and-ham dish. Who would Jess call if she went into labor? The answer was never him. But who would she rely on? She needed friends.

It was after eight. Too early to go to bed. Jess had probably finished unpacking by now.

From the shell-shocked look on her face earlier, she was probably in the bakery's kitchen, baking something.

"Need to go out, girl?"

Goldie groaned a negative.

"Let's take a walk." He put his boots and jacket on.

Goldie dutifully followed him out the door.

"We'll go down Main Street and come back." No stops.

But when they came even with the bakery, his feet planted. The space in front of Jessica's was empty. Vera's bakery had outdoor tables, planters with cheerful flowers and personality. Jess had personality aplenty, but none of it spilled out here.

There was a light on in the downstairs kitchen, outlining the swinging door. A timer buzzed faintly. She'd be inside, pulling warm cookies or something equally tasty out of the oven.

Goldie stood on her hind legs and put her front paws on the door, peering inside. She cocked her head up at him, barked once and then bicycled her front paws on the glass as if trying to dig a hole through it.

The door from the kitchen to the front room swung open. Jess stood in the doorway, looking tired, worried and a sight for sore eyes. "Duffy?" Her voice was muffled.

Busted. He should wave and move on. But his boots had taken root. He wasn't going anywhere.

She flipped the lock and opened the door. "Hey."

"Hey." Duffy hunched his shoulders against a sudden gust of wind, breathing in the smell of warm sugar and cinnamon. "I thought you might be baking."

"Am I that obvious?" She inventoried his features, but it didn't feel as if she were searching for Greg. It felt as if she were drinking him in, storing him in her memory. "Cookies just came out of the oven. I could use a taster."

Jess. Her baby. The elderly town and their fix-it needs. Duffy wanted to be free to do what he wanted when he wanted. But the tug toward Jess was strong. Toward her arms and her warmth and her sweet kisses.

When he didn't answer, she said, "Never mind. Thanks for checking on me."

"I wasn't…" He had been. Of course, he had been.

The look in her dark eyes said she knew it. "Goldie probably needed to stretch her legs."

"Her owners haven't shown up yet."

She smiled sadly. "She's found her forever home."

Duffy was going to disagree, but when he looked down, Goldie was in her familiar spot—sitting next to him, one foot on his boot. His life was spiraling out of control. Neighbors and dogs and babies and mush. This could not be his life. This was not the way he wanted things to be.

"You were great today, rescuing me when I needed it most." She placed a soft hand on his cheek, brushing over his stubble to rest on his neck.

One pulse of her fingers, one gentle tug of her hand, and he'd take her into his arms.

A kiss. He wanted one. To soothe, to console, to—

She released him. "Good night, Duff."

Before he knew it, the door was locked. Before he knew it, he was back home. Before he knew it, he was alone.

He was in his own place, a decent place. He had a good job. For once, he wasn't burdened with credit card debt or the responsibility of making sure his parents could make ends meet. He should be happy. He should be fulfilled. He shouldn't want.

He did.

CHAPTER EIGHTEEN

JESS FELL ASLEEP reading the recipes and commentary in the Martin family binder. It smelled of chocolate and cinnamon and history, like a beloved cookbook should.

She dreamed of banana nut bread and happy babies and a smiling Duffy. She awoke before dawn to Baby giving the binder a good kick. Baby should have been kicking Jessica's dreams aside, at least the ones regarding Duffy.

When he'd stopped by last night, she'd assumed he'd come by to talk. And when he'd looked at her as if he didn't want to communicate with words, she'd reached for him. But he'd frozen at her touch. Nothing had changed. There would be no more touches. No more dreams of his smiles.

The people in Harmony Valley had stocked the bakery's kitchen before Jess had arrived. To avoid the stigma of charity, Jess insisted on repaying them with baked goods this morning. She'd made snickerdoodles and cream cheese brownies last night, trying to calm her nerves. It wasn't enough to fill the bakery case.

She smoothed a hand over the cinnamon roll recipe. The page was lightly dusted with flour. Written in the margin were the words *Satisfies a crowd.*

Jess hoped some of the Harmony Valley residents would come by this morning. She'd love to give back by giving them a taste of what her bakery would eventually become. "Because we don't take handouts," she told Baby, who wiggled into a more comfortable position as Jess sat up.

After a quick shower, Jess was downstairs hard at work baking cinnamon rolls. Baby was being an easy rider this morning, so she also made vanilla scones. She arranged her offerings in the bakery case on the colorful pottery serving plates the ladies claimed to have found in the cupboards. Jess still had her doubts about the plates. They were too beautiful to have been left behind. She suspected they were charity, as well. Charity would end today.

Jess set the coffeemaker to brew and then unlocked the front door. Someone had deposited two oblong planter boxes made from redwood in front of the window. They had no dirt or flowers, but Jess doubted that situation would remain for long if she didn't put a halt to things. Enough was enough.

"We are not in need. We can do stuff on our own." Jess stood in the doorway, pressing her thumbs into the small of her back, enjoying the brisk air and sunshine.

A familiar green Buick turned onto Main. Agnes parked, calling out the open window, "We're here to help. People should be stopping by soon."

Jess had suspected as much. "We're not taking any money," she said firmly. "I don't have any licenses or permits."

"That won't stop the community from dropping in. Or leaving tips." Rose flitted to the sidewalk, leaving Eunice to help Mildred out of the backseat.

"Did you fill out the paperwork?" Agnes removed Mildred's walker from the trunk and locked the sides into place. "I can review it before everyone gets here."

"Everyone?" Baby moved in a way that made Jessica's equilibrium shift forward. Like face-plant forward. She gripped the door frame.

"Yes." Agnes watched over Mildred as she seemed to be watching over Jessica. Step by slow step.

Jess had wanted to be part of Harmony Valley because people were so inclusive. But she didn't want to be a burden, someone people like Agnes or Duffy felt obligated to help.

Duffy's truck turned onto Main. They all waved to him as he passed. Goldie peeked out the window at them.

Jess felt a pang of something she didn't want to name, a pang she had to find a cure for. Duffy wasn't hers and never would be.

"He likes you," Eunice announced with a flourish of her hand, as if this were breaking news.

"He prefers to be alone." Jess led the women inside.

"He likes you," Eunice insisted. "He brought you these planters he made a few weekends ago."

Jess stopped. "Duffy made those?"

"Didn't you know?" Eunice tugged at a purplish curl. "They were in his backyard just beyond the back steps."

"I didn't see him drop them off." Perhaps he'd done so while she was in the shower. Or while she ran the mixer. Classic Duffy. He couldn't help himself. He was programmed to take care of people with a generosity that rivaled the selfish greed of his twin. And yet, she didn't feel cared for. She felt like an albatross around his neck.

"Duffy is a shy one," Mildred said, positioning her walker at a table. "Remember when we were at his house last weekend? He barely spoke a word."

"He keeps to himself." Rose sashayed past the window as if it were a stage. "I asked him about Jessica the other day and he just grunted."

"I'm agreeing with Eunice on this one," Agnes said. "He likes you. He just doesn't know how to tell you he likes you."

Jessica knew Duffy didn't lack the skill to express his feelings. In fact, he preferred to avoid them.

Eunice put her face inches from the bakery case, and fluffed her bangs in her reflection. "I'll tell him it's okay to approach you directly. Valentine's Day is around the corner."

"You'll do no such thing. I think you're all blowing this out of proportion." Baby chose that moment to do the shimmy-shake. "We're friends." Or they would be when she set down clear guidelines. No late-night visits. No touching faces or tucking hair behind ears. And absolutely no kisses. "I don't want to hear any more nonsense about it."

The elderly ladies shuffled around in their orthopedic shoes, muttering to each other about romance and oak trees and traditions.

Jess brought down the supply of coffee mugs. They were large and white and smelled of dish soap. One had a price tag on the bottom. She sighed.

"Have you picked out a name for the baby?" Eunice tugged on the hem of her teal crewneck sweater.

The women didn't wait for Jess to answer.

"How about Clarence?" Rose glided on her toes closer to the bakery case, peering inside. "He was a circus clown when I was a high flyer. Big muscles. Hair as black as night."

"Shirley." Mildred sat in her walker. "I always wanted a daughter named Shirley."

"Her baby's name should mean something to Jessica." Eunice leaped back into the fray. "Respect for the loss of a loved one or honoring a dear, dear friend."

"Well said." Agnes nodded.

Rose bounced on her toes. "She just wants Jessica to name her baby girl Eunice."

A timer went off in the kitchen and Jess

left the women to argue. She hadn't decided upon a name for Baby because she was with Eunice—she wanted the name to mean something, to be linked to family. She'd have to ask Duffy about family names. And wouldn't that conversation go over well?

She removed a tray of mini chocolate muffins. The voices in the front room dropped to whispers.

"What are you ladies talking about?" If it concerned more donations, Jess was putting her foot down.

"Nothing," they chorused.

Flynn and his wife entered the bakery, followed by Slade and Christine.

And then the bakery was a crush, as if it were the most popular restaurant in New York City.

Jess had never felt so happy. The only thing missing was Duffy.

"NO DISEASE?" DUFFY looked at the results again. He sat at his desk upstairs in the winery, examining the numbers in a chart with tiny print.

Christine took the report from him. "Ryan, are you sure we sent them a sample from the last row of the vineyard on Parish Hill?"

"I'm beginning to sense doubt in my abilities." Ryan placed his elbows on his desk and tapped the folder in front of him with his fingers. "I walked to the bottom of the vineyard, just like you said. I took samples from the smallest vines, just like you said. I sent the samples in to the lab we use in Davis, just like you said." His smile lacked his usual easygoing charm.

Duffy had been so sure the vineyard was infected. He stared at Goldie's small head resting on his boot. She clearly had every confidence in him. He went back to trying to identify what they'd missed. "And you requested they test via RT-PCR?" A reverse chain reaction laboratory test.

"Yes...no." Ryan's smile faded. "That test was überexpensive. I had them test using the ELISA method."

That explained it.

"ELISA is enzyme-based and not all the leaf-roll virus enzymes have been identified," Christine said gently.

"So we test again?" Ryan looked as sad as Goldie when she didn't get table scraps.

"We test again," Duffy confirmed.

Ryan grabbed his coat and told them he

was headed out to Parish Hill. "And here I thought I was saving a few bucks."

"We appreciate it," Christine said. "But we need the broader test."

Goldie raised her head to watch Ryan hurry down the stairs.

"Nice dog." Christine placed the test results in the trash. "You got lucky with her."

"I'm merely a foster home until her owners show up." A foster home. Goldie didn't treat him like a foster parent. Or his home as if it were temporary. She had a water bowl in the kitchen and a pillow by the fireplace. He'd found a tennis ball in the Mionetti's vineyard that she somehow got her small jaws around. She loved playing fetch. Was this how Jess had been in foster care? Had she settled in, firmly intending to stay with a family? Only to realize that she was just a number on a balance sheet?

Another set of footsteps mounted the stairs. Shelby, the wine cellar manager, appeared. Goldie trotted over to greet her, sniffing her boots with interest.

"She smells my goose. Don't you, girl?" Shelby knelt to pet Goldie.

If there was one thing Duffy could rely on, it was the unpredictability of Harmony

Valley residents. Though he hadn't expected it from someone under the age of seventy. "You have a goose?"

"Yep." Shelby stood, drawing her sweater over her baby bulge. "She mothers the kittens I rescued from the wine-cellar walls a few months ago."

"Shelby will take in any animal." Christine looked up from her email. "She could take Goldie for you until someone comes to claim her."

Duffy's mouth went dry.

"You having trouble with this girl?" Shelby's voice pitched high. "I don't believe it. My husband might make a fuss, but I'll take her."

Duffy had to swallow twice to work up enough saliva to speak. "She's fine. No trouble at all. I'm sure her owners will show up any day now."

"Be careful." Shelby's features tightened and twisted into an expression that betrayed unresolved wounds. "When the original owners show up, it's devastating to let them go."

"It's only a dog," Duffy said. But he felt the lie in his words. Foster care. Goldie deserved better than that. Jess deserved better than that. They both deserved a permanent home and unconditional love.

"If you change your mind, let me know." Shelby dropped a folder on Christine's desk. "Here are the wine readings you wanted."

The two women began discussing sugar quantities and fermentation levels as if they were reviewing the latest fashion trends. Duffy's eyes crossed just listening to them. He mumbled something about checking the vineyards and headed out, Goldie at his heels. They drove by the bakery, but it was shut up and dark. Jess was most likely in back getting all her business paperwork taken care of. The empty planter boxes he'd dropped off earlier looked…well…empty.

Duffy needed to pick up some supplies from Cloverdale. He knew of a nursery along the way.

JESSICA WAS BAKING when she should have been resting. But her nerves were jangled and her head was fuzzy from all the paperwork she'd filled out with Agnes.

Her cell phone rang.

Jess jumped. Baby jumped. Even the pan of biscotti she was filling seemed to jump.

It was a robocall. A prerecorded message.

"This is a reminder that your Lamaze class starts this coming Friday night."

Jess had forgotten about Lamaze. Or, like everything else, she'd put it to the back of her mind, which had, of course, lost it.

"Remember to bring a yoga mat or a blanket and pillows. You will be working with your partner on the floor. See you soon!"

Jess had been meaning to ask Vera to help her through childbirth. That was no longer an option. She was left with Eunice or... Dare she consider Duffy? She'd prefer Duffy's steadiness. He'd most likely agree, not because he wanted to, but because he felt obligated to.

Movement out her front window drew her attention. She set the timer and hurried to the front door, where Goldie danced on her hind legs for attention.

Jess knelt to oblige. The sidewalk was cold beneath her knee. She swept Goldie into her arms, and stood. "Flowers?"

Duffy finished potting some geraniums and stood, wiping the dirt from his hands on a small towel. "Bakeries need flowers."

"How much do I owe you? For the planters and the flowers?" She couldn't afford to pay him, not when the bakery needed an

298 A MEMORY AWAY

espresso machine and Baby needed a crib.
But the flowers were colorful and cheerful.
They made the bakery look loved.

"Nothing. It's a gift."

She was weary of accepting charity under
the guise of such an innocent word, resent-
ful that *gifts* kept showing up. "Take them
back to your house."

"No."

"How much?"

She recognized that determined tilt to his
chin, but was equally adamant that people
began to respect her boundaries. "You want
to pay me for these?"

She nodded.

"Fine. Let's barter." He smiled, but it wasn't
a smile of compromise. It was the smile of a
conqueror. "I'll take payment in coffee and
a Danish."

She clutched Goldie so tight, the poor dear
whined. "That's not enough to pay for all
this."

"Okay." His eyes took on a mischievous
glint, the one that melted her heart. "Coffee
and Danish for a week."

It still wasn't enough. She put Goldie down
so she could cross her arms and glare at him.

His smile dimmed. "Coffee and Danish every day until Baby's born?"

"Deal. Thank you for doing business with me." She pressed a kiss to his cheek. It seemed natural until he looked at her with that same look of longing he'd had in his eyes last night.

Her chest fluttered. Baby bumped her back into the doorway, because Baby knew she didn't need to make a fool of herself.

"Have you had dinner yet?" Duffy's gaze dropped to her lips.

Her lips. Her lips. Her hungry-for-a-kiss lips.

"Uh…no." Pregnant brain was back in control.

"I'm roasting eggplant with potatoes." His gaze cooled, which did nothing to stop the nervous fluttering in her chest. "Baby needs sustenance. Every time I come by you're baking. You're probably in pregnant-brain mode and have forgotten to eat real food." He paused, looking as if he hadn't realized he'd just invited her to dinner. And then he rushed on. "What do you say? Vegetables? My house? Fifteen minutes?"

"I have…uh…biscotti." She looked over her shoulder. She had biscotti somewhere.

"In the oven." This was good. She'd completed a sentence.

"Okay. You get there when you get there. I'll keep dinner warm for you." He gathered up the empty flowerpots and bags of potting soil, and walked away with Goldie, whistling.

Jess hurried back into the kitchen, Baby bouncing enthusiastically all the way. "Don't get any ideas, Baby. He's your uncle."

But it wasn't Baby she needed to worry about.

DUFFY SET THE TABLE. He loaded the dishwasher. He took out the garbage. He lit a fire.
What am I doing?

He was acting as if Jess was coming over for a date.

He'd given her planter boxes. He'd given her flowers. He'd given her an excuse to kiss his cheek.

What? Was he so lonely he was willing to forgo his long-awaited freedom?

A knock at the door. Goldie pranced eagerly in the foyer, as if she knew it was Jess.

Duffy made a decision. He'd open the door and pretend as if everything was the way it had been the first night she'd stayed here. He'd open the door and be cool.

He opened the door and felt a grin split his cheeks. "Come on in." Inward groan. He sounded first-date happy.

She had a dusting of flour at her temple. Without thinking, he wiped it off with his thumb.

Their eyes met; a flicker of memory seemed to pass through hers that had nothing to do with Greg. Duffy's heart accelerated. This was so not in line with a carefree lifestyle.

One ear cocked up, Goldie looked from one human to the other. Then she thumped her tail. Even the dog was in league with Duffy's ill-timed feelings.

Duffy turned away. "Have a seat at the table." While she did so, he plated the food and brought it over.

She ate in silence. This wasn't exactly how he'd pictured dinner. He did a quick rewind, from the time she'd confronted him planting flowers to the present. Other than that chaste kiss, nothing seemed silent-treatment-worthy.

"Tough day at the office?" he asked.

"I don't think I've ever done so much paperwork." Her gaze was troubled. "My brain is feeling a bit mushified."

"Mushified? Is that like pregnant brain on steroids?"

That got a smile out of her, but it didn't reach her eyes. "Something like that." She gestured toward a plastic container with brownies. "I brought dessert."

Duffy should have let her distant mood go. He couldn't. "Have you remembered something about Greg that upset you?"

"No. For the most part, my memory is back. It's just…" She set her fork on her plate and met his gaze levelly. "I need a Lamaze partner."

Lamaze. Labor. Childbirth. Situations men didn't normally aspire to be a part of.

"I was thinking of asking Eunice," she added.

"I…" Duffy had been preparing his speech to turn her down when her words sank in. "Eunice? My next-door neighbor?"

"Yes." Her smile was small and sad, and made him disappointed in himself. "She's retired. It won't be a burden for her to help me."

"What if she faints at the sight of blood?" Eunice faint? What about Jess? She got queasy at the sight of bodily fluids. "You have no idea how Eunice performs under stress."

"Work with me here, Duff. I don't have many options."

Duff. He opened his mouth to volunteer, but stopped himself. This was a serious commitment. He'd be on call. There'd be no spontaneous trips out of town for the next few weeks.

His heart wanted to say yes. His head wanted to erase their conversation from her memory.

Because she hadn't been given a table scrap, Goldie groaned at his feet, and raised her gaze to his.

Who was he kidding? Until Goldie's parents showed up, there'd be no trips out of town anyway. "Is there a reason I couldn't be your Lamaze partner?" *Is there a reason I can't keep my mouth shut?*

"Other than you don't want to do it?" She stared at her plate. "Eunice likes being with me."

This is good. This is exactly what I want.

"It's not that I don't like being with you," Duffy hedged.

"I don't want to be an obligation. We're *friends.*" Jess said it as if she'd announced she was making broccoli with dinner. Unemotionally, as if she had no idea his insides were in turmoil—wanting to be there for her was having a skirmish with not wanting to commit. "You don't want to do this, so don't ask."

"Despite my determination to be commitment-free, I still manage to help out here and there." He rapped on the table with his knuckles. Not hard, but hard enough to rattle Goldie, who stood and cocked an ear at him. "The other day I helped Flynn and Slade remove the tree from Rutgar's property."

Jess chuckled. "Someone guilted you into it. I know you didn't volunteer."

"How do you know that?"

"Because." She laid a hand over the top of his fist. "Of all the empty houses in Harmony Valley, you chose to rent one with stairs in front and back."

"I chose it because of its size and central location. I can be at any vineyard in minutes." She didn't think he'd volunteered because he had stairs? What did that have to do with anything?

"Duffy." Her other hand wrapped around his. "Your father's in a wheelchair. You have no ramp. No way for your father to come in-side."

His pulse pounded in his temples, rushing past his ears to do so. "I…uh… I was going to build a ramp. I bought redwood, which is resistant to rot."

"And you made planters instead," she said gently.

The room funneled down to her eyes. He could read so much in their depths. Compassion, understanding. She saw the truth he'd buried so deep he hadn't known it himself, hadn't seen it in the mirror every morning. He didn't want his parents to come over. Or at least, he hadn't. Not at first. And now, weeks later, he'd put it out of his mind.

Dad must hate me.

No. If he didn't hate Greg, Dad would never hate Duffy. But he'd know. He'd know and it would be another disappointment Dad chose to bear.

The blood rushing to his head made him dizzy. He was grateful for Jessica's touch, for her understanding. He barely understood the implications of his actions, but he knew he had to make things right with his dad. And perhaps, with Jess.

Without knocking, Eunice let herself in.

She carried a cake pan with aluminum foil over it. "I made butter cake." She set it down next to the brownies, and claimed a seat, oblivious to the tensions at the table. "If you like it, I can give you the recipe, Jessica."

"Is it a favorite of your mother's?" Jess didn't let go of his hand. It was probably the only thing anchoring him upright.

"It was a favorite of my father's." Eunice was in full-on self-absorbed mode. He knew when she got like this, she didn't see anything but herself and her own needs.

So like me.

The thought shocked Duffy backward in his seat. Jessica's touch melted away and as it did, his heart pounded harder.

This could be me in fifty years.

Never married. No children. Parents and siblings gone. He'd be a dotty old man. Okay, maybe not dotty and desperate for attention like Eunice. He'd more likely be the hermit in the neighborhood, the one who complained about neighbors who didn't put their trash cans away the moment the garbage truck left the street, the one who shouted at children who played on his grass, who...

He'd listened when his father and Jess spoke of how wrong it was that he isolated himself, but he hadn't moved beyond the justification behind why he was doing it.

Duffy reclaimed control of the conversation, butter cake be damned. "When is this class of yours?"

"Are you going back to school?" Eunice studied him with wide eyes. "I always wanted to get a degree."

"It's a class to learn how to give birth," Duffy said firmly. "I'm going with Jess."

"It's a class to learn how not to panic while giving birth," Jess corrected. "And Duffy isn't going with me. I was going to ask you, Eunice."

"Me?" Eunice preened. There were eye blinks and hair fluffs. "I'd love to go."

"Then it's settled. The three of us will go." Duffy speared a bite of eggplant. "I'll drive."

CHAPTER NINETEEN

JESS LUMBERED DOWN Duffy's front steps like an old cowboy after a hard ride. "You don't need to walk me home, Duff." Just like he didn't need to go to Lamaze class with her. She'd been unable to talk him out of it.

"We're walking you home." He and Goldie.

Eunice was already climbing the steps to her place. Her butter cake had been surprisingly tasty, although the piece Jess had eaten felt like it was already clogging her arteries. Or perhaps that was the frustration she was feeling over Duffy's sudden caregiving streak.

When she'd pointed out the inaccessibility of his house to his father, she'd expected him to rationalize his choice behind his need to live a carefree lifestyle. Instead, he'd grown silent.

"I've been meaning to ask," Duffy began when he reached her side after locking up.

"What happened with your job in Santa Rosa?"

Jessica shoved her hands in her jacket pockets, fisting them on either side of Baby's bulge. "Do we have to go there?"

"My parents and I went by yesterday and… well, Vera was weird about your leaving. She thought we were your lawyers."

Wasn't that peachy? Duffy's mother must think the world of Jess.

"I made a mistake. I thought my boss was my friend." She'd positioned Vera in her heart as a mother figure. "She lied to me." Saying it out loud hurt all over again, the achy, bring-you-down hurt that was hard to overcome. "Vera knew about Greg and the chance to own my own bakery. She didn't tell me because my baking had become popular. She wanted to keep me there. Knowing that, how could I stay?"

Duffy said nothing. No doubt he was thinking how could she risk an income when she was about to have a baby?

"I tried to get other jobs, but no one would hire me." She sighed. "It was a rash decision and it could have been disastrous."

"If not for the offer here." He put his arm over her shoulder. And although she didn't want to need his strength, she took it anyway. "You made a decision because you had a backup option."

"I made a decision because I couldn't stand the thought of being used for profit. It was a stupid gut reaction. I didn't spend enough time considering my responsibility to Baby."

They were almost to the planters now. Almost to the parting of ways for the night. Parting. With hugs. With kisses.

Or not.

Jess fumbling in her pocket for the keys.

"I'm sorry," Duffy said as they reached her door. His arm fell away.

"For what?"

"There's a long list. Starting with my distrust of you and ending with this." He drew her close.

Jessica's belly bumped him. "Lamaze chauffeurs don't kiss their passengers." A weak, awkward attempt at humor and avoidance of what could only lead to more weak, awkward moments. But she didn't move from the shelter of his arms.

"You're a strong, principled woman, Jessica Aguirre. And I'm proud to call you..." His smile slipped.

"Friend," Jess finished for him, taking the

opportunity to rise up on her toes and plant a kiss on his cheek. She stepped back, and he let her go.

She waited until she was upstairs to admit to Baby that she was disappointed.

DUFFY AND GOLDIE were at the bakery before Jess unlocked the door in the morning. It was nippy, but the sun was out and there was a promise of warmth in the air. He hoped the warmth would carry over to human interactions.

Jess opened the door. "I didn't make Danish, but you can have lemon loaf or Bundt cake."

"I'll take whatever came out of the oven. It smells awesome." He stepped inside, then grabbed a couple of chairs and took them out front.

"What are you doing?"

He carried a table out next, attaching Goldie's leash to a table leg. "I called my parents last night. They're coming today." Best tell her and rip off the Band-Aid quickly.

"Now?" So much panic stuffed into one word.

"In a few minutes." Duffy noticed the

empty coffeepot. "I'll make the morning joe."

"I'll have the nervous breakdown." She wasn't kidding. She stood in the middle of the bakery, pale and still.

Duffy wanted to take her in his arms and tell her everything would be fine. Instead, he tucked a strand of hair behind her ear. "My mom has made progress since you saw her last. She wants this." At least, Mom wanted to want this. There was the release-of-claim paperwork, which Duffy was sure Jess would object to. But he knew better than to try to stop his mother once she'd made up her mind.

"That's what you told me before and Linda didn't want any part of Baby or me." She gazed up at him with liquid eyes. "And I said all those awful things."

"You spoke from the heart." As she always did. "And my family took it to heart."

She didn't look as if she believed him. A timer went off in the kitchen, a call to action she didn't ignore.

By the time the coffee was done, Duffy's parents were pulling up. He helped them get settled at the outdoor table, told Jess they'd arrived, brought them coffee and slices of Bundt cake.

"This is the best cake I've ever eaten," Dad proclaimed.

"Is she coming out?" Mom had the contract in her lap.

"She's in the midst of making something. She'll be out soon." Duffy was glad they had time alone. He needed to clear the air. "Dad, I owe you an apology."

He scratched his head. "For what?"

"I rented a house here without thinking about you and your needs." The words came out of Duffy's throat as if they'd been scraped from a barrel bottom.

Mom stared into her coffee.

Great. She'd known it, too.

Dad went with pretending he didn't know what Duffy was talking about. "It's your place, son. I don't know why—"

"The stairs, Dad." Duffy's throat was threatening to close. He had to work to get the words out. "I never should have rented a house that wasn't wheelchair accessible."

"You should always do what's right for you." Dad reached for Mom's hand. "We'll get by."

Duffy appreciated the sentiment, even as he realized it might not always be possible.

"I'm going to build a ramp on my back stairs today. So you can come inside anytime."

Jess joined them. She set a plate of biscotti and shortbread cookies on the table. Her gaze bounced everywhere. "Thank you for coming."

"It must be exciting to open your own bakery," Mom said carefully. "And be your own boss."

Jess risked a look at Mom's face, risked a small smile. "I hope my experience makes me a better boss. When I'm in a position to hire someone, that is."

"Sit down, my dear," Dad said. "You're putting a kink in my neck."

Jess sat with a mumbled apology.

"I'm joking," Dad said. "Everyone puts a kink in my neck. Hazard of my condition, I'm afraid."

"Oh, Thomas." Duffy's mother raised her gaze skyward, and then she smiled at Duffy. "I don't think we would have made it through the lean years without your father's humor."

Duffy nearly fell out of his chair.

Mom's gaze brushed over all three of them. "He's as quick with a quip as I am with a barb."

"We're all a work in progress." Dad's sunny

smile infected Mom, infected Jess, infected Duffy. They all smiled at each other.

A green Buick parked nearby. Agnes poked her head out the window. "Is this a private party? Or can anyone come?"

"The more the merrier." Dad waved them over.

"Welcome to Harmony Valley," Duffy said under his breath. But this time his nosy, overly friendly neighbors didn't seem so bad.

JESS RETREATED TO the kitchen as soon as she heard a timer buzz. She had nothing in the oven. She'd set it as an excuse in case she couldn't handle Duffy's mother.

Agnes, Rose and Mildred had invited themselves to sit with the Dufraines. It had taken the pressure off Jess, but she welcomed a little breather.

Linda walked in, holding a tightly rolled set of papers. Clips held her too-dark hair smooth and tight away from her face. She wore a button-down that was buttoned up, every last button. Everything about her screamed controlled unhappiness. "Need any help?"

"No, thanks." The words came out like a nervous twitter. She swallowed and tried again.

"Do you need anything? Coffee? Water?" *A wooden stake to drive through my heart?*

A glance at the photograph with three generations of Martins decorating a wedding cake calmed Jessica's nerves. She was safe here. She belonged. Nothing Linda could say could take that away. Besides, she seemed to have taken her nicey-nice meds today.

"I do need something." Linda unrolled the papers and handed them to Jess.

A gaping pit formed in Jessica's stomach and dropped in front of her toes. "What's this?"

"A peace treaty, of sorts." Linda's smile was equal parts apology, embarrassment and determination, making her seem like she had a soul.

Jess began to read. The gaping hole at her feet widened. Vertigo set in. Jess felt as if she were teetering on the edge, fully expecting to be pushed into the abyss from behind. The contract proposed she sign away all rights to Greg's assets. In exchange, she'd receive one thousand dollars. And a happy grandmother for her child.

"I brought my checkbook," Linda said softly.

Jess felt the shove, felt the tumbling nausea of defeat. And then her gaze found the wedding cake photo, the one with three bakers working in harmony. She held on. "Does Duffy know about this?"

"In theory." Her lips barely moved. "He advised me against it."

If Jess signed, she'd have everything she ever wanted for Baby—grandparents and a family. If Jess signed, things would be easier between Duffy and his mother. If Jess signed, she'd be selling out, dropping into the abyss where principles were bought and sold as quickly as red velvet cupcakes on Valentine's Day.

Jess ripped the sheets of paper apart. Her head cleared. Her stomach steadied.

"What are you doing?" Linda cried.

Jess handed the remains to Duffy's mother. "I don't place conditions on relationships. I can't be bought or sold. If you want to be involved with my baby, it'll be because you've found a place in your heart for Greg's child, not because we signed a contract. Excuse me." Jess escaped up the stairs, shut herself in the pink bathroom and sat on the pink toilet. Her limbs shook and her breath came in ragged gasps.

Footsteps announced a visitor. "Jess?"

"Go away, Duffy."

Too late, she realized she hadn't locked the door.

Duffy entered and sat on the edge of the pink tub. "Mom's leaving," Duffy said quietly, his expression grim. "Dad said to thank you for your hospitality."

Jess drew on every ounce of willpower she had to remain silent. She stared at pink tiles and willed herself to be calm. She'd have thought all that pink would ease her stress. Pink was such a mellow, happy color.

Duffy sighed. "I told her you wouldn't sign, but Mom's kind of a learn-by-mistake woman."

"She's afraid."

"We're all afraid, Jess. Even you." There was compassion in his gaze.

She wanted none of it. "Don't lump me in there. I made my peace with Greg."

"Yep." He nodded slowly. "But you haven't made peace with your past. You view every gesture of friendship as having strings."

"That's not true."

"Jess, I couldn't even give you flowers." He touched her knee. A brief connection that he immediately broke. "At some point, you're going to have to take your own advice. Move past the fear and let go." He left her, shutting the door behind him.

Leaving Jess wondering if he was right.

"I'VE NEVER SEEN so many pregnant women at one time," Eunice said upon entering the Lamaze classroom. "And they're all so…so… big." Most were bigger than Jessica. "Where are the chairs?"

Jess followed Eunice into a room at a health clinic in Santa Rosa. Five couples were laying blankets on the carpeted floor. Duffy was the last to enter, carrying Jessica's comforter and a pillow.

Jess took one look at the couples and turned to Duffy, placing a hand on his chest. "You can wait in the car."

"I'm Kiki, your instructor." A tall woman smiled fast and sweet, a flash of teeth against her dark skin. "This must be Jessica. And your partner is…"

"Me." Eunice introduced herself with pride. "And that's our driver. Duffy."

Kiki gestured toward an empty space on the floor. "Partners can sit there."

"I can't sit on the floor." Eunice would never get back up. "I thought I'd have a chair and Jessica would lie in bed."

"Wouldn't that be ideal?" Kiki's smile never wavered. "Unfortunately, we don't have room for beds in our classroom." She gestured again toward the floor, as graceful as if she were a model on a game show featuring a coveted prize. Hand up, graceful flick of the wrist, hand down. A real pro.

"You can sit in a chair, Eunice." Jessica took the comforter from Duffy and spread it out. "I'll take the floor."

"I'll sit with you." Duffy wasted no time sitting next to her, despite Jessica's protests.

Eunice didn't know whether to be jealous—*she* was supposed to be Jessica's partner—or pleased—Duffy and Jessica were clearly meant for each other. Helping Cupid would be almost as satisfying as helping to deliver Jessica's baby.

Kiki brought Eunice a plastic chair that was as uncomfortable as sitting on the wrought-iron bench in the town square. And then class began.

After introductions, Kiki presented a diagram of the birthing process, and then showed a brief video of a live birth.

"Oh, my," Eunice whispered. Her stomach felt like the time she'd tried eating sushi. She raised her hand. "Excuse me. As coach,

I wouldn't be on the tail end of this business, would I?"

Duffy shot Eunice a look of disbelief.

"Good question." Kiki clearly enjoyed her job. She smiled all the time. She seemed to smile bigger when she looked at Eunice, most likely because Eunice was a good student, always had been. "What do you think, class? Where should your support partner be during delivery?"

A pretty blonde who looked like she was carrying twins said, "Wherever Mom wants you to be."

"That's right. Mom's doing all the work. She gets to decide who goes where." Kiki moved on, demonstrating breathing techniques and basic types of massage to relax Mom-to-be, and then encouraged the partners on the floor to practice massage. The first position was sitting cross-legged, facing each other.

Jessica glanced up at Eunice, who shrugged and said, "I lost my ability to sit like that at least twenty years ago. Tag." She poked Duffy's shoulder. "You're it."

Duffy had a serious look on his face. Eunice couldn't tell what he was thinking, but she hoped he was going to take advantage of this opportunity to win Jessica over.

Jessica and Duffy turned to face each other. Jessica planted her hands on either side of her hips as if she needed stabilization so she wouldn't fall over backward.

Duffy reached out. Jessica started when Duffy's hands touched her belly. Eunice would have started, too. Duffy had big hands and a big temper. No wonder Jessica had asked her to come. She looked as if someone had plugged her into a live socket. Her face was flushed as red as Eunice's cornmeal mush.

Eunice leaned down and whispered, "If you need to practice on me, Duffy, you can." Because, clearly, he needed practice.

DUFFY'S PALMS MADE small circles on Jessica's enormous belly, sending a myriad of signals—all of which Jess tried hard to ignore.

His touch soothed Baby. His touch heated her skin. His touch magnetized her gaze to his.

There wasn't surprise in his eyes. Or detachment.

There was heat and interest and a bit—just a hint—of mischief.

It was the deviltry that got to Jess. They'd been dancing around this attraction of theirs. Now they were waltzing right into it with intimate touches, soft sighs and a hint of a grin. Right there! At the corner of his mouth.

Didn't he realize that they needed to get past this? Didn't he understand that she valued him more as Baby's uncle rather than a boyfriend? If they kissed, if they dated, if they spent time together as a couple, there was no guarantee that it would be long-term.

And then there was his aversion to commitment and his declaration that she didn't know how to accept help or gifts from friends. They were as incompatible as bananas and ham and hollandaise sauce.

Jess drew a breath, prepared to stop this.

"Time to change positions." Kiki was the harbinger of good cheer. She had no idea that Jess was on the verge of a panic attack. "Supporting partners are going to sit with their legs in a V, knees bent for support. Moms will sit in that V, which is a great position to relieve the stress of back labor by receiving deep massage."

Jess felt no stress relief from the first po-

sition. She doubted she'd feel any more relaxed from the second position.

"Need help?" Duffy asked when Jess didn't
move to sit with him.

Again, she prepared to call this off.

Eunice leaned forward, whispering, "This
is more physically demanding than I realized. I'm going to have to go into training
and lift weights or something."

Duffy had his back to Eunice. His grin.
So rare.

Without a word, Jess moved between his
legs. She carefully kept her distance, looping her arms around his knees, looping a
hold on her heart.

Kiki talked about different massage techniques and focal points.

Jess had a focusing thought: *Baby needs
an uncle.*

At Kiki's instruction, Duffy's fingers
kneaded the muscles of her shoulders. "Geez,
you're tense."

You think?

At Kiki's instruction, Duffy ran his big
hands up and down her arms. "Tell me if
this bothers you."

It bothered her peace of mind.

At Kiki's instruction, Duffy used his

thumbs to loosen the muscles at the small of her back.

Heaven, help me.

"Give me my pillow. I'm ready for bed." Jessica's confession gave everyone in the room a good laugh.

Somehow, Jess made it through the rest of class without making a fool of herself. Somehow, Jess made the drive without interrupting Eunice's monologue about the raw nature of the birthing process and how hard it was going to be to assist her. Somehow, Jess didn't protest when Duffy dropped Eunice off first.

And then they parked in front of the bakery.

Duffy helped Jess out of the truck and walked her to the door.

Jessica's blood was humming. And the tune wasn't a lullaby. "Good night," she said, fumbling with her keys.

Duffy took her chin in his hand and turned her to face him.

Now was the time to protest. Now was the time for common sense to prevail.

Jessica's eyes drifted closed as Duffy's lips neared hers.

Their first kiss had been a surprise, a reaction. It had been spontaneous and unexpected.

This kiss was as deliberate as the man himself. A gentle meeting, a warm greeting. And then the kiss deepened. His arms came around her as she sagged against him, clung to him for support, gave herself up to the moment and the man.

This, her heart murmured. *This man.*

She knew she could love Duffy, but she'd been holding back. Images flashed in her head, not of Greg, but of Duffy. His hand on hers as he helped her down from the truck. His smile when she said something he found humorous. His words of encouragement, even when her choices made him uncomfortable. This man. He was a man to love, a man to risk for.

I love him.

Baby kicked in agreement.

He was kissing her. That had to mean he'd gotten over his relationship phobia. They'd go out on Valentine's Day. She'd swallow her pride and cook for his parents on Easter.

Love extended the kiss, dragged time to a standstill, fogged her brain.

He drew back, his face lost in disorientating shadow. Greg or Duffy?

Was she dreaming? Her pregnant brain groped for memory and context. She was in Duffy's arms. She loved Duffy. It was a love that forgave and trusted. She hadn't loved Duffy's brother, not like she was supposed to, not with faith and confidence, not like a man deserved to be loved.

"Oh, Greg," she whispered, saddened.

Duffy's arms stiffened and then he released her, striding back to his truck.

"Wait. It's not what it sounded like." She stumbled forward, thought better of it and placed her feet solidly on the ground. "I didn't think you were Greg."

"That's not what it sounded like." His voice. She had knives that weren't as sharp.

"I just realized something about Greg that I should have before." Her heart seemed to have dropped to the vicinity of her baby-heavy belly. She placed a hand there for support. "It's pregnant brain."

"You were thinking about my brother while I was kissing you." He opened the door. "No man wants to hear that."

"But…wait… I…" What else could she

say? That she'd just realized she loved him?
That was the last thing Duffy wanted to hear.

   As requested, Duffy stood. Waiting.

   Until he couldn't wait anymore.

CHAPTER TWENTY

IT WAS LIKE Greg stealing Dad's money all over again.

The pit in Duffy's stomach. The pounding in his temples. The broken record in his head: *This isn't happening.*

He'd tried to set aside his aversion to obligation, and look where it had got him. Bested by Greg.

His brother must be laughing wherever he was.

Duffy stayed away from the bakery. He threw himself into his work, bringing in extra crews so he'd be exhausted by day's end. The one vineyard he didn't work was Parish Hill. If it was infected, Duffy didn't want to risk spreading the disease.

On Monday when he opened his front door, he found a thermos of coffee and a bag with a warm Danish on the porch. On Tuesday, he found a travel mug full of coffee and a bag with a chocolate chip croissant.

By Thursday, he was expecting a morning payment. It was just like Jess to stick to their deal for payoff of the redwood planters. They hadn't spoken since last Friday. Duffy had to make a decision about Lamaze class Friday night. Would he live up to the obligation he'd begun with her or bail?

The easy route was to bail. But Duffy had never bought into easy outs.

"The results are in." Christine ran down the stairs to where Duffy was rinsing out his travel mug. She waved a sheet of paper. "It's leaf roll, just like you suspected."

Ryan came down the steps, sitting midway, gangly legs stretching toward the first floor. Goldie trotted over to sniff his sneakers.

"I'm sorry I was right." Almost as sorry as Duffy had been to have kissed Jess and hear her murmur his brother's name.

Christine didn't seem to be bummed out by the news. "The university wanted to know if we're open to experimental treatments. I told them yes."

"It's the perfect location," Duffy agreed, not able to work up the enthusiasm Christine had.

"Isolated." Christine nodded.

"If you don't count Rutgar," Duffy said. The old man was going to be a pain to whoever went up there.

"You can handle Rutgar." Ryan grinned as if they shared a secret. "He likes you."

Oh, no. "He likes Jess."

Christine laughed. "A way to a man's heart is through his stomach. And Jessica's scones can soothe the savage beast. Take her up there and break the news to him gently. He's going to be invaded on a regular basis and we don't want him to chase anyone away."

Duffy only agreed because he feared Rutgar might take his shotgun to deter a stranger from hanging around up there. It had nothing to do with it being an excuse to talk to Jess.

He found her balancing on a ladder, writing on the chalkboard behind the pastry case.

Duffy's heart leaped into his throat, leapfrogging higher and higher, until his voice—when he needed it most—was low and croaky. "What are you doing?"

She grabbed at the top rung of the ladder, sending him racing across the room, ready to catch her if she fell.

"Get down." He couldn't look her in the eye, afraid she'd recognize Greg in his features. "Get down before I have a heart attack."

She didn't move. "I need to change the sign. It's February. I'm not making pumpkin scones and that's what it says the special is." Her voice. Amazingly put-together considering Duffy was about to unravel.

"Get down." The bullfrog was back. "I'll do it. Whatever it is. I'll do it."

Jess came down the ladder slowly. "I'm done."

"Next time, call me. I'll do it." He still couldn't look her in the eye. Goldie sat at his feet. Her he could look at.

"Do you have neat handwriting?" Jess asked.

"People can read it."

"Customers prefer lettering with character. It says you put thought into what you're going to say and what you've baked."

Well. He was no calligrapher. He didn't even have good penmanship.

Goldie cocked an ear, as if by doing so she could hear the undertones of the dead-in-the-water conversation. Duffy saying you hurt me. Jess admitting being unable to tell the difference between him and his brother.

"Thanks for stopping by." Her feet disappeared into the kitchen. "Goldie looks good. Take care."

He looked at Goldie. Goldie padded toward the swinging door and looked back at him.

Duffy desperately wanted to leave, to protect his wounded pride. He didn't. Instead, Duffy pushed through to the kitchen and the awkward conversation that awaited him. "I didn't stop by to be the safety police. I need a favor." He should tell her about the flour on the floor near the sink.

"I don't grant favors to people who can't look me in the eye."

He'd missed her straight-shooting talk far too much. He manned up and met her gaze squarely.

"Much better." She gestured toward a plate of cookies and a glass of milk. "You can view that as my peace offering or a bribe to get you to stay while we talk this through."

"I don't want to rehash the crime."

"Now, see. That's where we differ. I made a mistake, but it wasn't a crime." She was joking, until she wasn't. "I was befuddled."

"You confused me with Greg." He didn't touch her supposed peace offering.

She wrapped her arms around her belly,

which seemed to be sagging more than it had nearly a week prior. "I didn't. I was lost in your kiss. So lost that I found something I'd been hiding away from myself." She worried her lip, before having the courage to say, "I have feelings for you and when I compared them to how I felt for Greg, well…my feelings for him came up wanting."

Duffy took a step back, nearly stumbling over Goldie. This was worse than he thought. "You said you loved Greg."

"There you go. I knew you'd have that reaction." Other than the deep blush on her cheeks, she didn't betray any form of lovesick emotion or disappointment in Duffy. "It's why I didn't want to fall for you. I mean, just look at me. I'm a package deal. And you want to sow some wild oats and maybe settle down without so much as a goldfish in the house."

"I'm flattered." And terrified. "And confused. What does it mean?"

"Nothing." Her voice flattened. "Just because my feelings for you run deeper than they ever did for your brother means nothing."

Duffy was sure needles poking in his eye might be less painful.

"Greg was my first true love and of course I'd get it wrong. But I was so desperate to be with someone that I didn't recognize how shallow what we had was. And so when I looked up at you that night, when your face was in shadow and I was tired and floating in a state of awe over everything I'd realized, I felt the need to apologize to Greg."

"To Greg." Croaker was back.

She nodded. "He deserved better than what I gave him."

"He stole from you!" Duffy would never understand this woman. "He lied to you. He betrayed your trust. He chose his path. You should hate him."

"What good do those feelings serve? They make me sick to my stomach. Greg is dead. Struck by lightning. Maybe the same thing happened to my mother." Jessica's voice pitched higher. Her determination to be strong was enviable, the tremor in her words wrenching. "Maybe my mother's alive and enjoying her life, the one she got from a do-over by abandoning me. Maybe I should go on forever letting the choices of someone else eat at me and eat at me until there's nothing left inside. Is that how I should live? Hating the man who let me buy his affection? Hating a mother who disappeared? Hating you because you can never love me back?"

He didn't think she had a hateful bone in her body.

She sagged against the island counter, spent and gasping for air. "I'm just so tired, Duffy. I'm tired of being used. I'm tired of being pitied. I'm so tired that I... I wish I could get over these feelings I have for you."

Duffy felt run-through-the-ringer tired, too.

"Listen." She took a cookie and the glass of milk. "You keep people at a distance to avoid obligation. I'll do anything to bring them closer. And I want to be in on the closeness too as long as I'm included because I've earned a spot in the crowd. And not just because people are being nice to the pregnant woman." A hint of sadness passed behind her eyes. "We're not compatible. So don't worry. I'll move on from this...*infatuation*."

Infatuation?

"Baby will never know." She took a generous bite of cookie, and then washed it down with milk. "I'm not going to be a burden to you, Duff. I probably shouldn't have said a word about how I feel, but I couldn't let you go on believing I was thinking about Greg when I was kissing you." She finished her cookie.

"Thanks. I think." Honestly, he didn't know what to think. He'd never had a woman tell him she loved him before, much less apologize for it and promise to fall out of love with him. All without the drama of tears. If it had been any woman other than Jess, he'd—

"Now, what was this favor you came to ask for?"

JESS SUPPOSED THERE came a point in your pregnancy where you lost all decorum and bared everything, stretch marks and all. Without jaw-dropping embarrassment or heart-stopping mortification. Hadn't she seen it in the live childbirth video the other night? That woman had spread her legs to the camera and then bared her breast when it came time to breastfeed.

Jess had done the same thing with Duffy. Laid herself bare. Emotionally, that is.

She hadn't expected him to wrap his arms around her and declare his love.

Neither had she expected him to calmly stick to his beliefs and ask her to go to Rutgar's, without much more fuss than the suggestion that she "bring the cookies."

And so she stood next to Duffy on Rutgar's front porch, a plateful of cookies in hand and her heart hanging by a fraying thread.

The door swung open. "Well, well, well. You brought your woman to see me." Rutgar's voice was like a bullhorn. "And bribes, too."

"Glad to see you didn't greet us with the shotgun." There were equal parts levity and gravity in Duffy's voice.

Having been on the business end of Rutgar's shotgun and agreeing with Duffy on the import of keeping university researchers safe on the mountain, Jess put on her sweetest smile, her sweetest voice and revealed her sweetest creation—death by chocolate cookies. They were still warm. "You're right. We're here to bribe you."

Duffy rolled his eyes.

"I like you." Rutgar claimed a cookie and took a bite, swallowing half. "Him, not so much."

"He grows on you."

"He can't have grown on you too much. Didn't put a ring on your finger. Haven't heard you're moving in together." Rutgar shook his shaggy, gold-gray mane. "Stubborn, that one. Can't take advice."

"All true," Jess agreed, because it was. "Some people take longer to get to the truth than others."

Duffy made an unintelligible noise.

"And some people get smart and don't wait around." Rutgar popped the rest of the cookie in his mouth and reached for another. "If you're ready for a real man, you just let me know. I'd renovate my house for a woman like you."

Annoyance fell off Duffy like fall leaves in a windstorm. He exhaled deeply and shifted his stance.

Jess ignored him. "You'd get rid of all the dead animal heads, Rutgar? That is true love."

Since Duffy didn't seem able to convey why they were here, Jess did, emphasizing the importance of the visiting researcher's work—not that she understood what it was exactly—and the need to keep whoever it was safe.

"I see now why he brought you," Rutgar said, accepting the plate of cookies. "And I accept your bribe." He closed the door on them.

Baby did a bladder bounce, confirming Jessica's assessment. "I declare our trip a success. Time to go." She waited until they got in the truck to deliver the hard news. The decision that cracked her heart in places she hadn't known she could hurt. "I've decided Eunice should be my Lamaze partner. You don't need to drive us."

He didn't argue.

DUFFY WAS TRYING to watch a movie, but mostly he was staring at the screen and stroking Goldie's fur on Friday night.

Jess loved him.

He glanced at the empty couch corner. The thought should have scared him. Instead, he felt oddly at peace, as if he was adrift in space, but tethered by this one thought: Jess loved him.

Eunice charged inside. "I need your help." She ran around the couch, blocking the television with her purplish hair, which nearly stood on end.

"Who died?"

"No one died." She shook her head. "Now I know how Agnes feels." Stomping her foot, she exclaimed, "It's Jessica. I need your help with Jessica."

Duffy rocketed to his feet, sending Goldie

tumbling to the couch. "Did something happen at class tonight? Is she in labor?"

"She's fine. It's me. I need help being her coach." Eunice put a hand over her stomach. "They showed a film on C-sections tonight. I almost lost my meat-loaf surprise."

"Is that all?" Duffy sat back down, body drained from a false alarm.

"No." She shook a finger at him. "I couldn't make her relax. I tried to help her breathe and nearly passed out myself. I panicked. Kiki had to take me out to the corridor. I am *not* cut out for this job."

"She doesn't want me," Duffy said, which was a half-truth. She wanted more from him than he could give. And since he couldn't dislodge that lump in his throat, he couldn't give her anything.

"She may not want you, but she needs you. *I* need you." Eunice got down on her knees, blinking her eyes wildly. "I can't have this baby alone," she wailed.

"Calm down." He patted her shoulder clumsily.

"No." She did the pendulum head shake. "You don't understand. I've never had a baby. I may be a woman, but I am not made for childbirth."

"Okay. All right. I'll talk to her."

Eunice threw herself at him. She smelled of hair spray and lemon drops. "Oh, thank you. Thank you."

He managed to set her on her feet. "Don't thank me until I talk to Jess."

But Eunice was ecstatic. She practically ran out the door yelling, "I'm saved! I'm saved!" The door slammed and then almost immediately opened again. "Don't forget. Tomorrow is the baby shower."

Duffy knew he should have felt apprehensive about talking to Jess. Instead, he felt an odd sense of anticipation.

CHAPTER TWENTY-ONE

"Much as I like hanging out with you," Shelby said to Jess Saturday afternoon, running a hand over her midsize baby bump, "shouldn't you be working?"

Jess had her feet up on a chair outside the bakery. "I didn't pass the health inspection. Turns out the state now requires a bigger sink or two sinks for the size of my kitchen."

Before that shock had time to demoralize her on Friday, Agnes had been on the phone to Mayor Larry, demanding he install a second sink. Jess had offered to pay, but Agnes wouldn't hear of it. "It's his responsibility to get you set up for business."

To repay Mayor Larry, she'd be baking scones for him every week for two years.

Flynn was in the kitchen with a plumber. Jess was outside trying not to feel like a mooch.

After all the rain, they were having an unseasonably warm February. It was seventy degrees outside. Birds were singing. Baby was peaceful. And hopefully she'd be able to pass inspection next week. Otherwise, her savings would be taking a hit. There was only so much free baking a budget could stand.

Only so much a heart could take, too. She might feel as if she belonged in Harmony Valley, but there was an ache that Duffy alone seemed able to fill. Rejection sucked. And to be rejected by both Dufraine men? Demoralizing. Her heart had taken its share of hits. She'd get over Duffy. Somehow. He was a good man. An honorable man. She just wasn't the woman for him.

As if conjured by her thoughts, Duffy rounded the corner and headed their way, Goldie at his side.

From this distance, she could identify the mismatched colors—red and burgundy—and admire his confident stride. She could also pull herself together after her heart recovered from its initial Duffy-love flurry.

Her pounding pulse must have awakened Baby. There was shifting and shimmying, causing Jess to adjust in her chair. She wasn't looking forward to a conversation with Duffy, but at least she had Shelby as a buffer.

"I should be going." Shelby stood. "My baby

is in the mood for a nap. Maybe next week you can give me a lesson on how to make scones."

"Or we could start out with something easier," Jess said, having heard of Shelby's lack of skill in the kitchen from more than one Harmony Valley resident.

"Don't forget. I'm bartering that bag of flour for your services." Shelby headed toward Duffy at a brisk pace. A fat white goose that had been settled in the planter box hopped to the ground and honked, waddling after her.

Jess wasn't fooled. She'd already had four people drop off ingredients today. Eggs. Butter. Flour. Sugar. Every person had said they'd take a batch of cookies or brownies in exchange for stocking her larder. It was charity. And charity was a hard lump to swallow. But she was trying to view each addition to her stock as a show of friendship. Friendship could be repaid with kindness rather than money.

The baby was practicing its soccer kicks now. Over and over.

Jess sat up. "Ow."

Duffy jogged the last twenty feet to her side. "Contraction?"

"No. Just kicking." She levered herself to her feet. "I need to walk Baby back to sleep.

Don't let me keep you from wherever you were going." *Coward.*

"I was coming to see you."

Drat. Jess walked faster. It felt more like the waddle of Shelby's goose. "Give me a break," she muttered, missing her femininity, longing for the days of belted blouses and feminine heels.

"What'd you say?" Duffy caught up to her.

Had she been walking that fast? Or had he been slow to catch up to her? "How are your parents?" *Deft change of subject, girl. Pat yourself on the back.*

"Fine." He glanced over his shoulder. "Do you have time to talk? We can take Baby on a walk around the block."

"I kind of thought we talked through everything the other day." How much more could they rehash things? She loved him. He didn't reciprocate. End of story.

"Something new always comes up."

Be still her foolish heart, the one that hoped he'd learn to love her.

They reached the barbershop with its spinning pole. Phil, the elderly barber, sat in one of the chairs inside. He lowered his newspaper and nodded to them as they passed.

Who was she kidding? Love wasn't an option on his radar. "If you've decided to give up on Goldie, it's too late. That dog is yours. Even if I could keep her at the bakery—which the health inspector would not approve of— she'd run straight back to you."

Duffy looked aghast. Even Goldie seemed to give her a wide berth.

"Well, I'll be…" Jess chuckled. At least one girl had won his heart. "You're a dog owner. I never thought I'd see the day."

"I live in fear that her real owners will show up." He was slow to admit it.

"You're her real owner now."

They rounded the corner, working their way down the block toward the sheriff's office. Baby was no longer a kicking machine.

"How was Lamaze class without me?" Was that longing in his voice? Or relief?

Jess glanced at his face. There was something she wasn't getting here. "Turns out, I'm very good at breathing. Eunice, not so much."

"Did she get kicked out of class for good?"

"Ah, she told you." That explained the guarded look in his eyes. "She wasn't kicked out. She was put in time out."

They rounded the next corner. Harmony Valley being a historic town, the buildings weren't long or wide. Therefore, the blocks weren't long or wide.

She noticed he didn't rush to volunteer to be her backup Lamaze partner.

And then a contraction hit. Hard. Her stomach solidified. Her legs stiffened. Her entire body felt like it was in a compression chamber. She walked like a pregnant Bride of Frankenstein.

"Whoa. Your face has turned beet red." Duffy led her to a bench in front of the winery's wine cellar.

Jess sat like a plank of wood on the bench. There was no relaxing.

"Can I do anything for you? Get you water? Remind you to breathe?"

Breathing. Air. Duh. Jess did several rounds of hee-hoo.

The contraction eased. She practically collapsed against Duffy. "I am so out of shape. If they pass out grades for labor, I'd predict mine to be a D minus."

JESS WAS A WRUNG-OUT, sweaty mess. A beautiful, wrung-out, sweaty mess.

Duffy was supposed to keep her away from the bakery for another twenty minutes while the ladies prepared for her baby shower and guests arrived.

She sat up and tried to put herself back together—smoothing hair, wiping her face, trying to smile. Her hands began massaging her stomach in big, slow circles. "Pregnancy is not for the lighthearted."

Duffy could relate. She'd scared him there, turning so red he thought she might pass out, until she began her Lamaze breathing.

"Unbelievable. Baby's awake." Her palm stopped moving. "Do you want to feel Baby kick?"

Feel something inside of her? "You're making me uncomfortable."

"I hear babies do that to men." She smiled reassuringly, and held out her hand. "Come on. Be brave."

"Baby doesn't scare me." The child within her shared Duffy's genetic makeup. Babies were a fact of life, a propagation of the species. Duffy gave her his hand, scooting closer.

Not to be left out, Goldie hopped into his lap.

Jessica's touch was gentle, yet she pressed his palm firmly against the fullness of her stomach.

"Nothing." That wasn't exactly true. Duffy

felt the warmth of Jessica's body, the strength of the muscles cradling the child and the contrasting softness of her skin.

"Baby can be shy." Jess chuckled.

And then her stomach moved beneath his palm. Not a seismic shift, but more like a gentle flick of a tiny fist against his hand. And again. And again. And again.

The detachment that Duffy had been trying to uphold fell away. "There's a baby in there." His gaze rose to meet Jessica's.

She smiled broadly. "You betcha."

And not just any baby. Greg's baby. A part of Greg.

His father's words upon first learning the news returned to him: *a do-over*.

Greg, the brother he loved. Greg, who'd changed the lives of everyone he loved and then opted to live alone. Greg, whose crap lifestyle and lies had given Duffy Jess and Baby.

"Holy moly." Duffy had just found two good reasons for forgiving Greg: Jess and Baby.

Goldie turned and licked his chin.

He grinned. It felt brighter than the sun, that grin. "This is awesome."

Jessica's face was near his. She was smiling and beautiful. She was making this do-over possible for Greg.

And then his gaze dropped to her lips. They were kissable lips. She was a kissable woman.

He remembered kissing her, drawing her body close, sheltering her from…from… She didn't need sheltering from anyone. She just needed to be loved.

Holding her created a wanting, a longing and something that seemed like it could be love. As she'd said, his beliefs were a product of fear. The fear of the unknown was melting away. There were no more fears that Greg would return and bilk them out of more money. No more fear that he had to watch every penny in order to keep a roof over all their heads. No more fear that the connection he felt to Jess would drag him down, would be a burden. Loving Jess and Baby would be a privilege.

Am I too late?

Jess stood, breaking their connection. "I'd like to get back. They should be done with my sink."

"Hang on." He captured her hand with his, holding Goldie in his lap with the other.

She looked down on him. How easy it was

to imagine him on one knee asking her to make a lasting commitment.

The old Duffy—*the scared one*—scoffed at the idea. People dated for years before they moved in together, waited years more before marriage. He'd known her for weeks. And yet, he knew her better than he knew himself.

The new Duffy—the one with an earth-shaking, wondrous feeling in his heart—gripped her hand tighter, was reluctant to let go. Had he ruined any chance with her by hiding behind the walls of fear?

He didn't know. He couldn't seem to ask. How would he start down this path to commitment?

Slowly.

"Sit back down." When she didn't, he added softly, "Please."

She sat, raising a brow.

"It's Eunice. The pressure of being your only Lamaze partner is too much for her." *That's right. Come through the back door.*

"Come on. She's a trouper."

"And she trooped right into my house after you dropped her off last night." He was still holding her hand. That was success, wasn't it? "It was the C-section video that did her in."

Her free hand crept up to cover her mouth. "It was intense."

He didn't want to imagine. He'd never been a fan of slasher movies. All that blood. "If you let me back on the team, she can do it."

She wanted him. He could see it in her eyes. But her defenses were up. "I don't want to be another responsibility to you."

"You wouldn't be. I'm a changed man." *Trust me.* "I have a dog."

"Ha! You cheated. I forced her on you." She shook her head. "Nope. I'm already the town's project, and I'm trying not to let it kill me. Therefore, I can't do the same to you. I can't be your obligation." She stood, but instead of releasing him, she tugged him up with her. "I keep saying we're going to be friends."

His gaze met hers. He thought about loving her until they were old and gray. The idea didn't scare him. "Friends don't let friends have babies alone."

"Now you're just reaching." But she was smiling as they walked the rest of the way around the block. She smiled when he claimed Goldie needed a potty break in the town square. She smiled until they opened the door to the bakery and saw all the people, the decorations, his mother.

"Surprise!"

A BABY SHOWER?

Jess didn't know whether to laugh or cry.

There was Eunice, blinking her eyes and posing by the cake, which had been decorated with amateurish pink and blue lines of icing. Agnes, Mildred and Rose stood near the door and a gift table. Flynn and Slade. Shelby and Christine. Duffy's parents.

She turned to Duffy. "You knew?"

He held up his hands. "Guilty. I made sure we had pizza instead of meat-loaf surprise."

Eunice grabbed Jessica's arm and towed her to the back of the room where they'd set up a white baby crib. "We all chipped in. I made the baby quilt." It had baskets of flowers in blues and pinks.

"You shouldn't have." The old resentment reared its head, snapping against the idea of charity. But it was for Baby and these gifts were from her new family in Harmony Valley.

"We wanted to." Agnes hugged her. "You've brought so much pleasure and excitement to town."

"It's not the Taj Majal of cribs." Rose patted the rail. "But it's sturdy enough to hold an infant having a meltdown."

"Rose," Agnes scolded.

Rose crinkled her brow. "Kids have tantrums."

"I love it," Jess said.

Eunice grabbed her arm again and towed her into the kitchen. "This is from me."

A wooden rocking chair.

"Eunice, it's beautiful." Blond wood. Sturdy wood. Expensive, for sure. "But I can't accept. It's too much." She could accept small gifts or gifts where everyone had chipped in. But the rocker was worth something.

"I don't see why you can't accept it." Eunice frowned. "If you don't take it, when I die it'll go to charity."

"Wrong word, Eunice." Duffy came up behind them. "She didn't mean it like that, Jess."

"Well, I could have said it'd go to the dump." Eunice ran a hand lovingly over the chair back. "It was my mother's rocker and I'd like to come over and rock a baby. Why is this a bad thing? Did I miss something?"

A family heirloom? Jess forgot to breathe.

"Can you give us a minute, Eunice?" Duffy put his hands on Jessica's shoulders and guided her into the rocking chair. "I know what you're thinking."

Jess didn't want to answer, much less move, but the chair had other ideas. She began to rock in a gentle motion.

His gaze captured hers. "You're thinking these people look at you and see a poor pregnant woman, one who needs help."

He wasn't right. She'd gone past that. But he was touchably close and so dear about her feelings that she had to let him run with the idea. "Isn't that what you saw the first time we met?"

His grin held that trace of mischief her heart was so very fond of. Was he on to her? "I saw a swindler, not a destitute pregnant woman."

"I'm not destitute." But she was far from middle-class.

"I know that. They know that. But you don't seem to know that." He held on to the rocker handles, stopping the chair, staring her in the eyes. "This is a town full of grandmothers and grandfathers—or in Eunice's case, a should-have-been-grandmother. Their grandkids aren't around to spoil. They want to spoil you. And if, occasionally, the gift seems a bit extravagant, instead of immediately getting your back up, be gracious and accept."

It was a beautiful speech. It meant a lot to her.

"It's just… They don't know me," Jess said in a small voice.

"They know you well enough. I know you well enough." His hands moved to her knees. Warm, steady. "And you knew them well enough to move in after only being here two days."

He was right. He was right. The rightness of it punched the lights out of the belief that had kept her sane over the years. It wasn't enough to bite her lip and accept kindness. Accepting kindness did not define who she was.

Duffy grinned. "That's my girl."

Maybe she was. Maybe she always would be. If he smiled at her like that every once in a while, she'd live with a broken heart.

Linda entered the kitchen. She wore a flowery dress today. Her too-dark hair color had faded.

Duffy took one look at her face and said, "Don't do it, Mom."

"I have a gift for the baby." She handed Jess a card.

Jess was overwhelmed with images of spinning wheels and spindle pricks. She opened the card and discovered a check for one thousand dollars. Whatever she'd just learned in the past few minutes did not apply to Linda's check. "I can't accept."

"If you don't take it, I'll just open up a college fund for the child." Her voice became spindle thin, ready to break when in their past dealings it had been honed to a strong, sharp edge. "Please take it. It would make me feel like I did something nice for Greg after all these years."

"A gift of love," Jess murmured.

Linda's features softened into a smile, a genuine smile, a smile of a kindhearted grandmother who knew how to forgive.

CHAPTER TWENTY-TWO

His mother making nice with Jess was a good sign, right?

Duffy slung an arm around each woman and brought them back to the party.

The elderly women of Harmony Valley were drawn to Jess like bees to the queen. They preened and pressed small gifts into her hands, edging Duffy back. Laughter and advice filled the air. Duffy ended up against the back wall, crossing his arms and watching over the mayhem.

Eunice appeared at his side, placing a hand on his forearm. "Is she okay?"

Two spots of color dotted Jessica's cheeks. Her gaze sought his. Hers slightly panicked. His reassuring.

"She'll be fine." He raised his voice to be heard above the ruckus. "Ladies, we're all *friends* here. Why don't we sit down and let Jess breathe?"

"Perfect," Eunice murmured, rushing off

to direct a circle of chairs be made around the mom-to-be.

Shelby was sitting in the corner next to Christine. Her hand rested on her baby bump. "Remind me to have you run my baby shower."

"I have a wedding that needs planning, too," Christine added with a sly smile.

"Not a chance," Duffy told his coworkers. "This is a onetime deal." For the woman he loved.

Eunice called him over to help. He asked Mildred to move over and make room for his mother in the circle. He doled out slices of pizza. He handed out glasses of punch. He sent Jess bolstering smiles. He cut the cake and distributed pieces. He was being an all-around supportive guy while the women played baby shower games and shared birthing stories that made him cringe.

He loved Jess. Everything was going to be all right.

Outside the bakery, Flynn and Slade sat with Duffy's dad and Goldie. Duffy joined them. It was quiet and peaceful. Duffy hadn't recognized the tension in his body until he sat down and the stiffness in his shoulders drained away.

"We were wondering how long you'd last

in there." Goldie sat in Dad's lap and the breeze tousled his graying hair. Although Dad always put on a happy face, for once, the lines around his smile seemed less forced.

"You're a brave man." Slade set his cell phone on the table next to a bottle of beer. "Able to wield power tools *and* a cake knife."

"Same skill set," Flynn ribbed, handing Duffy a beer from the cooler at his feet. "Did you teach him that, Thomas?"

"Nope. Michael's always been self-sufficient." His father's gaze was filled with pride. "If the mower needed fixing, he took it apart to diagnose the problem. If the car wouldn't start, he was the first one under the hood." He patted Goldie's head. "He was the son that wanted to be left alone while he figured things out."

Duffy opened his beer and took a sip. Inside, the women laughed. Soon there'd be the voice of a baby added to things in Harmony Valley.

"Of course," Dad said, "some things took longer for Michael to figure out than others."

Slade gave Duffy a sideways glance and a smile. "Such as…?"

Dad was more than happy to fill in the

blanks. "How Santa made his rounds on Christmas in twenty-four hours."

"Rocket-powered sleigh?" Flynn grinned.

"Time warp?" Slade asked.

Duffy played along. "Fairy dust. Slows the space-time continuum."

"And girls." Dad chuckled. "It took him a long time to figure out girls."

Duffy glanced through the window. "I'm still working on that one."

"We're all working on that, my friend." Slade reached over and tapped his beer bottle against Duffy's.

"But his biggest challenge…" Dad's voice gentled. "Was to understand why his brother made so many wrong choices."

The table fell silent. Duffy shouldn't have been surprised that Flynn and Slade knew about his brother. This was, after all, Harmony Valley.

"Do you have an answer to that last one?" Duffy asked, not caring that he had an audience. "I'd like to know."

"Because I let him down." Whatever had buoyed Dad's spirits up to that point deflated, and along with it, deflated him. Dad slouched and hung his head. "I was providing you boys a good life. When I was injured, that life disappeared. He was angry and I was foolish." Dad mustered a small smile. "I let an eighteen-year-old handle my finances. He wasn't mature enough to resist temptation."

"It wasn't your fault." Duffy's voice was almost a whisper. "Greg chose money over family."

"It doesn't matter what he took," Dad said, reaching for Duffy's hand. "He gave us back so much more."

They both looked inside. To Jess and what would soon be a baby.

"WANT TO COME over for dinner tonight?" Duffy asked as he put the last of the chairs back where they belonged.

Jess was still in a state of awe from the friendship and caring those in town had shown her.

Thomas and Linda had long gone home. The ladies had left, even Eunice. They'd taken home leftover pizza and cake. Eunice's chocolate avocado cake had been a big hit, possibly because she didn't tell anyone what she'd put in it until after they'd all taken bites. Flynn, Slade and Duffy had carried the crib and rocking chair upstairs, along with the baby clothes, quilts and blankets she'd been given.

All that was left was to wipe down the tables, which Jess was doing. "I may head upstairs for a nap. And I may sleep through until tomorrow morning."

"And deprive Baby of dinner?" Duffy leaned on a chair back. The heat was in his eyes, as if he'd forgiven her for invoking Greg's name after their kiss a week ago. "Come over to my place and nap on the couch while I make dinner. We can practice for Lamaze class." This last was said with intimate smoothness.

The friend boundary gave off a sharp intruder alert that had Jess standing upright and giving Duffy her full attention. "*Friend*. Baby is going to be delivered with Eunice by my side."

"Didn't we solve this a few hours ago?" The combination of his frown and the authority in his tone rubbed Jessica all wrong. "I'm back on the team."

"No. You made a suggestion, which I turned down." It was getting harder to keep her voice neutral. "Why the change of heart? Being a Lamaze partner is a responsibility. You don't do responsibility."

He glanced over his shoulder at Goldie, tethered to a table outside. "I felt Baby move. It moved something in me." He closed the distance between them, taking her hands and holding her gaze with a look that she'd never seen in his eyes before. It was kind and warm and…*loving*?

"I don't understand." Not his change of heart. Not that look in his eyes.

"I realized today that I want you in my life. Both of you. Forever." His smile would have filled her with joy if he'd said those words days ago when she confessed her feelings to him, if he'd said he loved her.

She'd hoped to hear those words, but they didn't spark joy. They weighed heavily on her heart, because she couldn't believe him. "Careful, now. Don't get carried away."

"We can do this, Jess. We can make a home for Baby and Goldie." His smile had a forced quality, as if it was his job to convince her. "We can share diaper duties and baby-sitting. We can share cooking and cleaning chores. Two paychecks can stretch much further than one. I'll have your back and you'll have mine."

The pieces that had once been her broken heart seemed to crack and fall to the floor.

"You sound like you're looking for a room-mate." She yanked her hands away. "You feel responsible for my child now that you've felt Baby move. I don't want to be chained to you. You'd only resent me and my child."

"You're…you're turning me down?" Some of the aloofness she'd seen the day they'd met returned to his face.

"Yes. You've presented a very compelling business deal. Unfortunately, I already have a business." She gave him a gentle shove out the door. "When I said I had feelings for you, I meant love, Duff. Love, not a fondness that might keep us together for a few months or a few years. I meant love. The kind of deep feeling that binds two people together for a lifetime." She shut the door and locked it.

He rattled the knob. "I love you. I do."

There were the words she'd longed to hear. His words slowed her steps, slowed what was left of her heart. Jess turned. "You can't love anyone if you can't sacrifice for them," she said sadly, giving him one final chance to prove he loved her. "What have you gone out of your way to do for anyone lately?"

His palms were pressed against the glass. He didn't have an answer.

Jess had hers.

JESSICA'S DAYS WERE FILLED, even if her heart was empty.

The health inspector came by and gave her a passing grade. Martin's Bakery was officially in business. Orders came in for birthday cakes, specialty breads and cookies. El Rosal placed a weekly order for dessert trays. Mornings at the bakery bustled with activity. Her case was always empty by noon.

Jessica's worries about the profitability of the bakery were put to rest.

Duffy didn't come by for a week. And then one day Jess unlocked the front door and discovered a flyer taped on the bakery's window. It was a picture of Goldie and Duffy. The caption read A Man and His Dog. At the bottom was the instruction "Please return this flyer to Martin's Bakery."

Jess took it down.

She shouldn't have bothered. The talk in the bakery that morning was all about Duffy.

"He posted these all over town." Agnes added hers to the growing stack on the counter.

"He's lost his mind since Jess dumped him." Eunice gestured toward Jess with her coffee mug.

"You can't dump someone if you weren't

a thing in the first place," Jess said, sounding as grumpy as the Duffy of old.

A few days later, the town was blanketed by another flyer.

"I thought Duffy was a confident man." Rose unfolded her copy of the flyer and placed it on the growing stack on Jessica's counter. "But this tells me he's definitely got something to prove."

The flyer featured the headline Committed to Helping Our Community. There was a picture of Duffy replacing the siding on Bessie Harrington's mobile home. And the instruction to return the flyer to the bakery.

"Is he running for office?" Mildred asked.

"He's lobbying for Jessica's heart," Eunice said.

Jess pressed her lips closed.

The third flyer went too far.

"'I'm lobbying for Jessica's heart,'" Rutgar read the caption. "He's serious. I took this picture." Of Duffy, down on one knee, next to the bench in the town square, holding a ring box toward the camera.

In addition to the usual instruction Duffy had printed on the bottom, he'd added, "If you think that's a good idea, let Jessica Aguirre know."

"You helped him, Rutgar?" Jess felt betrayed. And embarrassed. Her customers got some good laughs out of it. And then there was her heart, which had somehow managed to reassemble a piece or two and root for Duffy. "I thought you were on my side."

"I admit the boy has a habit of rubbing me the wrong way." And then Rutgar leaned over the counter and whispered, "But he's changed."

"He told you to say that." Jess slapped a few coins into his humongous palm.

Rutgar straightened and drew himself to his full, massive height. "Nobody tells me to do anything."

Jess pressed her lips together as Eunice edged beneath Rutgar's arm. "I told him not to do this. It goes too far, asking you to marry him on a flyer."

"You knew?"

"I helped him pick out the ring." Eunice hunched her shoulders as if in shame, but her smile belied that notion. She was enjoying Duffy's campaign.

Jess couldn't believe he'd won over the town and bought a ring and hadn't come by in days!

"Same time tonight for Lamaze class?" Eunice asked.

Jess nodded tightly. For the first time since moving to Harmony Valley, she longed for the anonymity of working in a large town.

But she couldn't help but wonder what Duffy had in mind next.

CHAPTER TWENTY-THREE

THE CALL CAME in the middle of the night at a time when sleep was its deepest.

Duffy fumbled with his cell phone and managed a bleary answer. "Yeah."

"Duffy?" It was Eunice. She spoke in a small, scared voice, a whisper really. "It's time."

"For Baby?" He swung his feet out of bed and ran a hand across his face. "I'll pick you up in five minutes."

"No, Duffy." Eunice continued to whisper. "We're already here. At the hospital."

"What?" Duffy flipped the light on and searched for a clean pair of jeans. "The plan was you'd call me when she called you."

"I know," Eunice said miserably. "But she went into labor during Lamaze and we went directly to the hospital next to the class-room." Her voice become muffled and hard to make out, as if she'd put her hand over the phone. "I thought they were sending us home, but the doctor came by and…"

There was a wail in the background.

"Get here, Duffy. Get here." Eunice hung up.

Duffy dressed, took Goldie out and was on the road to Santa Rosa in record time. He parked and ran into the hospital. All he could think about was Jess panicking in labor, forgetting to breathe, and Eunice passed out next to the bed. Jess needed him! Eunice needed him! Baby needed him!

Once inside the hospital, everyone was helpful in directing him to Labor & Delivery. And then he ran into a snag.

"Your relationship to Ms. Aguirre?" the Labor & Delivery nurse asked.

"I'm her fiancé," he lied, trying to catch his breath.

The nurse glanced at a sheet of paper. "Ms. Aguirre doesn't have you listed on those permitted inside the delivery room. Not your name, not even the word *fiancé*."

"Okay, okay. We had a falling-out." Duffy lowered his voice. "But I love her. I love her. And she's in there right now with our good friend, who is squeamish and may pass out during touchdown time." He tried to look harmless and helpless and sincere. "Please.

Just ask her if I can come in. She needs me. And I need her."

Something about his plea must have worked, because the nurse nodded and headed down the hallway, ducking into a room. There were blank sheets of paper in the printer. Duffy took one, along with a pen, and began writing.

"YOU CALLED HIM?" Jess couldn't keep the anger from her voice. Her body was a knotted ball of fire. She'd been in labor for hours and was exhausted. If this was how babies came into the world, she was never having another one.

The nurse slipped out the door with Jessica's answer: *No. Duffy was not allowed inside.*

The birthing room had bright green walls and pictures of carousels and airplanes. Cheerful things that contrasted against Jessica's pain.

Eunice held Jessica's hand, a worried look on her face. Her purplish hair had long-since flattened from Eunice tugging nervously on the ends. "Yes, I called him. He may not be your rock, but he's mine. I need him."

"Oh, Eunice." Another contraction was building. Jess could feel it at the base of her spine. She glanced at the monitor, but it hadn't even begun to climb.

"Please let him in."

The muscles about Jessica's abdomen began to tighten. "He doesn't love me. I'm just a responsibility to him." She clenched her teeth.

The nurse came back in. "He said to give you this note."

The contraction was reaching its peak. Jess clung to Eunice's hand as if it was the only thing keeping her on the bed.

Eunice cringed. "Ow. I think you just broke a bone."

The nurse loosened Jessica's grip. "Breathe."

Oh, yeah. Jess often got lost in the pain and forgot her hee-hoo. "How much longer?" she asked when the contraction subsided and the nurse finished checking the history of her contractions and how far she'd dilated.

"You should read the note," the nurse said. "For her sake." She pointed toward Eunice, who was sagged in the chair next to the bed looking as if she'd just given birth. She fanned herself with Duffy's note.

Jess couldn't read it. Her brain function had fallen so far below pregnant brain, she doubted she could read. "Eunice, can you read it?"

The old woman wiped her forehead and unfolded the note. "He's making you an offer to be part of the baby's life. How sweet."

"How much?" Jess ground out. "How much is my baby worth to him?"

"Priceless," came a deep voice outside her door. "That baby is priceless."

You bet. "How much, Eunice?"

Eunice held the paper up for Jess to see. "He says, 'I give you and Baby my heart. No obligation. No charge.'"

A solitary tear spilled onto Jessica's cheek. "Come in, Duff. Please come in."

He came into view. Her same, solid Duffy, hesitating by the door. "I love you, Jess. You don't have to marry me. Just let me love you and Baby. That's all I ask."

Brimming with love, Jess held a hand out to him. "It's enough." Enough to get her through birthing this baby, enough to last for years to come.

"Thank heavens." Eunice scurried out of her seat and claimed one farther back against the wall. "The cavalry has arrived."

Duffy closed the distance between them and cradled Jessica's hand in his as another contraction gathered steam inside her. "I'm so glad I'm here to make this memory with you, love."

Jess nodded, losing the ability to answer as the contraction sent its shuddering tentacles up her body.

The nurse returned with the doctor. Things got hectic after that.

But Jess held on to the memory of Duff holding her hand, of Duff coaching her to breathe, of Duff's wide and wondrous smile when Baby came into the world.

Duff called it a miracle.

Thomas called it a do-over.

Jess called him Gregory.

* * * * *

LARGER-PRINT BOOKS!

GET 2 FREE LARGER-PRINT NOVELS PLUS 2 FREE MYSTERY GIFTS

Love Inspired®

SUSPENSE
RIVETING INSPIRATIONAL ROMANCE

Larger-print novels are now available...

LARGER-PRINT BOOKS!
GET 2 FREE LARGER-PRINT NOVELS PLUS
2 FREE GIFTS!

HARLEQUIN

super romance

More Story...More Romance

YES! Please send me **The Montana Mavericks Collection** in Larger Print. This collection begins with 3 FREE books and 2 FREE gifts (gifts valued at approx. $20.00 retail) in the first shipment, along with the other first 4 books from the collection! If I do not cancel, I will receive 8 monthly shipments until I have the entire 51-book Montana Mavericks collection. I will receive 2 or 3 FREE books in each shipment and I will pay just $4.99 US/ $5.89 CDN for each of the other four books in each shipment, plus $2.99 for shipping and handling per shipment.*If I decide to keep the entire collection, I'll have paid for only 32 books, because 19 books are FREE! I understand that accepting the 3 free books and gifts places me under no obligation to buy anything. I can always return a shipment and cancel at any time. My free books and gifts are mine to keep no matter what I decide.

263 HCN 2404   463 HCN 2404

Name	(PLEASE PRINT)	
Address		Apt. #
City	State/Prov.	Zip/Postal Code

Signature (if under 18, a parent or guardian must sign)

Mail to the **Reader Service**:

IN U.S.A.: P.O. Box 1867, Buffalo, NY 14240-1867
IN CANADA: P.O. Box 609, Fort Erie, Ontario L2A 5X3

READERSERVICE.COM

Manage your account online!

- Review your order history
- Manage your payments
- Update your address

> *We've designed the*
> *Reader Service website*
> *just for you.*

Enjoy all the features!

- Discover new series available to you, and read excerpts from any series.
- Respond to mailings and special monthly offers.
- Connect with favorite authors at the blog.
- Browse the Bonus Bucks catalog and online-only exculsives.
- Share your feedback.

Visit us at:

ReaderService.com